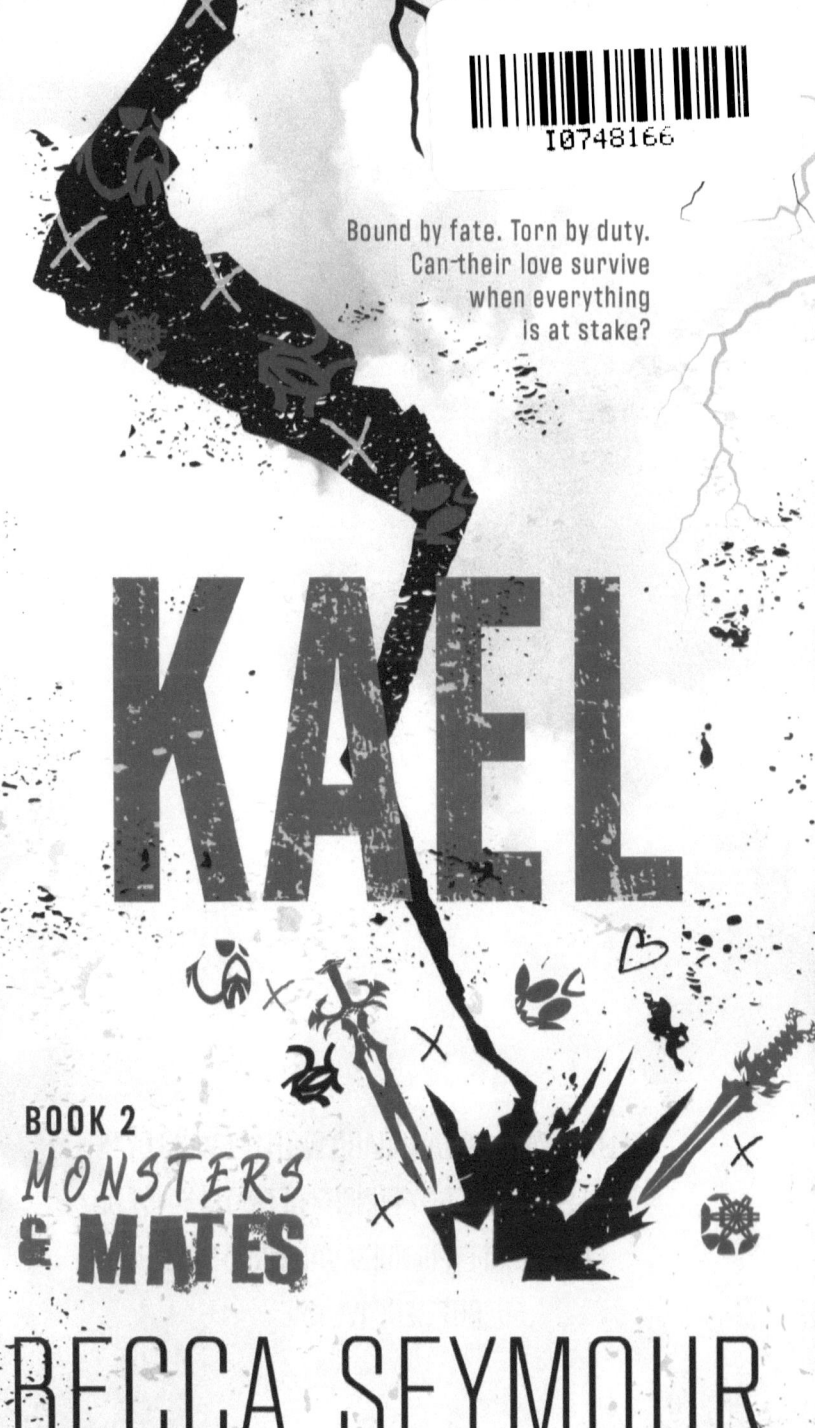

Bound by fate. Torn by duty.
Can their love survive
when everything
is at stake?

KAEL

BOOK 2
MONSTERS
& MATES

BECCA SEYMOUR

FALLING FOR A ROYAL GUARD WITH GLOWING EYES
AND A LETHAL ENERGY PUNCH? DEFINITELY NOT ON
MY TERRAFEARA SURVIVAL BINGO CARD.
BUT HERE WE ARE.

KAEL

BOOK TWO
MONSTERS
& MATES

BECCA SEYMOUR

COVER DESIGN: BOOKSMITH DESIGN

EDITORS: HOT TREE™ EDITING

E-BOOK: 978-1-923252-37-0

PAPERBACK: 978-1-923252-80-6

CHAPTER
ONE

EVERY DAMN TIME THE LIGHTNING FLASHES through the green sky and cracks this world apart, I wince. On the inside obviously. Not a chance in hell that I'll let any of these fuckers see even a hint of weakness.

Being a "fragile" human got old fast the day I got dumped unceremoniously into this world. It's why it's been my mission to toughen the hell up. I barely hold back my snort, thinking my dick-for-brains "uncle," a.k.a. my mum's latest loser bogan boyfriend before I was purged from Earth, would be proud.

I'd put up with over a year of being called every homophobic slur under the sun, complete with all the "effeminate" bastardisations he could come up with. If only back then I had the skills I have now. Not a chance the piss-poor excuse for a man would utter a word if he saw me on the training mat, let alone got up close and personal with the newly formed muscles I hadn't thought I'd been capable of developing.

I suppose that was the thing with being vulnerable and legit the weakest species in this dimension. I'd quickly figured out it was a kill-or-be-killed world. Or at least, toughen up and survive—no matter what it takes. Day five of being here all those months or years (fuck if I know how many exactly) ago, I'd lost count of the number of times I'd almost been eaten or murdered, and all it took was a chance run-in with Varek for me to know I didn't want to die.

And yes, by "chance run-in," I absolutely mean the Riftborn Rebels' group leader took pity on me and saved my arse. I'd been wedged behind a rock, trying to escape an eyeless monster I'd since discovered was a *nullmaw*.

As it turns out, those little suckers might be blind as a bat, but it's as easy for them to scent out a quivering human as it is for me to head into Woolworths—a big-arse supermarket in Australia (that's assuming they're still in business)—and buy myself a cooked chicken on my way from work.

Fuck, now I want roast chicken. I wouldn't even mind chasing after one and plucking the damn thing myself. Ask anyone: Chasing food, hunting, preparing, cooking—it's most definitely not in my skill set. But I suppose the point is moot since Terrafeara is a dimension without our tasty feathered friends. Which means, once again, I'll be stuck eating whatever Decca and Molsi have cooked up for us.

"You beautiful bag of dicks, what's cooking?" I greet as I enter Dathanor's mess hall. Okay, when I say "mess hall," think less "insert whatever popular Hollywood Army movie here" and more Dungeons & Dragons had a baby with *Insterstar Trek*, or whatever it's called. Listen, I hated sci-fi and especially monster-slash-horror movies when on Earth. I'm just impressed that I know what Dungeons & Dragons is—courtesy of a deliciously geeky ex–fuck buddy of mine.

But back to the hub of Dathanor. It's a second-floor cave—above ground level—and the only one that has good airflow out the back for fire pits. But the biolumi-nescent green-and-blue veins here do also channel some sort of energy that can be used to cool as well as heat. Or so I've been told. Honestly, I wouldn't put it past either Decca or Molsi to have made that shit up.

Decca flips me off with all four of her middle fingers —something I take great pride in having taught her. And just to be clear, yes, she does have four hands. And arms. Molsi, though, they arch their super-pointed monobrow at me—again, something I taught them to do—before they scrunch their nose, saying in perfect English (they even manage a touch of exasperated affec-tion), "Sonny, I'm not sure 'a bag of dicks' can be used as a term of endearment."

"No?" I step close to the large plank used as a countertop here—a barrier between the Riftborn and Decca's sharp knives she's threatened me with more than once. "I beg to differ. If someone handed me a bag of dicks right now, I'd be pretty fucking set for the night."

Molsi's scrunched nose remains in place. "A bag of severed dicks would give you... joy?"

The fuck?

I backtrack quickly. "Fuck no, Molsi. Bloody hell. Who said anything about *severed* dicks?" My already-soft cock shrivels in my pants. "I was thinking more like dildoes. Vibrators, you know?" I slam my mouth shut, because of course Molsi doesn't know what a vibrator is.

Like 99-point-whatever percent of the population here in our rebel hideout, Molsi is not human. Nor is Decca or the majority of individuals I feel like I have something in common with. Or at least who I can shoot the shit with.

At the moment, there are a staggering six humans, including myself—though I did hear that another two have joined us. I have exactly zero more details than that since they pretty much left again as soon as they arrived. At some point this morning, the newcomers joined Shanae—a badass Southern woman who, quite honestly, I could fall in love with if I wasn't, you know, gay and if her mate wouldn't eat me if I looked at Shanae wrong—on some sort of mission. No doubt because of that massive lightning rift that had me wincing earlier.

And the other four humans... unsurprisingly, they're wrapped up in their mates, stuck like glue to their bonded. And if I sound petulant, that's because fuck yes, I am. Being the exception to every damn rule is not my idea of a good time.

Varek has this theory that all humans who've crossed the rift into Terrafeara have a destined mate just waiting to be discovered and bonded to. Everyone except me that is. And it's not even like it's down to a waiting game. Every other human here—and other humans who Varek, Shanae, and literally every creature and species here have come across—have met their fated within a week of the rift.

So that either means my mum's scumbag boyfriend was right (that I'm a cunt, destined to be alone) or my fated mate is dead. Okay, so there is, I suppose, the very real possibility that I've already met them, and when they realised who they were going to be tied to, they ran as fast and as far as their furry, maybe even clawed feet could take them. Which, I think, technically, would lead me back to the first explanation.

But also, fuck all that.

Or at least, back to me fucking a bag of dildoes. Now, wouldn't that be something special? But it's best I keep these thoughts to myself, especially if I want something decent to eat that's not going to turn my hair orange (a story for another time—*never*). Plus, if anyone knows anything about the newcomers and why they went off with Shanae and her crew, then Decca or Molsi does.

They hear and see everything. Well, they seem to get all the good gossip at least. And since my duties here are pretty basic and I still haven't got to swing a sword or pummel a monstrous beastie or even anyone from the royal guard who are enemy number one—not for lack of trying, I will pointedly add—I have enough time on my hands to hear all the juicy goodness usually before anyone else.

"Let's go back to 'what's cooking,' both in that pot over there and where Shanae's headed off to." I flutter my eyelashes, which, to be honest, rarely works with most folks, but Decca loves that shit. Not having eyelashes or brows herself makes her think my fluttering is sweet, so obviously I use it to my advantage.

Decca lets out a snort and stirs the bubbling pot with one of her many hands while another tosses a handful of something red and wriggling into a sizzling pan.

"Tonight, we're having a lovely stew of krigworm and arlak root," she announces. "Nice and thick. Should keep your human belly full for a few hours."

Molsi adds, "And fried silkstalks. Don't worry, we drained the venom first."

"Comforting," I deadpan. "Just what every growing boy needs: protein, starch, and the ever-looming possibility of food poisoning."

Decca cackles as she stirs, the thick brownish-green

sludge in the pot making a noise that I refuse to describe. My stomach is already on thin ice.

"Speaking of digestible horrors." I lean in, resting my forearms on the wooden plank. "What's the deal with the newcomers? Two humans, yeah? And some other species?"

Molsi gives me a sharp look, their pale silver eyes glittering under the bioluminescent glow. "Shanae took them out with two others. One Pyronox, the other... unidentified."

My eyebrows shoot up. "Pyronox?"

Pyronoxes aren't exactly common. I've only met one in my time here, and he was a walking inferno with muscles to match. Massive, skin like molten rock, bright bloody red, and capable of setting an entire camp ablaze with a sneeze. Pyronoxes are basically the last creatures you want to invite to a bonfire unless you want the whole damn forest to go up with it.

"And the human? The adult one?" I ask, trying to keep my tone casual.

Molsi tilts their head, considering me. "Mated to the Pyronox."

There goes that hope.

Not that I was about to run off and throw myself at the guy, but still, I wouldn't mind a nice, simple "down to fuck" situation. Instead, it looks like he's already wrapped up in an infernal love story. Lucky bastard.

"They left almost immediately," Decca chimes in,

flipping whatever she's frying. "Hours ago, actually. Apparently, they're searching for evidence of the latest rift and whatever came through it."

My gut tightens.

Of course, I can't help but wonder—hope, even— that whatever slipped through might be my mate. But that thought is fucking ridiculous, and I hate myself a little for even considering it.

Still, I tap my fingers on the counter, frowning.

"Any clue what the unknown creature is?" I ask. Though, in truth, it could be a whole town, not just one unfortunate bastard.

Molsi shakes their head. "No details. But it must be important if Shanae took them all out there herself."

Interesting. Shanae is no fool. If she's personally escorting them, something about this situation is worth investigating. Saying that, the lightning storm seemed to last longer than usual.

"So, what you're saying is, I should be prepared for some fresh chaos?" I muse.

Decca grins, all teeth and mischief. "Aren't you always?"

Fair point.

I grab a wooden bowl as Molsi ladles some of the questionable stew into it. As I take my first hesitant bite, my mind is already turning over the possibilities. New rift, new creatures, and two more humans added to our ranks. One of them, at least, definitely not mine.

But what about the other?

And why do I get the feeling that everything is about to change?

A sudden commotion outside makes me pause, spoon halfway to my mouth. Heavy footsteps thunder through the hall, voices rising in an urgent, tangled mix of Glowranthian and English.

"Sonny!" A tall Trefite bursts into the mess hall, breathless. Their dark scales shimmer under the glow of the cave's veins. "A human has been taken to headquarters."

My stomach clenches. Headquarters isn't here—it's a short trek away, hidden but more exposed than our rebel accommodation.

"Taken?" I ask, standing. "By who?"

"They were found unconscious. Strange clothing— no pants, like many humans seem to favour. Shanae's party found them. She went ahead with the majority of her crew. Sent two back with the unconscious human." The Trefite pauses. Up close I recognise him as Dreink. "Varek sent for you."

A sharp thrill rushes through me. I've been waiting —practically begging—for a real job here. Something with purpose, not just the usual errands or menial tasks that keep me from going insane. Back in Sydney, I worked as a nightclub promoter, which, let's be honest, was mostly talking my way into free drinks and making sure drunken idiots didn't vomit in VIP lounges.

Not exactly a skill set that translates well to surviving a rebellion in a monster-filled dimension. It's why I've thrown myself into training, pushing my body, learning to fight. If war ever comes—hell, it's already on the horizon—I want to be ready. Because as a human, a Riftborn, I'm a target. The ruling realm's queen sees us as property, assets to be used however she damn well pleases. Captured, enslaved, experimented on.

No fucking thank you.

I slam my bowl down, appetite forgotten. "Let's go."

Decca and Molsi exchange a glance, but they don't stop me or even ask me to clear up after myself. They know better. And yes, that means I'd sulk pretty phenomenally if I'm delayed.

"Thank you," I throw over my shoulder as I follow Dreink out into the tunnels, my pulse thrumming.

A new human. Found unconscious. Taken to headquarters.

Something tells me this is exactly the kind of excitement I've been waiting for.

The tunnels twist and shift, damp air curling against my skin as we move. Bioluminescent veins pulse gently along the rocky walls, casting eerie blue-green shadows that flicker with each step we take. The path is familiar —I've made the trip to headquarters a handful of times —but there's always a sense of unease travelling this far from the heart of our makeshift town.

Once we're out of the tunnels, we're exposed. Not

just to the creatures that lurk beyond the cavern walls but to the ruling queen's spies.

"You got any details?" I ask, my voice hushed despite the steady crunch of my boots against the stone floor.

Dreink glances at me, their overlong tongue flicking out briefly, tasting the air before we leave the confines of the covered tunnels and step into the daylight. "Only what I told you. The human was found unconscious. No obvious injuries, but their arrival is... odd."

"Odd how?"

They hesitate. "Fredole, who brought them back to base, mentioned their body temperature was lower than normal. Plus, there was a dead Dlanwik nearby."

I frown. "Strange." Sure, there's a lot of heat in this part of Terrafeara, but there are snowcapped mountains in the distance. I've never got close to them myself, but Shanae told me the snow is almost identical to that on Earth. The main difference is the flakes are more like tiny shimmering crystals, almost translucent in the sunlight, rather than the soft, fluffy flakes we know.

A dead Dlanwik close is also bizarre. They're venomous creatures, and if one had bitten the human, they would definitely be dead rather than just unconscious.

Does that mean the human managed to kill it? Impressive as hell if they did.

But hold on. Did Dreink say they weren't wearing trousers?

I roll my shoulders, anticipation tightening my muscles. The human's unconsciousness could mean anything. Not everyone coming through the rift handles it well. Some freak out, others attack whatever they see, and a few just go into some kind of stupor, completely zoned out. Me? I wasn't exactly graceful. Those first five days of trying to survive were a mess. I'm pretty sure I spent half that time hiding in a bush, shaking like a leaf, and trying not to get eaten by whatever local wildlife thought I looked tasty. But hey, at least I eventually figured out the whole "don't die" thing.

This poor bastard? Seems like they didn't get the chance to figure it out.

As we break through into the open field leading to headquarters, my eyes land on the structure in the middle of it all, and as always, I have to suppress a laugh.

The fucking bowling alley.

Of all the places that could've been ripped from Earth and spat out into Terrafeara, it had to be this. A dated, neon-lit, old-school bowling alley straight out of an American suburban fever dream. The first time I'd seen it, I thought someone was screwing with me. A piece of Earth wedged into a monster dimension. But now? It's headquarters. A beacon in the underground. A joke and a safe house all wrapped into one.

We step inside, past the dusty reception counter and the ancient vending machines filled with nothing but dust balls and rust. The place is dimly lit, the blacklight glow catching on the scratched-up walls where neon lights still flicker. The lanes have long been repurposed, except for one—most are now training spaces, while other areas have been turned into war rooms and makeshift quarters for those being assessed.

At the far end, past the gutted snack bar, a small group is gathered outside the door to the small healing quarters. Varek stands at the centre, his imposing frame making the others look small in comparison. His vibrant purple skin shifts slightly under the glow, his silver eyes sharp as he turns to face me.

"Sonny," he greets me, voice a deep rumble. "Good. We need to talk."

My attention snaps to the cot inside the room.

A man.

He's stretched out, unconscious, his chest rising and falling in slow, steady breaths. His dark hair is damp, clinging to his forehead, and his skin is pale—too pale. His lips are also chapped. But the thing that catches me most?

No trousers.

Not in the fun, sexy way. More in the "I got yanked through a rift mid-something" kind of way. He's wearing a thin vest and boxers. I squint. Are those snow-boots?

I step closer, my curiosity outweighing caution. "They've been unconscious this whole time?"

Varek nods. "We checked for injuries. There are none. No bruising, no marks. But something isn't right."

I glance at the others in the room—a scout; Aeroth, our medic; and Reat, one of Varek's trusted advisers. All watching. All waiting.

Something about this feels... different.

I swallow hard, pushing away the strange sense of familiarity crawling up my spine. "What do you need from me?"

Varek exhales, crossing his arms. "Shanae isn't here. You understand humans better than anyone. We need you to talk to them when they wake."

Excitement flares in my chest. It doesn't matter that I'm the second choice. This is a real job. A real purpose. Something more than running messages or helping cook whatever the hell I just abandoned in the mess hall.

"I can do that," I say, my voice steady.

Varek studies me a beat before he nods. "Find out what you can and keep them calm. I want to know who or what killed the Dlanwik."

I bob my head. "I can do that."

Without another word, he retreats, and I'm left with Aeroth, whose language—a bunch of clicks and hums —I can't decipher. She can speak English, as well as

Glowranthian, but I understand why she doesn't like to if hand gestures can do just as well.

Time crawls as I sit by the unconscious man, watching for any sign of movement beyond the slow, steady rise and fall of his chest. Nothing. Not even a twitch of fingers or a flutter of eyelids.

The only thing that shifts is my patience.

I risk a test, pressing the back of my hand against his forehead. An icy chill clings to him. His skin is so much cooler than mine, but his lips aren't blue. That has to be a good sign, right?

With a sigh, I push to my feet. No point in hovering. Aeroth will let me know if something changes.

I step out, leaving the dimly lit room behind, and wander towards the back of the bowling alley, where the seating is actually comfortable. If I'm going to wait, I might as well do it with a book.

I barely have time to settle into a battered old chair, cracking open the latest novel I scavenged from one of the storage rooms, when a commotion stirs in the main area. Raised voices. Heavy footfalls. The unmistakable tension of something important arriving.

Peering around a small partition, I take in the newcomers.

A man. A kid—maybe ten, maybe fourteen? I've never been great at guessing ages. They're accompanied by a Pyronox, the glow of their ember-like skin unmistakable, and a creature I've never seen before.

But what really grabs my attention are the two Glowranthian figures.

I suck in a sharp breath, my gaze falling on the shorter one first. Light blue skin, almost pearlescent under the dim lights, intricate symbols marking his uniform—royalty. Likely one of the princes.

Holy fuck. What the fuck is a prince doing here?

My heart kicks up a notch, but I don't have time to dwell on it before my attention shifts to the Glowranthian beside him. This one is huge—towering and broad. His glowing bioluminescent markings are subtler than the prince's, nearly hidden in the shadow of his massive frame.

A bodyguard.

Everything about him screams danger, from the way his nostrils flare as he scans the room to the way his muscles tense beneath his dark armour. The effect is both hypnotic and infuriating.

Before I can dwell on that thought, the human man turns and starts walking towards the room where the unconscious one is being kept.

That's when it happens.

The Glowranthian bodyguard's gaze snaps to mine, luminous eyes locking onto me with an intensity that pins me in place.

What the fuck?

Something sharp flickers across the prince's expression, his lips pressing into a thin line. Then the bodyguard's eyes flare slightly before his entire posture shifts, his muscles tightening as his expression darkens. He turns to the prince, murmuring something low in their native tongue, and then—just as quickly as he met my gaze—he looks away.

Pointedly.

My stomach twists.

Well, fuck you too.

But the interaction stirs a deeper unease in me, a reminder that since arriving in this world, royalty—the realm itself—has been my enemy. *Our* enemy. And yet here they are. Here, in our supposedly hidden head-quarters.

What the hell is Varek doing letting them in here?

CHAPTER
TWO

A TWITCH OF HIS FINGERS AND A LOW MOAN alerts me to the man waking. I sit up, placing the Mills & Boon circa 1975 down before standing and closing the door. While the headquarters is no longer a flurry of activity—the prince, his royal guard, plus the humans and the Pyronox gone (to where I have no idea)—I don't know how the guy is going to react when he fully wakes.

He's warmed up, at least, his skin no longer cool to the touch. The poor guy has the worst case of chapped lips, though. A blanket is tucked up to his chest, covering his bare legs, and his snow-boots, which Aeroth and I removed, are on the floor near the closed door.

Aeroth is out of the room, which is probably a good thing. We have no idea who this man is, when he arrived, or what he's been through. Though based on the gossip I've heard while waiting, I think he came through at the same time as the guy wearing an Akubra (so I assume he's Aussie) and the kid who's with him, which means he's *not* from this morning's rift. But that's not even the *big* gossip.

Apparently, this guy is the prince's mate.

Like, what the fuck? For one, poor guy.

The prince and his family—the queen in particular—are the reason why we're at risk, are hiding, and this whole rebellion was formed in the first place.

And two? He's found his fated mate, or at least, his fated mate's found him. Not to sound like a jealous bitch, but how the fuck is that fair?

Okay, so maybe I'm feeling a little hard done by. Not that it's his fault, so I'll keep my self-pity locked away tightly.

But back to the guy who's slowly waking up. Trying to keep him calm while promising him he's safe and building his trust so I can get answers is my job... my mission. And I intend to impress the hell out of Varek.

Doing so might actually get me away from being a general dogsbody. Not that I'm not willing to support the settlement however is needed, but still, being pulled in so many directions is frustrating.

Another groan and his eyeballs move rapidly behind his eyes before his lids flicker.

"Hey," I say quietly, wanting to forewarn him that

he's not alone. "You're safe. Just take your time opening your eyes, but know that you're in our compound and you're safe here."

He stiffens. Completely. Like a deer caught in the headlights, or more accurately, like a bloke waking up in an unknown place, surrounded by God knows what, and realising he might be royally screwed.

Yeah, that tracks.

I hold up my hands in what I hope is a universal I-come-in-peace gesture. "Hey, mate, you're safe. Just breathe, yeah? No one's gonna hurt you."

His breathing is shallow, chest barely moving beneath the blanket, his wide eyes darting around the dimly lit room. When he spots the boots by the door, his whole body tenses further, like he's bracing for something.

Right. Reassurance time.

"Look, I get it. This place is weird as hell. Trust me, I had a full-blown existential crisis when I landed here. Thought I'd actually carked it and was in some kind of purgatory for all the times I skipped paying my club bar tab. But, nah, turns out, it's just another world. Lucky us, right?" I give a dry chuckle, hoping humour might break through whatever terrified spiral he's in.

His gaze finally flicks to me, wary but slightly less frozen. I take that as a win.

"So, uh, I'm Sonny. Aussie. Club promoter from Sydney. Got sucked into this joint thanks to a lightning storm that nearly made me crap my undies." I gesture vaguely to the ceiling. "Long story. But the point is, I know what it's like to wake up here and have no bloody clue what's going on."

His throat bobs as he swallows. He's still tense, but some of the sheer panic is fading from his face. That's good. He's listening.

"How about you? You okay?" I ask. "Or, well, as okay as someone can be when they've just been yeeted through dimensions?"

His lips part, and for a second, I think he might stay silent. Then, finally, he speaks. "I'm okay. Achy, but I'll live." The sound of his voice makes me jolt.

Australian. No mistaking it.

Well, bloody hell. He definitely must have come through with the other Aussies.

"Where in Aus you from?" I ask, leaning forwards slightly. "Sydney? Melbourne? Please don't say Brisbane, or I'll have to start treating you with mild suspicion."

He hesitates, then rubs a hand over his face, fingers lingering at his temples like he's nursing a headache. "Western Australia," he finally says, voice hoarse. "Yallingup."

I blink. "Never heard of it. Sounds made up." I keep my voice light and teasing.

His lips twitch—like, the tiniest fraction of a smirk. If I weren't paying attention, I might've missed it.

"It's real," he mutters. "South of Perth. Small town."

I nod like that means anything to me. "All right, so what were you doing when you got rifted?"

His brow furrows. "Rifted?"

"Yeah. That's what we call it when the big flashy alternate-dimension storm tears through the land and effectively hoicks it out and swaps it for a piece of Terrafeara. Makes it sound less horrifying."

He exhales sharply, then shifts under the blanket. "Terrafeara?" His skin pales. "What the hell kind of name is that?"

A snort of a laugh bursts from me. Okay, I think this guy and I are going to get along just fine. "Stuff of night-mares, right? As far as dimensions go, its name pretty much sums up the kinda monsters out here. The good news is, they're all out there and can't get into this place."

He nods, looking mildly less horrified. "I wasn't in WA when it happened," he says. "I was in Portugal. Serra da Estrela. Heading out to snowboard."

I stare at him. Then at his snow-boots. Then back at him.

"You're telling me you were in Portugal? Like, actual Europe? On a mountain? About to have a bougie little ski trip? And then—poof—you wound up here?"

He nods slowly, like he's piecing it together in real time. "Yeah. One second, I was putting my gear on. Next, there was a storm, and I was... here. But still there? Like a piece of the mountain came with me and was planted in a forest that was humid as gloopy soup."

I let out a low whistle. "Damn. That's new." I focussed on his location rather than the burning question about his cool temperature when he arrived.

He frowns. "New?"

"Yeah. As far as we know, the rift's only pulled people from the same general area back home. Usually a couple of kilometres. But Portugal, another continent? That's a first." I pause. "Also, you snowboard?"

His frown deepens. "Yeah?"

I shake my head, mildly offended. "What is it with WA guys and extreme sports? You blokes just come out of the womb ready to climb cliffs and throw yourselves down mountains?"

His shoulders relax—just a little, but enough for me to notice. "We like adventure."

"Mate, there's adventure, and then there's getting sucked into an alternate universe where monsters roam and some prince bloke apparently wants to claim you as his soul mate."

His entire body locks up again. Oops. Maybe I shouldn't have dropped that last part just yet.

"Right. That's another thing we need to talk about," I mutter. "But first, what's your name?"

He hesitates, then finally says, "Dawson."

I nod. "All right, Dawson. Let's figure out what the hell's going on with you."

I study Dawson as he shifts slightly under the blanket, his face screwing up like he's only just realising how sore he is. "You hurting anywhere in particular?" I ask. "Or is it an all-over kind of ache?"

His brow furrows, and for the first time, his eyes—deep brown and currently suspicious as hell—land on me properly. "Bruised, I think. But... not dying."

I snort. "That's a pretty low bar, mate. Hungry? Thirsty?"

At the mention of thirst, he swallows thickly. "Water. Please."

"Coming right up," I promise, pushing up from my seat. "You want food too? Something bland to start?"

He hesitates, like he doesn't trust the idea of eating yet, but then nods. "Yeah. That'd be good."

I make it halfway to the door before his voice, hoarse but steady, stops me.

"I, uh... I got attacked."

I turn back, raising a brow. "That's... not shocking. This world is basically a wildlife documentary where everything wants to eat you, electrocute you, or melt your face off."

He lets out a laugh—dry, short, but it's something. "Yeah, well. This thing nearly had me." His gaze flickers, like he's reliving it. "Freaky-looking bastard. Skin all grey and blotchy, arms too long, big creepy mouth but no lips."

I stare at him. "Oh, mate. You ran into a Dlanwik?"

"A what?"

"Dlanwik. Fast, sneaky, and venomous as all hell. If one of those things bit you, you wouldn't be having this conversation. You'd be...." I mime keeling over dead.

His face loses a bit of colour. "Oh."

"So how the fuck did you kill it?" I ask, because now I'm really curious.

Dawson shifts awkwardly and clears his throat. "Uh. Pure luck."

I cross my arms. "Do tell."

He lets out a slow breath. "I was kinda backing up. Trying to keep distance, 'cause the thing was fast and all wiry, like a pissed-off spider with arms. And then I tripped on a tree root."

I wince. "Shit."

"Yeah. Fell flat on my arse. And the thing pounced at me. So, in pure panic, I grabbed the first thing I could find and just swung as hard as I could." He pauses. "Turns out, I grabbed a rock. A very large, very jagged rock. And I swung it straight up as it lunged, caught the bastard right in its creepy mouth."

My eyes widen. "You bashed its face in?"

"Pretty much. Brain trauma, I guess? Thing made this awful gargling sound, flopped around a bit, then stopped moving." He makes a vague motion with his hand. "I just sat there, hyperventilating, trying to figure out what the fuck I'd just done."

I blink, then burst out laughing. "You one-hit KO'd a Dlanwik with a rock?"

He mutters, "Not my proudest moment."

"Mate, that's amazing. That's like some 'caveman defeats alien invader' type shit. You should be proud."

Dawson just shakes his head, mumbling something about how this world makes no sense.

"And how'd you end up unconscious?"

"Must have knocked my head when I fell. I know I walked away from where I killed that thing. Not sure how far I made it before everything went black."

I wince. "Well, you're here now. Sit tight. I'll get that water and food. And hey—no more wrestling monsters, yeah?"

He lets out another dry chuckle, but when I turn to leave, his body goes tense again.

"You're leaving?"

I pause, glancing back. His hands are gripping the blanket, knuckles slightly white.

"I'll be right back," I say. "No one's coming in, I promise."

His jaw works, like he's trying to tamp down his reaction, but I can see it. The sheer fucking exhaustion, the fear lingering under his skin.

"There aren't... other things here, right?" he asks.

I sigh, leaning against the doorframe. "Okay, here's the thing. Yeah, there are other beings here. But we don't call them 'things' or 'monsters.' Most of them are what we call Riftborn, while the dominant species here are Glowranth. Each species here is intelligent, living their own lives, just like us. Yeah, some have fangs or claws or magic, but that doesn't mean they're out to get you."

He swallows. "And the ones that are?"

"We keep them far away from the compound." I meet his gaze, making sure he knows I'm not bullshitting him. "You're safe here, Dawson."

His shoulders relax, just a fraction.

"Good," he mutters. "I don't have the energy to fight off another one."

I chuckle. "Yeah, let's not test your caveman survival skills again just yet." With that, I head out.

The second I step into the hall, Varek is there, arms crossed.

"Sonny," he says, all business. "Report."

I sigh. "He—Dawson—is awake. Banged up but fine. No major injuries. He killed a Dlanwik with a rock."

Varek actually raises a brow. "A rock?"

"Yep. Man's a menace."

He exhales through his nose, like he doesn't have time for my shit. "Good. And his memory?"

"Seems intact. He remembers coming through the rift, being attacked, nearly shitting himself." I hesitate. "Also, he's Australian."

Varek narrows his eyes slightly. "Interesting. That makes three who arrived through the same rift."

"Yeah, I was thinking that too." I shift on my feet. "He says he was in Portugal when he got pulled through, though."

He frowns. "That's not the same place as Australia?"

I shake my head. "Nope. Complete opposite side of the wo— Holy shit, opposite side of the world. Like, my Earth geography is not the best, but I'm pretty sure if you looked at the globe and placed a ruler against it—through it—" I shrug. "—I'm pretty sure the other side is Portugal, maybe Spain. But considering where Dawson said he was, my money's on Portugal.

"Hmm... unexpected."

"Tell me about it."

Varek studies me for a beat, then says, "The prince is demanding to see him."

I wince, barely holding back my sneer at the mention of the Glowranth. Fuck. "Already?"

He tilts his head. "Why does that sound like a problem?"

I clear my throat, not about to admit I might've let it slip that Dawson is apparently the prince's fated mate. "Varek, we both know humans don't have 'fated mates.' That's fantasy novel bullshit."

Varek's expression doesn't change. "You need to prepare him."

There's something in his tone that sets me on edge. I narrow my eyes. "Prepare him for what, exactly?"

He doesn't blink. "For the bond."

I stare. "Oh hell no."

Varek's mouth tightens. "Sonny—"

"No." I cross my arms. "If you're thinking of nudging him towards this 'fated mate' thing to flip the prince to our side, you can fuck right off."

He exhales, but I see the flicker of guilt in his expression. "It would be advantageous—"

"To who?" I snap. "Because it sure as shit wouldn't be to Dawson."

Varek studies me, probably weighing whether to argue. But then his shoulders ease just slightly. "You're protective."

"Damn right." I lift my chin. "Spent enough years in the club scene seeing people get pressured into shit they didn't want. Not on my watch."

There's a long pause. Then—

Varek sighs. "You're right."

Wait, what?

He gives me a small, approving nod. "I respect your stance. And I appreciate your loyalty to your own kind."

I blink. "You—are you actually apologising?"

Varek's mouth twitches. "Don't push it."

I smirk. "Noted."

Then, rubbing the back of my neck, I add, "Look, I'll talk to Dawson. Get him up to speed. But no pressure, all right?"

He nods. "Agreed."

I exhale. "Good." Then I gesture towards the

kitchens. "Now, if you'll excuse me, I need to get our rock-wielding survivor some food before he passes out."

Varek actually huffs a quiet laugh as he steps aside. And with that, I head off, already mentally preparing for how I'm going to support and protect Dawson. I make it about ten steps down the dimly lit hall before I run into a wall.

Not a literal wall. No, that'd be kinder. Instead, I find myself face to face with a Glowranth royal guard. Every part of me goes on high alert.

The moment he sees me, his entire body stiffens, shoulders locking, jaw tensing, like I've just personally offended him by existing in his vicinity.

All right, then.

I'm not looking for a fight—hell, I just want to grab food and get back to Dawson before he spirals—but something about the way this guy holds himself pisses me off immediately.

He's tall. Taller than me by a solid foot, which, fine, a lot of people are. But it's the way he *feels* tall that gets to me. Like the height's not just genetic luck but something he wields, something he knows makes him untouchable. Like he's been bred for it, trained for it.

And he *has* been.

He's not just any Glowranth. He's the prince's personal guard. That means he's not just strong—he's dangerous.

And an arsehole, apparently.

He's talking to Shanae, and she doesn't seem remotely tense. That throws me. She's relaxed, her arms loosely crossed, head bobbing slightly as she listens. She even greets me easily.

"How's the human?" she asks.

Not *the man. The human.*

Something about the distinction sticks, so I need to be careful with how I respond.

"Awake," I say. "Tired and scared, but I don't think badly injured. Trying to process."

The Glowranth doesn't look at me. But he speaks. "Is he ready to see my prince?"

The words are clearly directed at me, but he doesn't actually *face* me when he says them.

Something in my blood heats.

I take my time turning fully to him, dragging my gaze over him in a slow, deliberate sweep. And okay, yes, *fuck*, he's beautiful. Not in a delicate way. Not even in a traditional way. It's that kind of beauty that's all sharp edges and impossible angles, something cut from stone and meant to intimidate.

His skin is deep, dark blue—darker than the prince's —and gleams faintly in the dim light. Not just gleams. *Pulses.* There's a faint bioluminescent glow along the ridges of his arms, slow-moving veins of light beneath his skin. It's hypnotic.

Infuriatingly so.

Something in my chest tightens with an urge I can't

quite name. My fingers twitch before I can stop them, and his gaze *snaps* to mine.

Shit.

There's nothing subtle about it. The second my fingers move, his eyes lock onto me, pinning me in place with an intensity that makes my breath hitch. It's not just his size. It's not just the sharp cut of his jaw or the way his muscles shift beneath that perfectly fitted uniform.

It's the way he looks at me. Like he *sees* me. And not in a way I like.

It's assessing. Calculating. Like he's searching for something, *expecting* something, and coming up empty.

And it pisses me off.

The second my brain catches up to my body's reaction, my spine locks straight, and I fix my expression into something deliberately neutral. I refuse to let him rattle me.

I clear my throat and finally answer, "No."

His response?

Dismissal.

No acknowledgment, no indication that I've even spoken. Just a flicker of movement, a polite excuse to Shanae, and then he's gone.

Shanae watches him leave, brow furrowing slightly. "Well, that was weird."

I glare at his retreating form. "What a cunt."

She snorts. "Kael didn't do anything. He's been

nothing but chill and, honestly, down to earth. Well, until just now."

"He didn't have to." I shake my head. "That's the worst kind of arsehole. The ones who act like you're beneath notice." And "down to earth"? I barely hold back my snort. That's not the Glowranth I've witnessed.

And Kael? I grind my molars. That's the arsehat's name? Stands to reason his name sounds like a green veg that tastes gross.

Shanae hums, clearly amused but not arguing.

I exhale sharply and turn to leave, my whole body still humming with irritation. But then, just before I disappear down the corridor—

I feel him.

Not see. *Feel.*

A presence just at the edge of my awareness. Heavy. Pressing. I glance back, but the hall is empty. Still, I can't shake the feeling that he's watching. Somewhere. I roll my shoulders, shrugging it off.

If the prince is anything like his guard, we've got a problem. And if either of them tries to get anywhere near Dawson? They've got another think coming.

CHAPTER
THREE

AFTER DAWSON SPENT THE NIGHT IN THE infirmary, he woke looking more rested and a lot less freaked out. I've explained to him in more detail what I know about the rifts and how they work and told him that Jack—who I've since learned is the Aussie who got sliced into this world from Queensland with his nephew, Jamie—arrived at the same time.

Dawson is well enough to move, so I'm showing him around the headquarters. Varek wants to meet him and get answers before he's willing to welcome him offi-cially. It's the usual way of things here. Varek's bad-arse ability to siphon out the truth comes in handy when figuring out who to trust.

I can only assume that Prince Aelith and his dick-head guard, Kael, are here because Varek doesn't view them as a direct threat. Though Varek hasn't told them about the location of Dathanor yet either.

"You can trust Varek." I push reassurance into my tone and offer Dawson a kind smile. "He can be a bit intense, and I know it can be intimidating when you first meet him, but he has all of our best interests at heart." It's what I believe soul deep.

Varek has gone to bat for me so many times—and everyone in our community, including the arsehole members. It's because of that he has my loyalty. Not to say I'll roll over if I don't agree with what he's saying. Case in point is me not pushing Dawson to meet Aelith. I've yet to explain the whole "fated mates" thing, and for whatever reason, after my slip yesterday, Dawson hasn't yet brought it back up. Thankfully.

"Right. Sure thing." Dawson doesn't seem convinced, but the guy is taking it all in his stride.

He runs a hand through his messy light brown hair, eyes flicking between me and the hallway ahead. "So, this Varek guy," he says, voice still rough with sleep. "He's not gonna, like... do a mind probe on me or anything, right?"

I snort. "No, Dawson, he's not gonna mind-probe you."

He squints. "You said he can tell if I'm lying."

"Yeah, but not by, like, reading your brain."

Dawson doesn't look particularly reassured. "Right.

Just... by tearing out the truth like some kind of interrogation wizard?"

I sigh, rubbing the bridge of my nose. "I said siphon out the truth, not rip it out. He's not psychic. He just... has a way of knowing when someone's full of shit."

"Great," he mutters. "Guess I better not lie, then."

I shoot him a look. "You planning to?"

"No, but what if I accidentally do?" He spreads his arms in exasperation. "Like, what if I say something wrong and he thinks I'm shady? I've been here a day, mate. Half the time, I don't even know what the hell I'm talking about."

If that's the case, he's got a point.

I sigh and pat his shoulder. "Just be yourself."

Dawson tilts his head, considering. "You sure? Because back home, being myself mostly involves avoiding responsibility, snowboarding, and convincing tourists I know more about wine than I do."

I roll my eyes. "Yes, I'm sure. Varek will appreciate honesty."

He hums. "And if he doesn't?"

I flash him a grin. "Then we run."

He barks out a laugh, shaking his head. "Fantastic. Love that for us."

The door ahead slides open with a hiss, and we step into one of the private meeting rooms used for sensitive discussions.

Varek is already inside, his hulking form leaning

against the table, arms crossed. He straightens when we enter, those piercing silver eyes locking onto Dawson in a way that makes the poor guy visibly tense.

I don't blame him.

Varek is humanoid, but only just. His deep, iridescent purple skin shifts under the dim lights, an oil-slick shimmer rolling over his massive frame. His horns curve elegantly from his temples, framing a face that is both striking and unnerving.

It's not just his size that makes him intimidating—it's his presence. It commands. Like he could crush you without moving a muscle.

But instead of an immediate interrogation, he studies Dawson for a long moment, expression unreadable. Then his eyes flick to me before returning to Dawson. His voice is low, but not unkind. "You were unconscious when you arrived."

Dawson nods. "Yeah, apparently."

Varek tilts his head slightly. "And when you woke, you were... cold?"

Dawson blinks. "I guess? I dunno. I was more focussed on the whole 'where the hell am I' thing."

I frown. "Wait, so the whole cold thing wasn't because he'd been out in the snow?" As soon as I speak, I scrunch my nose, realising that it obviously wasn't since he'd been here, well away from the snow in Portugal, for a few days.

Varek's gaze lingers on Dawson before shifting back

to me. "When Aeroth examined him, his body temperature was noticeably lower than expected. Not dangerously so, but unusual."

I process that, recalling how cool Dawson was to the touch. "Okay... but why?"

Varek exhales slowly, as if choosing his words carefully. "I have a theory. The rift that brought Dawson here is... different."

I narrow my eyes. "Different how?"

He folds his arms. "Most rifts pull from a specific location. A singular tear, leading from one place to another. But this one...." He glances at Dawson. "It sliced across Earth itself, didn't it? Pulled from multiple locations?"

I nod, realisation dawning. "You think that affected him somehow?"

Varek doesn't answer immediately, but his expression darkens with thought. "It's possible."

Dawson raises a hand awkwardly. "Uh, just to clarify. You're saying I'm some kind of rift anomaly?"

Varek's lips twitch slightly, almost amused. "Potentially."

Dawson considers that. "Does that come with any benefits? Like, do I get laser vision or something?"

I press my lips together to keep from laughing. Varek, to my surprise, actually smiles—a rare thing. "Unlikely."

Dawson sighs dramatically. "Well, that's disappointing."

I shake my head, exhaling sharply. "Okay, but aside from his temperature being weird, is there anything we should be worried about?"

Varek studies Dawson again before answering. "Not immediately. But we should monitor him."

Dawson shrugs. "Cool. I'm fine with that."

There's a beat of silence, and then Dawson glances between us, rubbing the back of his neck. "So... what's the plan for getting me back home?"

I wince.

Varek doesn't immediately answer. His silver gaze flickers to me, as if checking to see if I want to handle this one. I don't. I don't want to be the one to break this to Dawson. But the weight of it already sits heavy in my chest.

Varek sighs, standing straighter, his massive frame casting a shadow over the room. "The rifts have been happening for over a human decade. Maybe even two." His voice is calm, measured. "No one knows why. No one has ever been able to control them. And no one who has come through has ever found a way back—that we know of."

Dawson doesn't speak at first. His fingers flex slightly at his sides, but his face remains steady. He nods once, slow and thoughtful, then exhales through his nose. "Right. So, stuck here, then."

It's not a question.

I can't help the way my chest tightens. Because even though I've been here for years, even though I've carved out a place for myself in this world, it still stings to hear it laid out so plainly.

Dawson takes it with a kind of quiet acceptance. No tears. No yelling. Just that same steady composure, like a guy who's too used to going with the flow to fight against the current.

He doesn't panic. He doesn't react the way most people would. It throws me a little.

Varek watches him closely, as if assessing, then nods approvingly. "You're taking this well."

Dawson snorts. "Mate, my life was already pretty weird. Now it's just... a different kind of weird."

I huff a laugh despite myself. "*Different* is one way to put it."

Dawson shrugs, shoving his hands into the pockets of his borrowed pants. "I mean, don't get me wrong. It's insane. But it's not like screaming about it is gonna change anything." He tilts his head, considering. "And it's not the worst place to be stuck, I guess. Got weirdly hot monsters—uhm, shit, no offence," he says quickly to Varek. "It's got weirdly hot different species and some solid hospitality."

I blink.

Varek arches a brow, clearly amused.

Dawson smirks. "Don't look at me like that. I'm just

saying, if I'd landed in some *Mad Max*, cannibal-infested wasteland, then yeah, maybe I'd be losing my shit. But this?" He gestures vaguely. "Seems all right so far."

My lips twitch. "You do realise we're literally in a rebel hideout, right? And didn't you nearly get killed just yesterday?"

"Yeah," he says easily, "but you seem to be doing okay, so how bad can it be, especially now I'm here?"

Varek actually chuckles, a deep, rumbling sound that I don't hear often. "You're an unusual one."

Dawson flashes him a grin. "So I've been told."

Varek shakes his head, the faintest trace of a smirk lingering before his expression sobers. "You should at least understand why we're fighting. You'll need to know what kind of world you're in now."

Dawson straightens slightly. "Yeah, I guess that'd be useful."

Varek steps around the table, his presence somehow even heavier when he moves. "We call ourselves the Riftborn Rebels. Most of us—myself included—are species that have been displaced, hunted, or forced under the rule of the queen."

Dawson's brow furrows. "Queen?"

"The ruling empire of this world. The one who decides who lives, who dies, and who gets used."

Dawson exhales, nodding slowly. "Right. Sounds bad."

Varek's expression darkens. "It is."

Dawson doesn't ask for specifics. Not yet. Instead, he crosses his arms, thoughtful. "So, what's the goal, then? Overthrow the evil overlord—lady?"

I grin. "Basically."

Dawson tilts his head. "And how's that going?"

Varek's jaw tightens slightly. "We're working on it."

Dawson watches him for a moment, then nods. "Well, if I'm not heading home, I can be down with that. But if it comes to any battle shit, like *Game of Thrones* meets *Lord of the Rings*, I'm not sure how handy I'll be."

I snort. "What, no sword-fighting experience?"

He scoffs. "Mate, I spend summers teaching rich Europeans how to snowboard and winters running ski tours in New Zealand. My muscles are strictly for balance and making beer runs."

Varek smirks. "We'll find another use for you."

Dawson laughs. "Great. Looking forward to it."

That's when the door opens again.

And Kael walks in.

My entire body stiffens on instinct. I haven't seen him since yesterday, and yet the second he enters, I feel him before I see him. Like an invisible pressure in the air, something weighty and charged.

His posture is the same as always—spine straight, shoulders squared, every movement measured and precise. He doesn't so much as glance at me before locking his piercing gaze onto Dawson.

And immediately, I don't like it.

I step in, shifting slightly so I'm positioned between them—not obviously, not enough to make a scene, but enough that Kael will have to look at me if he wants to continue this silent scrutiny.

It works.

His piercing gaze flicks to mine, unreadable and intense. A static-like charge prickles along my skin under the weight of it. He holds my gaze for all of three seconds before dismissing me entirely.

Arsehole.

Varek, to my surprise, doesn't immediately intervene. Instead, he leans back against the table, arms crossed, watching closely. There's something unreadable flickering behind his silver gaze, something sharp and calculating.

Finally, Kael speaks, and when he does, his voice is low and clipped. "The human has been requested."

I don't like the way he says it. "Requested?" I echo, tone flat. "By who?"

His jaw tenses, but his voice remains neutral. "Aelith."

Interesting that he doesn't call him *prince*.

Varek still doesn't jump in. He just watches. The pause stretches, and my gut tightens.

I know why Varek is holding back. He wants

Dawson to meet Aelith. That much was clear yesterday, even though he apologised for being pushy. The prince is valuable. His alliance could tip the scales.

And Dawson?

Dawson is the key.

The problem is, Dawson doesn't even know what the key unlocks. And the last thing I want is for him to be manipulated into something he doesn't understand. Kael's presence here means Aelith is already trying to get his claws in, which makes my hackles rise further.

I step forwards, shoulders squaring. "Why exactly does the *prince* want to see him?"

Kael's gaze sharpens. "That is not your concern."

I scoff. "Yeah, see, it kind of is."

Varek finally speaks, though his voice remains measured. "Kael. This is an unusual situation. It's understandable that there would be concerns."

Kael barely moves, but his energy shifts slightly— like he's acknowledging Varek's words without outright agreeing.

I press my advantage. "If Aelith wants to meet Dawson," I say, keeping my voice steady, "then I am concerned. And I want to know why."

Kael's bioluminescent ridges pulse faintly, and for a second, something flickers behind his gaze. Annoyance? Amusement? I can't tell.

I brace for a fight.

But then Kael simply exhales and says, "He wants to assess him."

That… is not a great answer.

Dawson looks at me. "Did you say prince, as in a prince to the evil queen?" His eyebrows are high by the time he stops speaking.

"One and the same," I add helpfully, even as a wisp of doubt forms in my gut. Should I be fighting them meeting so hard? They're fated mates, apparently, and even Prince Fuckwit wouldn't have the need to lie about that. But still, I refuse to allow Dawson to be railroaded. The snowboarder is sweet as pie. I would hate for the prince to sour any of that.

"Huh. No shit." Dawson shrugs and returns his focus to Kael. "Assess me how, exactly?"

Kael doesn't answer, which makes me really not like the implications.

I open my mouth to argue further, but Varek—who has been watching this entire exchange with rapt interest—cuts in smoothly. "Perhaps Sonny should accompany us."

Dawson, ever unbothered, just shrugs. "Yeah, cool. I can meet another blue dude like you. He's not gonna try to eat me or anything, right? My man Sonny here promised me I was safe. I am, yeah?"

There's something oddly trusting about the way he says it. Like he fully expects me to keep my word. And that does something to my chest. I exhale, nodding. "Yeah, Dawson. You're safe."

Kael straightens his huge form, raises his fisted hand, and pats it against the centre of his chest. "Dawson," he starts, his voice deep and heavily accented. "You have my oath that no harm will come to you while I am around."

Surprise sends my brows shooting high. Kael absolutely has my full attention. Oaths here are some serious shit, mixed with some special juju. That he's made such a bold oath is... honestly, it's interesting and kinda sweet. Words like that mean he'll protect Dawson from physical harm from everyone and everything, as long as it's within his power.

Including from his prince.

"Very cool of you, Kael. 'Preciate it." Dawson's grin is megawatt bright. His reaction, his honesty, and his complete acceptance of Kael's words loosen some of the tension that has kept my muscles taut since Kael entered the room.

Varek's gaze flicks to me again. If he's as surprised by the oath as I am, he doesn't show it. There's something careful about the way he speaks. "Good. Then we'll eat first. There's food available in the communal area."

With Kael's oath and Dawson's reaction, I don't know if I just got manoeuvred into agreeing, but somehow, we've got a breakfast to get through. And after that? Dawson's going to meet Aelith, and I have to go with him.

I'm just not quite sure how I feel about any of it.

BREAKFAST IS TURNING OUT TO BE A surprisingly pleasant affair.

I say surprisingly because, one: Kael has been with us this entire time, which I assumed would make my meal difficult to digest. And two: I just put something in my mouth that looks like the unholy love child of an octopus and a pufferfish.

It has tentacles.

But damn if it doesn't taste like the most tender, buttery scallop I've ever had.

The first time I ate on Terrafeara, I barely kept anything down. Between the weird textures, pungent smells, and the sheer wrongness of some of the colours (food should not be that shade of electric blue), I struggled. But now? Sure, I'd commit a felony—maybe light arson—for a sausage sizzle or a lamington, but my palate has adapted.

Mostly.

Still, food aside, the bigger surprise is Kael.

Somehow—don't ask me how—we end up sitting next to each other. It isn't planned, at least not on my end, and I'd rather rip my own arm off than admit how hyperaware I am of him the entire time.

Which is infuriating, because he hasn't so much as looked at me properly.

And yet he's strangely charming.

Not to me, obviously. No, the arsehole is still avoiding eye contact like I carry some kind of contagious disease. But with Dawson? Sweet as. He answers his questions, listens with what looks like genuine interest, and even cracks what I think is supposed to be a joke at one point.

And Dawson laughs. Like, full-bodied, head-thrown-back laughs. Which is probably the only reason I don't kick Kael under the table for being so insufferably likeable.

But just when I start to relax, just when I think I can actually eat in peace, his voice—low and deep—brushes against my ear. "So, how long have you been here?"

I jump.

Not a big jump, but enough that my knee knocks against the table with a dull thud.

His breath is warm against my skin. Close. Too close.

I turn my head slightly, but he's already angled away, staring straight ahead like he didn't just drop his voice an inch from my damn ear. His bioluminescent markings pulse faintly along his arms, betraying nothing.

Still, the question throws me.

Why would Kael be asking me personal questions? He hasn't to anyone else around breakfast.

"Uh." I clear my throat, trying to will my heart rate back to normal. "I don't know exactly. But fifteen rifts have happened since I got here."

That catches his attention. His gaze flickers towards me—almost.

"You track them?"

I nod. "They're a big deal. Sometimes humans come through. Sometimes...." I hesitate, then shrug. "Sometimes other species do."

Kael hums low in his throat, something thoughtful about the sound. Then he asks, "What was your life like on Earth?"

And that's what really surprises me. No one's ever asked me that before. Not really. People assume. People project. But Kael? He *wants* to know.

I shift, pushing my empty plate away. "I worked in clubs. Managed one for a while when my boss couldn't get a replacement."

Kael tilts his head slightly. "Clubs?"

I huff a quiet laugh. "Yeah, something called nightclubs. A place where people go to have fun, dance, move their bodies...." Here, I know I should stop for all the obvious reasons, but where's the fun in that? I continue, "Usually end up getting down and dirty... hooking up."

His lips twitch—not quite a smile, but close. "Down and dirty?"

"Sometimes people get dirty in a fun way that doesn't involve grime or mud."

Kael leans in slightly, his voice dipping lower. "Do you mean exchanging *bodily* fluids?"

There's something almost teasing about it. My brain short-circuits for a second. Is he...? No.

Nope.

I must have imagined it.

Except now I'm thinking about it. Thinking about *him*.

I don't know much about Glowranthian cities, what they do for fun, or how they unwind when they're not training or fighting. Kael is a warrior—his entire species is—but something tells me that as the prince's personal guard, he has no real concept of a good time.

How can he when his mission in life is to protect a prick of a prince?

But holy shit. Am I flirting with him? Is he flirting with me?

The guy asks me a couple of personal questions, shows some vague interest in my life, and suddenly I'm wondering if he's ever had a drink or danced or done anything remotely fun... and dirty.

Like I'm not supposed to remember that the sovereign state he protects is responsible for capturing Riftborn.

Kael watches me, his expression unreadable. "Did

you...? Is that...? I am asking if it was... an honourable profession."

I freeze. Something hot and sharp coils in my gut. The number of times I received flack for being in the nightclub industry was honestly tedious. And sure, I sometimes used to show my *ass*ets, because I have a great arse, and it was super bloody fun dressing up and getting attention. I certainly shook my butt when having a good time, and yes, a time or five I was mistaken for offering additional skills for a pretty sum—which, by the way, I never took.

But still, I'm not sure if he's taking the piss or implying something more. Either of those options has my guard shooting up.

"Why?" I ask quietly, my voice deceptively calm despite the fire licking at my chest. Because fuck him. As if anything he does for the almighty sovereign state is remotely honourable. "Would it be dishonourable if I did *sex* work?"

Kael tenses. His fingers twitch against the table.

For the first time since we sat down, he turns slightly—just enough for his gaze to flicker towards me before he catches himself and looks away again. And just when I think I'm about to get an argument, an excuse, something—

"I apologise," he says. "I did not intend to offend or even imply that you do not have honour."

It throws me off so hard that I forget to be mad for half a second.

Then Varek—who had definitely been listening—stands and stretches. "Time to move. We'll head to the east quarters."

Breakfast is officially over.

We leave quickly. It's a short walk, maybe just ten minutes to the east section of the headquarters' compound, just outside the bowling alley. As we walk, Dawson is ahead, chatting with Varek.

Kael walks beside me. I don't know why that surprises me, but it does. Especially after the way he threw me for a loop at breakfast. Admittedly, I may have jumped the gun a little with my interpretation, but with how quickly he apologised, maybe not.

I expected him to move ahead, keep his distance—he's been avoiding eye contact like it might set him on fire, after all. But here he is, his massive frame keeping perfect pace with mine.

For a while, neither of us speak.

Then, impulsively, I ask, "What's the process for bonding with a fated mate for Glowranth?"

Kael stumbles.

It's barely noticeable—just the faintest hitch in his step—but I see it. It's so damn unexpected that I stop walking entirely, just so I can soak in the moment. Kael stops, too, rigid as ever, his face carefully blank. But I'm watching him now, and yeah, that tiny flicker in his eyes? That's discomfort.

Interesting.

Slowly, finally, his gaze meets mine. There's something there—something uncertain, tightly wound, like he's treading carefully on unfamiliar ground. "I...." He hesitates. "It is... different for each species."

"I know that." I cross my arms, watching him closely. "That's why I asked."

His jaw tightens, and then—just for a second—his lips twitch. Not quite a smirk, not quite a frown. Just a flicker of something... teasing?

Kael? Teasing?

"Curious, are you?"

Oh, he has jokes now?

"Yeah," I say, leaning in slightly. "What, is it some big secret? You make a sacred blood pact? Dance naked under three moons? Maybe wrestle a two-headed bear?"

He exhales through his nose—a short, amused sound. "If only," he murmurs.

"Come on, then." I arch my brow in challenge, holding back my grin, not wanting to give him the satisfaction of knowing that I'm enjoying this way too much. "What's the deal?"

Kael glances away, then back again, like he's debating whether or not to tell me. Then, finally, he says, "There is a... recognition. A pull. It is immediate, though not always welcome."

I frown. "Not welcome?"

His fingers flex at his sides. "It is rare for the Glowranth." His voice is quiet. "I have only known of one in generations. The prince. And as you know, he is unbonded."

There's something in the way he says it. A weight. A tension so sharp, I could cut myself on it. And I swear—just for a heartbeat—I feel something ripple through the air between us.

Something warm. Tangible.

But then—

"Why do you ask?" Kael's voice is smooth, neutral. Too neutral.

I blink.

Damn. I did just ask that out of nowhere, huh? For some reason, I feel a little defensive now, which is ridiculous.

"No reason," I say, forcing a shrug. "I just... I've never met a mated Glowranth before, which I suppose makes sense since there haven't been any for generations." Which is weird, right?

Kael tilts his head, considering me in that unreadable way of his. "Would you like to?"

The way he says it makes my stomach flip, though I have no idea why. "Well, sure," I say, trying to sound casual. "Research purposes." But also, what the hell am I talking about? For one, I've seen the prince and am even on the way to see the dickhead now. Plus, he's not a Glowranth I want to get to know.

And really? *Research purposes?*

Kael makes another one of those low, amused sounds. As if sensing that I've got way too comfortable with this whole thing... with him—which, spoiler alert: I haven't since I'm full of shit—he straightens his posture, clears his throat, and promptly turns into a brick wall of avoidance again.

Damn it.

Before I can push further, we reach the east quarters. Dawson and Varek are already inside.

Kael exhales, steps ahead, and schools his face back into that unreadable mask of his. And just like that, whatever moment we were having is gone.

And I suspect, if Kael and Aelith have their way, I'll be meeting a fully bonded Glowranth as soon as Dawson's clued in and says yes.

CHAPTER
FOUR

I DON'T KNOW WHY I'M SURPRISED THAT I END UP with Kael while Aelith manages to steal Dawson away. Not that they've gone far—just a few metres across the communal space—but the prince's pointed look and his quietly uttered words in Glowranthian made it clear: *Kael, give us space.*

Which means I've been forced to sit here, across from Kael and Varek, with nothing to do but make awkward conversation or stare at the walls. Admittedly, I *could* just keep my mouth shut. But silence is not, and never has been, my strong suit.

Varek, for his part, made an effort at first. But once he saw that Aelith and Dawson were actually getting along—and, more importantly, once Dawson *laughed*— he decided his work was done.

And, just like that, he abandoned me.

His excuse was thin at best. Something about leaving the new human in *capable hands*. Mine, specifically. Then, with an infuriating smirk, he walked off.

So, once again, I'm left with Kael.

And honestly, I don't even know why I'm annoyed about it—beyond his casual rudeness, his clipped responses, and the fact that he rarely looks me in the eye. It's starting to get to me in ways I don't quite understand.

I huff a quiet sigh and lean back in my chair, tilting my head towards the ceiling. "So, this is fun."

Kael doesn't answer immediately. I expect silence. Instead—

"How did you come across the rebels?"

I blink. That... isn't what I expected. My gaze snaps to his, eyes narrowing with suspicion. "Why do you want to know? Looking for intel?"

If I'd been expecting a scoff, a glare, or even a dry, unimpressed *Really?*—none of it comes. Instead, Kael just shakes his head. "No." His voice is calm, even. "I only asked because I realise I never have."

His expression gives nothing away. But the way his glowing markings pulse—slow, steady—makes me think he means it.

I exhale sharply. "Fine. Since you're so interested." Though why he is makes no sense to me. We met—and I use that term super loosely—just yesterday.

His gaze stays locked on me. *Actually* locked. For

once, he isn't looking away, isn't staring past me or keeping his focus deliberately neutral. No, he holds my gaze—unwavering, unflinching, like he's peeling back layers I hadn't realised were visible.

It's unnerving. Intimate. And it makes it impossible to brush him off.

So, I tell him.

I don't embellish. I don't dramatize.

I just lay it out.

"I nearly died when I first got here."

Kael stiffens.

I pretend not to notice. "There was a...." I hesitate, then grimace. "I don't actually know what it was. Had the body of a panther—a big cat—but way too many teeth. And these ridges down its spine that kept shifting, like it was deciding whether or not to grow more."

Kael's eyes narrow slightly, his focus sharpening. "A Rithak."

"Great. It has a name." I tap my fingers against my abdomen. "Left me a nice little souvenir, though."

Before I can talk myself out of it, I lift the hem of my shirt just enough to reveal the scar that curves along my side. It's jagged, the edges rough, like something took a good chunk out of me. Which, to be fair, it did.

Kael's eyes snap to it. The glow from his markings flares, then dims. His hands tighten into fists against his thighs. "How did you survive?" His voice is quieter now, but there's an edge to it.

I let my shirt drop back down. "Something bigger got to it first. I ran."

Kael's frown deepens. "You were all alone for how long?" His voice is low, almost a growl.

"Five days." I lean back again, forcing a casual shrug. "I'm a hell of a lot more nonchalant about it now than I was back then. But if it wasn't for Varek saving my arse, we wouldn't be sitting here having this conversation right now."

Kael doesn't respond. Something about the way his muscles are locked, the sharpness of his jaw, makes me think he's *not* nonchalant about it.

I tilt my head. "What, you upset you weren't there to save me?"

His gaze flickers to mine, just for a second.

"Don't worry," I continue, trying to ignore the strange tension in his expression. "Since being here, I've worked my butt off getting stronger, learning to survive. I just need Varek to let me prove myself so I can head out there with one of the crew."

Something in his expression tightens—so unreadable that my stomach twists. It's like I've stumbled onto something I wasn't meant to. That, or he's laughing on the inside at the idea of me thinking I'm good enough to survive outside this safe haven.

I sit up straighter, breaking the moment. "What about you? How does one become the prince's ever-so-silent, ever-so-scowly bodyguard?"

Kael exhales slowly, as if deciding whether to humour me. Then "It is in my blood."

I wait. "That's it?"

He inclines his head slightly. "My ancestors have always served the royal family."

I frown. "You don't sound particularly proud of that."

His silence speaks volumes. Interesting.

I shift slightly, watching him. "Ever capture any Riftborn?"

He stills.

Subtle, I am not. But to my surprise, he doesn't bristle. He doesn't get defensive. His fingers curl against his knees, and after a long pause, he says, "I had to. As part of my training."

I study him closely, noting the way his glow dims. It doesn't seem like something he enjoyed.

"But you don't now?"

"No." His jaw tightens. "I never... took to that part of the job."

I arch a brow. "And yet you became not just part of the royal guard but accepted a position I suspect is high-ranking considering you're the bodyguard to the prince."

"I saved Aelith."

That catches my attention. "Really? Before you were on his protection detail?" I hold back my lip twitch. It sounds like I've been watching a whole heap of bodyguard movies. If only. Damn, do I miss movies.

Kael nods. "It was not my job, but... it happened."

I almost smirk. "Did you get in trouble for it?" I know enough about the Glowranth to understand what sticklers for rules they are.

His lips twitch. Just barely. "No."

And just like that, I start to see it—something deeper than just the prince's bodyguard. He trusts Aelith, sure. But Aelith *trusts him*. Enough to override whatever hierarchy was in place to keep him close.

I glance towards where Dawson and Aelith are still talking, laughter slipping through the space between us. Then, absently, my gaze drifts to the window. I let out a slow breath. The view is both familiar and deeply unsettling.

The green sky stretches overhead, streaked with ribbons of gold where the sun hovers low. The trees beyond the compound are *too* tall, their leaves *too* sharp, like blades waiting to slice through anything careless enough to brush against them.

And the fence—the heavy, reinforced line of defence that surrounds this place—is a necessity, not an aesthetic choice. Because out there? Out there, everything wants to kill you.

Kael shifts beside me, and I glance at him. His gaze is still locked on me, his markings still dimmed, but his expression is unreadable again.

I open my mouth to say something, then think better of it.

He exhales through his nose—almost a laugh, but not quite. Then, to my complete and utter shock, he says, "I could train you."

I almost fall off my chair.

Okay, no—I *do* fall off my chair.

It's not graceful. There's a very unflattering thump as my backside hits the floor, and across the room, Dawson chuckles. "You all right over there?" he calls.

Kael's hand hovers like he's considering helping me. But before I can process it, his fingers curl into a fist, and he pulls back.

Something tightens in my chest. I swallow it down, pretending it doesn't bother me. I push myself up, dusting off imaginary dirt, then fix Kael with a suspicious look. "You want to train me?"

His expression flickers—uncertainty, hesitation— but then he straightens, shoulders squaring. "Yes."

I wait for more, but he doesn't elaborate. I arch a brow. "Why?"

His jaw clenches. "I am here with the prince anyway. Aelith has no plans to leave—not with the increased risks to Riftborn. As long as he is safe, I may as well make myself useful."

I glance towards Aelith, a little surprised. He looks attentive, letting Dawson dominate the conversation. I can't hear what they're saying, but the fact that Dawson has his full focus is... unexpected.

Kael's voice pulls my attention back. "When I do leave with the prince and his fated, at least I will know you are safe."

Something about the way he says it—something in the intensity of his gaze—makes my stomach clench. Then, just as quickly, he looks away. The unease in my gut settles deeper. It must be the thought of Dawson being out there, alone with royalty.

Nothing to do with Kael. Nothing to do with the shitload of mixed signals he's sending me.

I take a breath, still studying Kael. He's hard to read, but there's something in the way he said it—*at least I will know you are safe*—that lingers. I don't know what to do with it, so I shove it aside. Instead, I roll my shoulders and cross my arms. "Fine."

His head tilts slightly. "Fine?"

I nod. "I'll take you up on your offer. You've got to be good at what you do, right? Considering who you protect."

His expression doesn't change, but I swear there's something different about the way he looks at me— something charged, like he's testing the weight of my words before deciding how to respond.

Finally, he inclines his head, as if my decision was inevitable. "We will start tomorrow."

I smirk. "Oh, so now you're making decisions for me?"

His eyes narrow slightly, but there's no irritation in them. "I assumed you would want to be prepared as soon as possible. Unless you are not as serious as you claim."

I bristle but bite my tongue. No way am I giving him the satisfaction of seeing me flustered. "Tomorrow, then," I say, lifting my chin slightly.

Something unreadable flickers across his face, but before I can even begin to pick it apart—

Aelith calls out.

There's a sharp edge of distress in his voice that sends a jolt through me. Kael is already moving before I fully register what's happening, his entire body snapping into action.

I twist towards the sound, and worry slams into my gut.

Dawson.

He's collapsed.

Aelith is holding him carefully, his expression carved with something close to panic.

I lurch forwards, my chair scraping against the floor as I shove past it, but Kael is already there, kneeling beside them. His bioluminescent markings pulse brighter, his sharp gaze raking over Dawson's unmoving form.

"What happened?" His voice is clipped, controlled.

Aelith shakes his head. "I don't know. He just—he was talking, and then suddenly—"

I don't hear the rest.

Dawson is *too* still. His face is pale, his lips almost blue.

A sickening wave of dread crashes through me. I shove past Kael, dropping to my knees. "Put him down," I demand, already reaching for Dawson.

Aelith doesn't move. His hold tightens, and his glowing eyes snap to mine, narrowed with something sharp and territorial. Protective. "No." His voice is low, warning.

I don't care. I push against him, trying to pry Dawson from his grip. "He's not breathing, Aelith. Let me help him."

Aelith growls, the sound curling around my ribs like an instinctive threat. His aura pulses—a presence pressing against me, telling me to back off. A flicker of fear claws through my chest. He's terrifying like this.

But I don't stop.

I can't.

Kael moves before I can even react. He steps between us, hand pressing firmly against Aelith's shoulder, voice low and even. "Let him go."

Aelith's glowing markings pulse bright, his chest rising and falling too fast, his grip still tight on Dawson.

"Aelith." Kael grips Aelith's shoulder. "Let Sonny help him. They are both human."

For a moment, I think the prince will fight him. That he'll shove me away and keep Dawson caged in his arms. But Kael doesn't back down. His hold is solid, grounding.

Something shifts.

Aelith blinks, his gaze flicking to mine. There must be something there—desperation, maybe—because he exhales sharply and lowers Dawson to the floor.

I don't waste time. I press my fingers to Dawson's throat. His pulse is there—weak, but there. But his chest isn't moving.

Not breathing.

I shove my panic deep, letting muscle memory take over. Nightclub work in Sydney—drunk idiots, overdoses, accidents. I've done this before. I can do it again.

I tilt Dawson's head back, open his airway, check for obstructions. Nothing.

"Come on, come on," I mutter, pinching his nose and sealing my mouth over his. I breathe for him. Watch his chest rise.

Again.

And again.

Aelith is silent after his first low warning rumble when I sealed my mouth over Dawson's. I glance up. Kael isn't watching Dawson. He's watching me. I feel the weight of his gaze, the intensity of it, but I can't afford the distraction. I focus and breathe for Dawson.

One, two, three—

A shudder jerks through Dawson's body. He coughs, his whole frame spasming as he sucks in a rattling breath.

Relief slams into me so hard, I nearly collapse. He's breathing. *He's breathing.* But he's still unconscious.

I press my fingers to his pulse again, steadying myself. "We need help. We need Aeroth. *Now.*"

Kael doesn't hesitate. He turns, calling for help—his voice sharp, commanding. Aelith doesn't move.

I glance at him. His expression is stricken, his intense eyes locked on Dawson's face like he can will him to wake up. Then, without a word, Aelith sinks to the floor beside him, his composure crumbling. He grabs Dawson's hand in both of his, bowing his head, his shoulders shaking.

It's not the reaction of a prince. It's the reaction of someone who cares.

Aeroth, our medic, arrives, kneeling beside me. I keep my voice steady as I run her through everything—pulse, breathing, response. She nods, moving efficiently as she checks Dawson over. Then she lifts him onto a stretcher brought in by a couple of Jigderias, Aelith rising instantly to follow.

Kael hesitates. He's looking at me.

I realise—too late—that I'm shaking. My hands won't stay steady. Adrenaline crash.

Kael reaches for me. His fingers hover just shy of my arm, like he's about to—

Aelith calls his name.

Kael clenches his jaw. Then, slowly, his hand tightens into a fist, and he pulls away. Without another word, he turns and follows his prince, leaving me sitting here alone.

Always a-fucking-lone.

I press my hands against my thighs, forcing in a deep breath.

Get it together, Sonny.

I glance towards Aeroth's retreating form. *See if they need help.*

Kael might be some elite warrior. Aelith might be a prince. But *I* know humans. Our medic found some books, sure—but I've watched enough *Grey's Anatomy* to pick up a thing or two.

And right now? That's going to have to be enough.

It's definitely enough to get my butt off the floor and make me stop feeling sorry for myself. Of course Aelith is terrified and needs his guard. Even though Dawson remains clueless, he and the prince are fated mates. From what I know, the prince will feel the bond acutely. Not so much for Dawson, who may feel some sort of attraction or pull, I suspect, to Aelith, but nothing hard-core or truly intense until they've completed the bond or at least some of the stages.

Or so I've heard. I can only assume it's the same for the Glowranth.

Drawing in a breath, I pull myself together. My

hands are still a little shaky, but I'm sure I'm not going to pitch over or make a twat of myself if I try to walk.

By the time I make it to the medical room—the same place I first set eyes on Dawson—I'm feeling more like myself. Aeroth looks up when I enter, the clicky language indicating she wants me here. I hold back my relieved sigh. I shouldn't feel joy knowing I'm useful, right? Especially not when a golden retriever of a sweet man collapsed and stopped breathing.

The thought sobers me up, and I take a moment to peer around the room.

Varek's already here, concern clear in the way he's holding himself. Aelith still has his hand clamped around Dawson's, and I assume from that—and him being in Aeroth's way—that he refuses to let go. My gaze shifts to Kael, and disappointment that's as ridiculous as it is real slams into me when I see his focus is completely on his prince.

I roll my eyes at myself before moving past them, not even giving a shit that I brush against—with a little more force than necessary—the hulk of a guard as I do. And fuck, the diva in me needs to wind his neck in. To be honest, I can't remember the last time I felt the need for my inner diva to step out. Certainly not since being in Terrafeara.

I kinda want to embrace it. I think that's what going without sex for so long has done to me—both addled my brain and made me be a petty bitch. Until I remind myself to do better and reluctantly put my claws away.

Right now, I should be doing just that, considering poor Dawson almost died.

Fuck, I'm a twat who needs to do better and ideally stop having inner meltdowns while a bunch of folks are standing around worried and apparently waiting for me to say or do something. Because yes, Aelith's eyes are on me.

"You saved him." His voice is gruff. The emotion trapped in his throat makes me squirm with discomfort.

"Uhm, hopefully. I got him breathing at least." The slightest of smiles forms on my lips, uncomfortable offering the prince any kind of sympathy. But I'm not a complete cunt.

"Save him again. Wake him up. If not, there will be consequences."

My brows shoot high at the heat, the cruel authority in the prince's tone. It's wrapped around what I'm sure is a very real threat. He's terrified, I know. But still... "What the fuck do you expect me to do? I don't have the ability to weave magic. I'm not a human doctor."

"You breathed life into him. Keep fixing him. If not—"

"Aelith." Kael reaches out and clamps his huge hand on his prince's shoulder. "Enough. Making threats will not work here. Sonny has done all he can. If there is more he can do, he will do so." He glances at me, his expression stoic, but there's emotion in his gaze that has me swallowing deeply and helps calm my irritation. "Right, Sonny?"

The question lacks demand, and the last of my ire falls away. "Of course I will."

Aeroth intervenes with a question I can only partially decipher, but it's enough for me to get the gist.

I nod at her and turn back to Aelith, whose luminous eyes are firmly on me. "Aeroth wants to know *exactly* what happened. When he stopped breathing, were there signs or clues?" I consider what else to ask to help him be as specific as possible. "Was Dawson talking, listening? Did you notice him eating anything different at breakfast?"

"Someone poisoned him?" Aelith stands abruptly, hand moving to where his sword should be. I'm kinda grateful Varek made them remove all their weapons as a condition of their entry.

But also, for fuck's sake. Dramatic and reactive much? I swear, there's only enough space for one drama queen, and I refuse to shed that title to a prince I wish would fuck right off.

The brush of a warm body pressing against my arm startles me. It's Varek. I hadn't even noticed him enter the room. His presence is immediately reassuring.

As I release a steadying breath, building up to call the prince a dickhead, I jolt at the gruff and absolutely menacing growl.

My gaze snaps to Kael in surprise. The fuck is he growling for? If he thinks for one second that his pain-in-the-arse prince can—

Varek's heat leaves my side, the growling cuts off, and loud pounding erupts in my ears.

What the holy fucking shit?

My eyes focus on Kael. He's staring hard at the place where Varek pressed against me.

That growl was low, guttural, and unmistakably possessive. I blink, barely processing the weight of Kael's stare locked on Varek before my brain jumps to the most ridiculous conclusion possible.

Holy shit.

Varek is Kael's mate.

It makes no fucking sense, but my thoughts latch onto it anyway. That's the only explanation for the primal sound rumbling deep in Kael's chest, for the way his body went rigid the second Varek touched me. Right?

Except... no. That can't be it.

Varek's been here for years, long before I ever stumbled into this world. And from what I understand, the bond doesn't wait. It doesn't delay. It sinks its claws in the moment the two fated souls are in the same space.

And Kael?

The guy has never looked at Varek with anything other than distant civility, the same way he regards every other person in this compound. Except for me when I think I'd have burnt to cinders a couple of times.

So then why the hell is he all growly and ridiculous?

There's a flicker of something sharp and unwanted in my chest, a quiet, ridiculous longing. Not that I want him to be my mate. Fuck that. I don't need some walking, brooding inferiority complex tied to me for eternity.

But if he were, I would know, wouldn't I?

I swallow, pushing the thought down, trying to ignore the way it needles at me. Humans don't feel the bond like others do. That's what I've been told. That's what I know. We don't get the soul-deep certainty, the overwhelming pull, not until the bonding starts.

Not that it matters. Kael is not my mate. And I don't care.

Before I can ask what the hell his problem is, the sharp, jerking motion of a body seizing pulls my attention back. Dawson convulses violently.

"Aelith, put him down!" My voice rings out, loud and powerful. I hadn't even realised he'd tugged him back into his arms.

The prince doesn't listen. His grip tightens on Dawson, as if sheer force of will alone will stop whatever is happening.

Aelith's snarl is absolutely inhuman. Monstrous. His glowing eyes snap up to me, and the weight of his fury is terrifying. His power crackles around him, a barely leashed storm. But I don't give a shit.

I shove forwards, only for Kael to move at the same time, positioning himself between us before Aelith can do something stupid. His voice is steady, calm in a way that seems to cut through the prince's spiralling rage.

"He is trying to help, Aelith." Kael's hand grips on his prince's shoulder, his hold firm but not forceful. "Let him."

Aelith hesitates. Just for a second.

It's enough.

I drop to Dawson's side as his body writhes, his limbs jerking in unnatural, painful spasms. My training kicks in, the old muscle memory of my first-aid courses and long nights working clubs in Sydney taking over.

"Shit—someone help hold him so he doesn't hurt himself."

Varek moves in first, his sheer size making it easy for him to keep Dawson's shoulders pinned. I shift to keep his head steady, my hands cradling it carefully to stop him from smashing it against the hard frame.

Kael doesn't move. He's still holding Aelith back. But his eyes are on me.

Not Dawson.

Me.

The fit continues, violent and relentless, and I bite the inside of my cheek hard to keep my own panic at bay. Seconds stretch unbearably long. Then, as suddenly as it started, it stops.

Dawson slumps, his chest rising and falling in uneven, gasping breaths. But he's breathing.

A heavy silence falls over the room. Everyone is looking at me, waiting for an explanation.

But fuck if I have one.

Aeroth crouches beside me, clicking something in her native language. Her brow is furrowed in frustration, her fingers trembling as she presses them to Dawson's pulse.

"He's breathing," Varek translates for her. "But this—this is not right."

No shit.

Aeroth is good. That much I know. She's patched up injuries, healed wounds I was sure would be fatal. But humans? That's different. And it's clear as she frowns down at Dawson's slack features that she's flying blind.

"I—" My mouth opens, then shuts. I don't know what to do. I don't know what's wrong with him. I don't know what caused this, and I don't know how to fix it.

But I know someone who might.

The reluctant thought settles, heavy and certain. "There's a human," I say, my voice measured. "A doctor. A surgeon. She passed through here a while back."

Varek's expression sharpens. "Iris."

I nod. "She bonded with one of the—" I hesitate, trying to find the right word. "—less friendly species."

Aelith exhales sharply, the tension in his frame shifting. "Where?"

"I know where they were heading. Her mate's territory."

Varek mutters a low curse under his breath. He already knows the problem. The species she bonded to doesn't play well with others. They're isolated for a reason. And if anyone else goes after them? They'll be killed on sight. No hesitation. No mercy.

"I'm the only one who might stand a chance at getting through to him," I finish. "Iris liked me. He almost tolerated me." The weight of that admission settles over the room.

Varek exhales, rubbing a hand down his face. "Sonny, you can't—"

"There's no other choice. Dawson needs help. We don't have the knowledge or resources here, but she might."

Aelith's sharp inhale draws my attention. He's calmer now, his earlier panic settled into something colder, more dangerous. "You're not going alone."

I don't have time to argue before he turns his attention to Kael.

"You'll escort him."

Kael straightens, his expression unreadable. There's the barest hesitation. The flicker of something I can't place in his gaze. Then he nods. "Understood," he says in Glowranthian.

And just like that, my fate is sealed, and I'm left wishing I hadn't been so eager to push myself and keep doing things for the greater good of the group. Why couldn't I have continued being a selfish prick?

CHAPTER
FIVE

I HAVE AN HOUR.

One fucking hour to get my shit together before I'm expected to haul arse with Kael, the Glowranth who can't decide if he wants to murder me or tolerate my existence. My stomach is in knots, but no way in hell am I making that obvious. I wanted adventure, right? I practically begged for it.

Well, here it is, and I'm one deep breath away from shitting myself.

As I make my way to my room, I leave the logistics of getting to Iris and her mate to Varek. The Hendroy are isolated for a reason—especially Iris's mate. If anyone else tried to get near him, they'd be dead before they even had the chance to wave a white flag. Lucky me, I'm the only one he might hesitate to rip apart.

Maybe.

Possibly.

Fuck.

It's a four-day walk at least. That's assuming we don't run into anything that wants to eat us, stab us, or generally make life miserable. And Dawson? He's barely hanging on. Will he even survive that long? I have no idea, and it's not a question I want to dwell on right now.

I need to focus. Packing. Right. What the hell do I even take? Everything I own is salvaged or traded for, and none of it is exactly ideal for trekking across God-knows-what kind of terrain while dodging certain death. Food? Water? Weapons? How many weapons is too many?

I'm nearly at my room when I run into the new guy who I haven't yet spoken to. Human. Tall. Broad shoulders. Wide grin. His eyes light up when he sees me, like he's actually relieved. It puts me at ease.

"You must be Sonny," he says, accent unmistakably Australian.

I blink, taking in the Akubra perched on his head. Shit, that makes me a little homesick.

"G'day," I say, reaching out to shake his hand. "And you're a tall drink of—" I stop mid-sentence as a massive red dude steps into view behind him. My brain short-circuits.

Pyronox.

I've never seen one in the flesh up close and

personal, but there's no mistaking the sheer size of him —all six-foot-plus, decked out in a leather kilt and strapped with more weapons than should be legally allowed.

I brace myself, half expecting him to snarl or growl or do something vaguely threatening. Instead, he beams at me.

"Humans are great," he says, voice deep as hell. "You could be Jack's friend."

Alrighty then.

Jack—the Aussie—shakes my hand, still grinning. "Jack," he confirms. "And you're Aussie too? Bloody hell."

"Small universe," I quip.

He laughs, but I don't have time to stand around and bond over meat pies and Vegemite.

"Listen, I'd love to stay and chat, but I've gotta move. The human you brought in—Dawson? He's not doing great. I'm heading out to find a doctor."

Jack nods, expression sobering. "You're going with Kael, then?"

I pull a face, not even surprised that he knows that. News travels fast here in Dathanor. "Unfortunately."

He looks surprised. "The Glowranth seems reasonable to me. Don't get me wrong, the prince is a prick, but his guard seemed like he was at least rational."

I snort. "Yeah, sure, if you like your reasonable with a side of broody and unpredictable."

Jack chuckles, and then his expression turns thoughtful. "How are you travelling?"

I shrug. "On foot." That's really the only way to go. There are other modes, but most require energy use that we don't have spare supply of here.

He whistles. "That's rough. You want my horse? Geralt's a good boy."

Geralt? Great name. But hell no.

"Appreciate it, but I'll pass," I say, grimacing. "Last time I dealt with a horse, I was seven. Bastard bit my fingers. Haven't trusted them since."

Jack shakes his head, but he doesn't push. Instead, he leans in slightly, lowering his voice. "From one Aussie to another—can we trust the rebels?"

I don't hesitate. "Yeah. There's some arsehats, and the politics are a mess, but Varek saved my life. I owe him everything."

He nods, mulling that over. "Good to know."

I grin. "Keep your room locked, though. Fringt— little grey dickhead, Dreting species—steals anything he can tie in knots."

Jack laughs, but if he knew what a nightmare it was trying to get by without a belt for a week while wearing pants two sizes too big because Fringt decided the leather strap was his new favourite toy, he wouldn't find it so funny.

Time's ticking. I clap Jack on the shoulder. "All right, mate. Gotta move."

"Wait," Jack says, and for the first time, his easy-going demeanour wavers. He hesitates, then glances at the Pyronox—his mate, I'm guessing—before looking back at me. "I—Solan and I—were hoping to talk to you before you left."

I frown. "About?"

"How you got here. And the rifts."

My stomach flips. Oh. I *get* it. He's new here. It's all overwhelming. But there's something about the way he asks that throws me. Something too intense. His mate shifts closer, his easy, fanged smile dimming.

Jack exhales. "I want to know how to get back."

My heart pangs. "There's no way to get home." My voice is quiet but firm. "Believe me. If there was, I wouldn't still be here."

Jack runs a hand down his face, looking frustrated. "It's not for me," he says finally. "It's for my nephew, Jamie. He's only twelve."

My chest aches.

I glanced at the kid who's stuck here yesterday, but twelve.... Fuck, that sucks. But thank *Christ* he has his uncle. At least he's not alone.

Jack watches me closely. "Do you know how the rifts are caused? If they're natural?"

I pause. "Natural? As in?"

He exhales sharply. "Could someone be causing them?"

Solan tenses, shooting Jack a wary look. "Careful," he warns.

Jack doesn't back down. Instead, he looks me dead in the eye and says, "Sonny is Aussie. If there's anyone I can trust, beyond you, Jamie, and Calythra, it'll be him."

My brain spirals. Jack thinks someone is responsible for the rifts? For bringing us here? My heart kicks up in my chest.

Who? Why? How?

It's too much to process. Not when I'm about to head out. Not when Dawson is possibly dying. Not when I'm already running on fumes.

Solan must sense it because he reaches for Jack's arm, gently pulling him back.

Jack exhales, giving me a reluctant nod. "We'll talk when you get back."

Well... at least *he* thinks I'm coming back. That's more faith than most folks will have in me, I suspect.

He nods, and I head off, mentally running through what else I need to grab before I'm stuck with Kael for four days of trekking through hell. Focussing on that at least helps me push what else he said to me away.

I shake off my unease and continue further into the heart of Dathanor. The cavern walls are rough beneath my fingertips as I trail my hand along them, the luminescent veins pulsing faintly in response to my touch. They hum with warmth, casting a soft glow that lights the narrow passageway leading to my room.

Before this place was in Terrafeara, it had been underground in another world. A hidden refuge ripped straight from one reality and stitched into another. Sometimes I wonder what it must have been like before, when underground, when surrounded by a floating lake or river. Amongst all the terror here, I can't help but wonder how life would have been if I'd ended up in a different dimension from this one.

But I don't have time to get philosophical about the cool, otherworldly badarsery of my surroundings. I have less than one hour before I'm expected to leave with a Glowranth who might very well kill me before the trip is even over.

Or worse—make me embarrass myself to death first. Because let's be honest, the big blue dude affects me, so of course my go-to is finding new and wonderful ways to humiliate myself.

I reach my room and start sorting through the mess I call belongings. Not that I own much. Everything I have, I either salvaged, stole, or traded for. And very little of it screams "appropriate for trekking through God-knows-what terrain while fighting off nightmares and trying not to get eaten."

Still, I do my best.

Clean undies. Because I may die, but I will die with dignity. Thick socks. Because blisters are a bitch. Sturdy walking boots I'd traded for something ridiculous (was it a broken radio? A spoon? Who even knows anymore). My weapons—because I'm not an idiot.

The dagger is my favourite. Small, deadly, and fits perfectly in the sheath at my waist. Close combat isn't ideal, but I'm short and wiry, which makes me fast. If I'm going to go down, at least I'll make it interesting.

With my pack mostly sorted, there's only one thing left to grab—food.

The mess hall is buzzing when I step in, and for the first time in my life, I seem to be the main attraction. Conversations lull, heads turn, and I hear my name whispered in the usual mix of concern, amusement, and barely concealed bets about whether or not I'll survive.

"Good luck," someone says.

"Try not to die," another chimes in helpfully.

Wow. So much faith in me. Really warms the heart.

Molsi and Decca are waiting for me near the food prep area, and the second they see me, I can tell they're anxious.

Molsi, their greyish skin shifting in patches of nervous agitation, clicks something in their native tongue before shaking their head. "You are going to get yourself killed."

Decca's fingers curl into fists as she exhales sharply. "You don't have to do this."

I wave them off. "Pfft. I'll be fine." Then, because I hate the lump forming in my throat, I add, "Besides, someone has to go save Dawson's cute butt. He's a sweetheart. Just wait till you meet the guy."

Molsi rolls their eyes but hands me a pack of food, the contents inside suspiciously lumpy and of unknown origin. I don't ask questions.

"Eat it," Decca orders. "Even if it looks back at you."

I take it with a theatrical grimace but with real gratitude. "You guys are the best. Kinda, maybe love you. Probably gonna miss you. Fuck off."

Molsi's lips twitch. "Touching."

But then Decca hands me a second pack, and my stomach sinks. "For Kael."

I stare at it. Then at her. Then back at the pack as if it might come to life and bite me. Something in my face must be hilarious because Molsi makes a delighted little noise, and Decca's eyes narrow in intrigue.

"So," Decca hums, all casual-like. "What's your deal with the Glowranth that's caused *that* reaction?"

"No deal," I say quickly. "There's no deal. I just— he's just—a dick."

"Uh-huh," Molsi drawls, clearly not buying it. "A sexy dick?"

I make a strangled noise. "That's not the point." And I really wish I hadn't taught either of them English words like *sexy*. I should have known my awesome teaching skill would come back to bite me on my own very *sexy* butt.

Decca grins. "Oh, but it is."

And just like that, I'm ranting.

It starts off strong. I say all the things I've been thinking. How Kael is the worst. How he keeps blowing hot and cold. How I don't understand him. How he represents the very thing that has slaughtered so many of the rebels.

And then.

Somehow.

It all goes downhill.

"I mean, I wanna punch him. Hard. Right in his stupidly perfect jaw."

Molsi makes an encouraging noise, clearly delighted.

"But also, God, is he sexy. And it's infuriating."

Decca outright cackles.

"And I don't even know if he has an arsehole!"

Dead silence.

"What?" Decca asks, breathless with laughter.

"I'm just saying! I don't know their anatomy! It's not exactly polite conversation to ask, is it?"

Molsi wheezes. "Hey, Kael, do you shit?"

I groan. "Shut up." But I'm not done. Oh no. I keep talking. "I bet he has a giant cock. It's always the broody ones."

Molsi is barely holding it together.

"Like, he could probably fuck me sideways with a smile. I'd come for days."

More silence.

I pause. Molsi and Decca are suspiciously quiet. Too quiet. A terrible feeling creeps up my spine.

Slowly, like a man who knows he's just walked into his own grave, I turn around. And there, standing with all the grace and amusement of a predator who has just caught his prey doing something deeply humiliating—

Kael.

Fuck.

I want to die. Just right here, on the floor. Let the luminescent veins in the stone swallow me whole.

Kael, to his credit, doesn't look angry. If anything, he looks entertained, which is almost worse. "I came for food," he says smoothly. "Didn't expect a full performance, though. Do continue."

I open my mouth. Then close it. Then open it again. Nothing. Why is he even here? *How* is he even in the main community? And when the hell did he start speaking so casually and inappropriately? Fuck, am I rubbing off on him?

Kael tilts his head. "Oh, don't stop on my account. I was particularly interested in the part where you were determining my... anatomy."

Molsi makes a strangled sound that might be laughter but is probably their soul leaving their body in second-hand embarrassment for me.

I am going to set myself on fire. That is the only way out of this.

Decca, ever the traitor, smirks. "Well, Sonny? Got anything to add?"

I clutch the pack of food to my chest like it's my only lifeline. "Nope."

Kael's lips twitch. "Pity."

And then, as if this couldn't get worse, he leans in—just slightly—and murmurs, "For what it's worth, you were right about one thing." He takes the second pack of food, throws it over his shoulder, and walks off.

I stare after him.

Molsi sucks in a breath. "Sonny."

I shake my head violently. "No," I say, voice hoarse.

Decca grins. "You okay?"

"No," I repeat, more broken this time.

Molsi pats my shoulder. "That was a lot. You gonna survive?"

"No."

But I have to. Because in less than an hour, I have to travel with that smug bastard, and I have a feeling I won't hear the end of this.

I DIDN'T THINK I COULD BE ANY MORE humiliated after Kael overheard me discussing his possible anatomical features.

Ha.

How fucking naïve of me.

"Nuh-uh. No way. You have to be taking the piss."

Varek somehow manages to keep a straight face, but I can tell—deep in his dark, scheming little soul—he wants to laugh. His lips don't twitch, but there's a certain smug glint in his eyes.

At least this time, there's no audience. No nosy rebels lingering to witness my further descent into disgrace. But, of course, the main offender is here, standing before me like this is a completely normal conversation.

Kael, deadly serious, holds up what can only be described as some kind of bondage harness.

I stare.

He stares back.

I glance at Varek.

Nothing.

Back to Kael.

Still serious.

Then back to the harness.

Leather straps, thick and reinforced with metal buckles. There are loops, padded sections, and a complex webbing design that could belong in a tactical gear store... or the darkest, most hard-core BDSM dungeon.

"You have *got* to be fucking kidding me."

Kael, the bastard, just tilts his head. "It's standard royal guard equipment. Used to carry wounded—"

"Oh, okay," I snap, throwing up my hands. "That's

so much better. You're not planning on slinging me around like a BDSM plaything—you just think I'm *injured*."

He sighs. "It's for efficiency."

"No, it's for humiliation."

Kael remains perfectly neutral, which only makes me more suspicious.

"What, is this payback?" I demand. "For the whole *arsehole* thing?"

His expression flickers *just* enough to confirm my theory.

"Oh, *fuck off*," I groan.

"This isn't about—" He exhales sharply, visibly recalibrating his approach. "Sonny, we don't have time for this."

I cross my arms. "Are you saying I can't keep up?"

Kael hesitates, which is the worst thing he could have done.

"Oh my *God*." My eyes widen in horror. "You *do* think I'm weak. You absolute—" I wave a hand at him. "—Glowranth bastard! I knew you were speciesist. I *knew* it."

"What? No—"

"You're saying I'm lame because I'm human, aren't you?" I press, pointing an accusing finger at him. "Well, fuck that. I've spent my whole life dealing with bigots, and I am *not* about to take it from some oversized flying cat—"

Kael's eyes widen in genuine horror. "That is *not* what I meant."

"Well, it sounded like that."

"I apologise," he says quickly—almost too quickly. "That was not my intention."

I narrow my eyes. He looks sincere. He sounds sincere—even went back to formal English. And somehow, I feel a bit mollified. But I'm still pissed.

And Varek? Varek, the traitorous shit, still isn't saying anything. He's just watching, arms crossed, expression unreadable. I know he's enjoying this. He probably has as much of a hard-on for Kael as Kael does for him. Which, frankly, is annoying, because Kael clearly does not deserve my leader's approval.

"I can keep up," I declare, lying so hard, I almost believe it myself.

Kael's lips press together, his eyes flicking over me like he's running calculations. He doesn't even have to say anything. The scepticism is palpable.

"We don't have time for ego," he finally says, voice low, steady. "Dawson had another seizure."

My gut twists. Shit. I can be a stubborn bitch, but I can't be a selfish one. I exhale sharply. "Fine. But I'm plotting my revenge."

Varek finally moves, stepping forwards with a smirk. "Make it creative."

"Oh, don't you worry," I assure him darkly. "I'm going to be so fucking creative."

He chuckles. The bastard.

Meanwhile, Kael is already adjusting the harness, and I finally get a good look at it.

It's a complex piece of gear, all sleek reinforced straps and custom padding, meant to hold a Glowranth securely against their carrier. No doubt useful in the heat of battle or the thick of rescue, but in this scenario? It's mortifying.

I eye it suspiciously. "You sure this isn't just some weird Glowranth soldier kink?"

Kael turns bright red.

Perfect.

I smirk, bolstered by his reaction. "Not into bondage, then?"

He makes a strangled noise. "Get in the harness, Sonny."

Varek snorts but wisely stays out of it.

I grumble the whole time, muttering about "If you're going to manhandle me, at least buy me dinner first..." and "I swear, if this gets weird, I'm biting you," but eventually, I let Kael strap me in.

And I immediately regret it.

Because the second he lifts me, it's alarmingly comfortable.

His body is warm, all solid muscle and infuriating ease, as though I weigh nothing to him. His weapons have been shifted to accommodate me, and I realise I'm carrying his supplies too.

Great. So not only am I strapped to him like some perverse backpack, but now I'm his personal fucking pack mule.

Varek watches the whole process with thinly veiled amusement. Then, just before we set off, he surprises me. "Remember your training," he says, voice softer than usual. "Stay safe."

I blink, caught off-guard. Varek doesn't do sentiment. Not really. For a second, something warm swells in my chest, and I actually consider hugging him. But before I can throw myself at him like a starving stray— which, yes, is impossible since I'm in a kink carrier— Kael growls.

Low. Deep. *Possessive.*

The fuck?

I glance at him in disbelief. "Oh, relax. Just because your dick is hard for my leader doesn't mean I should be denied basic human affection."

Kael, to his credit, looks absolutely mortified.

Varek?

Varek is fighting for his life not to laugh. "Right." He clears his throat, lips twitching. "You two should probably get going."

Kael doesn't wait. He turns sharply, yanking me with him like a bag of cargo, and strides towards the exit of the cavern. Varek gives me one last look—one that makes it clear he's definitely going to give me shit for this later. But there's something else there too.

Something serious.

And then, just like that, we're leaving. Leaving the safety of my home. Leaving everything I know. Finally, after all my talk, I'm actually doing something for the cause.

What the fuck was I thinking? I wanted adventure? Some grand, heroic journey? Please. I'm so far from being a hero, I'll probably trip over my own sword and accidentally impale myself before we even make it halfway.

Well, you know, if I could be trusted to bloody well walk.

CHAPTER
SIX

"You know, I'm absolutely sure this is a kink." Since I haven't been able to talk for the past five hours as Kael ran with me on his back, making it impossible to speak without biting my tongue, my filter has left me. My brain's also been jiggled around, which means all of my fucks have been bounced out of me.

Kael's usual grunt to my verbal diarrhea, which he's given me the past thirty minutes when he had no choice but to slow down to a walk due to the rough terrain, makes me grin. It's fun getting to him, each grunt like a tiny victory. A confirmation that yes, I am irritating, and yes, he is suffering. If I have to endure this undignified, bouncing backpack existence, then by God, I will make it as uncomfortable for him as possible.

Kael shifts me slightly, adjusting the straps of the ridiculous harness that keeps me plastered to his back like some kind of parasitic growth. "A kink?" he finally asks, his voice a smooth, stoic calm.

I nod, which he obviously can't see, so I make an exaggerated noise of agreement. "Oh yeah. There's definitely some depraved bastard out there who would pay good money for this kind of treatment."

He falls silent, which only makes it funnier.

"Seriously," I continue, trying to stretch out my legs —because damn, they're cramping—"some people would be so into this. Being strapped up, carried around, no control, just completely at the mercy of a big, strong Glowranth—"

"I'm going to drop you."

I cackle. "You won't."

"… I might."

I grin against his back. "Nah. You'd feel too guilty. You're all noble and honour-bound. I bet you'd have to do some weird Glowranth ritual of atonement if you did."

Kael sighs, long-suffering. "Do you always talk this much?"

"Do you always grunt this much?" I counter.

This time, he doesn't grace me with a grunt. He's silent, his long strides carrying us forwards over rough, uneven ground. I rest my chin on his shoulder—not exactly comfortable, but I'm so past caring at this point —and let my thoughts drift.

Curiosity gets the better of me. "So, how come you speak English so well?"

Kael exhales through his nose, and I get the sense he's choosing his words carefully. "I have always been... gifted with languages."

Huh. "That's convenient."

"It was necessary," he corrects. "As the prince's guard, it's my duty to understand and communicate with the many species of Terrafeara."

That's... surprisingly practical. "Still," I press, "English isn't exactly common here. Did you, like, study it? Listen to humans speak?"

There's a beat of silence. Then, quietly—reluctantly—Kael mutters, "Books helped when I was being taught by the royal guard."

I blink. "Books?"

Another beat. Another long, deep inhale. "I found... books."

Holy shit. "You learned English from books?"

"... Yes."

"Oh, that's fantastic." I shift slightly, trying to see his face. "What kind of books?"

Kael hesitates. He's clearly regretting this entire conversation. "It doesn't matter."

"No, no, it definitely matters." I grin, sensing an opportunity to get under his skin. "What kind of books, Kael?"

Silence.

"Kael."

More silence.

I nudge him with my chin. "If you don't tell me, I'm going to assume it was something really weird. Like... cookbooks. Or, bloody hell, children's books."

He makes a noise—something between a sigh and a growl. Then, so low, I almost miss it, he grumbles, "Romance."

I freeze.

Wait. What?

"Romance?"

Kael's grip on my thighs tightens slightly, and for the first time since I met him, he sounds genuinely embarrassed. "It was from a human dwelling. Many cycles ago."

I bite my lip, trying so hard not to burst out laughing. "So, you learned English from... romance novels?"

"They were well-written."

Oh, this is golden. "So wait, you're telling me you speak English fluently because you spent cycles reading books about... what? Star-crossed lovers? Forbidden passion? Torrid affairs?"

Kael makes another of those long-suffering sighs. "It was informative."

I lose it. I'm shaking against his back, gasping for air, my entire body convulsing with laughter. Kael mutters something in Glowranth under his breath. Probably a prayer for patience.

When I finally catch my breath, I wipe at my eyes, still giggling. "That's incredible. That's—wait, hold on." A thought strikes me, and I can't not ask. "Do you, like, understand human romance? Or did you just learn the words?"

There's a pause. "Both."

"So, theoretically," I say, fighting another round of snorting laughter, "if I described, say, a romantic date, you'd get it?"

"... Yes."

I cackle. "That's so fucking weird."

Kael ignores me. I shift slightly, thinking, and some-how, my brain takes a turn straight into personal territory.

"My mum used to read romance novels," I muse aloud. "Not, like, nice ones. Trashy as hell. But she wasn't really a nice person either."

Kael doesn't reply, but I can tell he's listening.

"She wasn't awful, I guess," I continue, sighing. "Never kicked me out. Even when I told her I was gay."

Kael slows slightly, glancing over his shoulder at me. "Gay?"

Oh, right. "Uh. Yeah. It means I'm into men."

He frowns. "Why is there a word for that?"

I blink. "What do you mean?"

Glowranth don't have eyebrows, but his ridges pull together in something close to confusion. "Attraction is attraction. We don't distinguish with labels."

Huh. That's... actually kind of cool. "So, Glowranth just, what? Like who they like?"

"Yes."

"Damn," I mutter. "That sounds nice. No bullshit."

Kael nods. Then, because he's apparently not done surprising me today, he says, "I think humans complicate things unnecessarily."

I snort. "Yeah, that's our brand."

For the first time since we started this hellish journey, Kael peers back at me, and his lips twitch.

I grin. "Was that...? Kael, did you just smile?"

"No."

"Oh, you totally did."

He picks up speed again, bouncing me just enough to shut me up.

I groan. "I hate this."

"Good."

I mumble something about turtles, because that's exactly what I feel like, and Kael actually pauses. "Turtles?"

I snicker. "You don't know what a turtle is?"

His silence is answer enough.

"Oh, this is so happening." I smirk. "As soon as we get back, I'm finding something to draw you a turtle."

Kael sighs, long and exasperated. "Why?"

"Because it's important."

"I doubt that."

"You don't know that."

He groans. "I regret engaging in conversation."

I grin, resting my chin back on his shoulder. "Too late, buddy. You're stuck with me."

Kael mutters something under his breath, and I swear, if I didn't know better, I'd think he didn't actually mind.

At some point, dignity has to take priority over efficiency. And right now, dignity is demanding a bathroom break.

"Okay, I need a minute," I announce. "Like, an actual, non-bouncing minute where I can remember what it feels like to stand on my own two feet and also, uh... handle some business."

Kael sighs, slowing to a stop with the reluctance of someone who is deeply, profoundly disappointed in me. "We're making good time," he mutters, but he kneels, loosening the straps and letting me slide off his back.

I stagger as my feet touch the ground. Everything feels weird. My legs wobble like a newborn foal's, and I cling to the nearest tree for support. "Fuck—I think my ass has forgotten what it's like to carry my own weight."

Kael crosses his arms, unimpressed. "I will allow five minutes."

I flip him off as I stumble into the trees. The terrain here is thick with foliage—tall, twisting trees with dark, smooth bark, their roots tangling like serpents over the ground. The air is humid, filled with the scent of damp earth and something sweet—almost floral, but not quite.

Beyond the trees, the land slopes downwards, revealing an expanse of still, glassy water. It stretches out further than I can see, the liquid dark and eerily purple, like ink spilled across a page. There's no visible shoreline on the other side. No rippling, no waves. Just... vastness.

After I pee, I frown, stepping closer. "Kael," I call. "What the hell is this?"

He's already pulling out supplies from one of the packs, moving with his usual efficiency. "A body of water."

"Yeah, no shit. Is it safe? Can we drink it?"

He glances up, following my gaze. "It isn't poisonous," he says, which is not the same as "yes, totally safe, go ahead and take a sip." "There are creatures in its depths, but they rarely come near the surface unless disturbed."

I do not like that wording. "Creatures?"

Kael shrugs. "Some are harmless."

"And the others?"

He doesn't answer immediately, which is answer enough.

I squint at the water. "So, this is like the sea?"

Kael tilts his head, clearly unfamiliar with the word.

"An ocean?" I clarify.

Recognition flickers across his face. "Yes. But without waves."

I frown. "Why not?"

He gestures towards the sky, then the land. "This region has no strong winds to push the surface. No shifting tides."

Huh. Weird. The ocean without waves feels… unnatural. But then, everything here feels unnatural.

I watch as Kael efficiently lays out food—something dried, something vaguely meat-like, and something that might be fruit if I don't think too hard about it. "I would like to travel a little longer before we stop for the night," he says. "We're making good progress, and the land ahead is not as rough."

"Fine by me," I say, but my focus is still on the water. Something about it makes my skin prickle.

And then it moves.

Just a flicker—a ripple breaking the otherwise-glassy surface. But it's there. My heart kicks. I straighten, eyes scanning the water. "Kael."

He looks up.

I don't look away from the lake—ocean—whatever the hell it is. My fingers curl around my dagger. "Something's moving."

The surface stills.

Kael is watching now, body tense, food forgotten. "Did you see what it was?"

I shake my head, stomach clenching. "Just a ripple. But it was big."

Silence. Then another ripple. Closer.

I grip my dagger tighter. "Tell me," I murmur, not taking my eyes off the water. "The creatures that aren't harmless... what exactly are we talking about here?"

The water ripples again, and before I can ask more questions, Kael's entire demeanour changes. His bioluminescent markings flicker excitedly, and his nostrils flare as he watches whatever's lurking beneath the surface.

His next word? Brimming with enthusiasm. "Food."

I blink. "What?"

Without another word, he's moving, stripping off his outer gear and stepping towards the water's edge like a hunter who's just spotted the perfect prey. And fuck me, I can't look away.

His physique is something else—not like a human's, but just as unfairly sexy. His muscles don't just sit beneath his skin; they shift with a fluidity that makes it impossible not to stare, like every movement is pure efficiency wrapped in strength. The markings across his body pulse faintly, tracing over the ridges of his arms, his shoulders, the powerful curve of his back.

He looks even bigger now, practically naked, which makes no sense—he's wearing less, not more, but somehow, without the extra layers, he seems larger than life.

I swallow. Hard.

And then he continues forwards, oblivious to my absolutely unhinged thoughts.

"Kael," I say slowly, watching as he crouches, eyes finally trained on the inky depths. "You're not seriously thinking—"

He dives.

"Bloody hell." I clap a hand over my mouth, half in horror, half in amazement, as he vanishes beneath the surface. A second later, there's a violent splash, then another, and then—pure chaos.

Turns out, Kael? Not a natural fisherman. Or whatever the hell the equivalent of that would be in this situation.

Water explodes around him as he thrashes, lunging after something just out of reach. He makes a grab—misses. Swipes—misses again. It's fast. Too fast. I can't see much beyond the flashes of movement beneath the surface, but whatever it is, it's big, and Kael? Kael is determined.

"You could just give up," I offer helpfully, watching as he narrowly avoids a faceful of lake-ocean-whatever-the-hell water. "Not everything is meant to be caught, you know."

He grunts in response, which I think means "fuck off," and lunges again.

Another splash.

Another struggle.

And then—somehow, miraculously—Kael emerges from the water, victorious.

Dripping, completely soaked—and now more purple than his usual deep blue—but he's triumphant. His bioluminescent markings are practically dancing with pride as he hefts his prize—a monstrous, writhing, abomination of a creature—out of the water.

And then he beams at me, looking more alive than I've ever seen him.

"I have caught it," he announces, like he's just won the bloody lotto.

I stare.

It's... horrible. The creature, not Kael.

The thing has too many eyes, scattered unevenly across its slippery, finned body. Its skin is a mottled mix of dark grey and something almost translucent, like an eel that got ambitious and decided to evolve into a nightmare. The fins are jagged, the mouth should not be that wide, and the worst part? It's still moving.

Kael thrusts it towards me, looking obscenely proud. "Take it," he says.

"Absolutely not."

His expression falters, and fuck, he looks wounded.

I sigh. "Fine." The second I grab it, I regret everything. It's so much heavier than it looks, and before I can brace myself, my knees buckle. "Shit!"

I go down hard, hitting the damp earth with an *oof*

as the weight of the thing completely overpowers me. For a moment, there's silence.

Then Kael laughs. Not just a chuckle. A full, chest-rumbling, unrestrained laugh.

"Oh, fuck you," I wheeze from the ground.

He hovers between laughter and concern, like he wants to keep enjoying my suffering but also maybe realises I've actually taken a hit.

Then my amusement fades. A sharp sting flares up my back. I wince.

Kael's laughter dies immediately. The shift in his demeanour is so fast, it's jarring. One second, he's amused. The next, his eyes flash, and a visible tremor runs beneath his skin.

"You're hurt." His voice is low. Rough. Like the words physically pain him.

I push myself up, rolling my shoulders as I leave the fish-thing to flop uselessly beside me. "I'm fine. Just a cut." I hope. It hurts, but I can't see it—not without twisting in ways that I definitely was not built for. The pain is above the waistband of my pants, a sharp sting that's already making my skin prickle uncomfortably.

Kael's gaze is locked on me. His nostrils flare again. His bioluminescent markings pulse.

I shift under his scrutiny, suddenly very aware that something about this has rattled him. "Kael?"

No response. Just intensity. The air between us

changes, something charged settling in his stance. And I have no idea why.

Then he moves.

Not just moves—*stalks*.

Every step is measured, predatory, his luminous eyes focused on me with an intensity that should have me backing up, telling him to calm the hell down. Instead, my breath catches, my skin burns, and holy shit, is it hot out here, or is it just me?

My fingers twitch at my sides, my pulse a chaotic drumline in my ears. I swear my throat's gone dry, but it's nothing compared to the heat coiling low in my stomach. His movements shouldn't be this hypnotic, shouldn't send a thrill down my spine, shouldn't make my body react.

And yet.

"Turn around," he rumbles, voice like the start of a storm, "and take off your shirt."

I blink. "What?"

His eyes flash. "Spin. Now."

I roll my eyes because fuck that tone, but before I can tell him he's being dramatic, he lets out a low, guttural growl.

My skin pebbles.

My dick? Hardens.

Oh holy shit.

This is wrong. So wrong. I think I might actually

come in my pants from the sound of his voice, which means something is fundamentally broken in me.

But I also do as he asks.

The second my shirt is off, I feel him close. So close. And yet he doesn't touch me. There's a moment of absolute silence before a noise rips from his throat—low, raw, pained. It jolts through me, a shock to my already-fried system, and I go to turn towards him.

I don't get the chance. His three-fingered hand lands hot and solid against my bare waist, stopping me in my tracks.

My breath catches. My brain? Short-circuits. And then—everything tilts.

The world spins, my vision flickers, and suddenly my limbs feel like dead weight.

Kael is immediately there, catching me, holding me close like I might crumble into dust. My fingers curl weakly into his arm as I fight against the dizzy haze clouding my mind.

"The hell just happened?" My voice is sluggish, my tongue heavy. "Why... why do I feel...?"

Kael's jaw tightens. "You fell on a rock."

I squint at him. "A rock?"

"A poisonous one."

Of fucking course. Because why wouldn't this place have poisonous rocks? Just another exciting new way for Terrafeara to kick me in the balls.

"So, what do we do?" I rasp, blinking against the fog rolling in.

He doesn't answer. But I feel it—his hesitation, his worry, the sheer reluctance radiating off him like waves.

"Kael." My tongue is heavy, my limbs going limp. "What's wrong?"

His grip tightens. "I have to draw the poison out of you."

I try to focus, try to push past the molasses in my brain. "As in... cut me open?"

Silence. Or... not silence. More like an implication so loud, it might as well be a scream.

My stomach drops. "Or—"

His next words wreck me. "If I do..."

I struggle to keep my eyes open. "Yeah?"

He exhales, voice tight. "It'll fully start the bonding process."

Scratch record. Freeze frame. *What?*

"The bonding fucking what now?"

Does that mean...?

"You're my mate," he says.

It's the last thing I hear before the darkness swallows me whole.

CHAPTER
SEVEN

HEAT CLINGS TO MY SKIN, COMFORTING IN A WAY that makes me snuggle deeper. Awareness comes slowly, a gentle unfurling rather than a jarring snap into consciousness. I feel... good? Which is weird as hell. My body is loose, my mind foggy but not in a poisoned way, more in a cosy, don't-want-to-move-ever-again kind of way.

It's nice.

It's warm.

It's—

Oh fuck.

The second I become fully aware, I also become horrifically aware of the fact that I'm not alone. There's a body beneath me. A strong, solid, immensely large body that's currently functioning as both my mattress and my pillow.

I still. My breathing changes. And I know—I just fucking know—that Kael notices.

The Glowranth's senses are too sharp not to. He hears things before they happen, scents changes in the air like a bloodhound, and yet—

He doesn't say anything.

I can hear his soft, measured breathing beneath me, feel the slow rise and fall of his chest against mine, but he doesn't move. And fuck me dead—I'm the one wrapped around him.

My arm is draped over his chest, my leg tangled between his massive thighs. One of my hands is currently resting over his heart—assuming that's where his heart is—like we're some sickly sweet romance novel couple who fell asleep gazing at the stars.

And then his words slam into me like a goddamn freight train.

You're my mate.

I go rigid.

My. Mate.

I have a mate.

Longing surges through me, hot and dizzying, my chest tightening with something too big to name. My gut clenches, my breath hitches, and for a moment—a brief, treacherous moment—I feel something close to bliss.

And then?

Reality backhands me across the face.

I've been here for years. Many, many cycles. If I had to guess? At least a couple of years, maybe more.

And Kael—

Kael would have known.

The second I was sliced into Terrafeara, the moment I bled onto this monstrous fucking world, he would have felt me. He would have sensed it—just like the prince did with Dawson.

And yet.

He didn't come for me.

He didn't find me.

He didn't fight for me.

What the actual fuck!

I react on pure rage-fuelled instinct, launching myself off him so fast, I stumble getting upright.

As I suspected, Kael is already awake. Of course he is. His eyes track every move I make, assessing, calculating, waiting.

Waiting.

And fuck if that doesn't just piss me off even more.

"You knew." The words rip from my throat, raw and furious, edged with something dangerously close to betrayal. "All this time, you fucking knew."

Kael doesn't speak. He just watches me, his face stoic, his markings dimming and flaring like they can't decide if they should give away whatever the hell he's feeling.

I shake my head, my vision swimming, my chest

tight. There's a pit inside me, a familiar one, deep and dark and gaping, the same one that's been there since I was a kid. The one made of loneliness, of never being good enough, of never being wanted.

It threatens to roll me, to swallow me whole—

But fuck that.

Kael moves. Not fast. Slowly. Like he's waiting to see if I'll bolt. Or maybe even stab him.

Honestly? I consider both.

I cross my arms, shoving all my hurt and rage behind a brittle shield of indifference. "Well?"

His lips part. He hesitates before he finally says, "I wasn't looking for a mate."

The words punch through me. A direct hit, right in the gut. My stomach twists, nausea clawing its way up my throat.

Didn't look for me.

Didn't want me.

I force my spine to steel, even as my entire fucking soul crumples in on itself. "Fuck you," I say, my voice steady, my tone deadly. "Seriously, go suck a thorny Glowranth dick and choke on it."

Kael winces.

Good.

And yet he still doesn't backtrack. Doesn't apologise. But for the first time since I met him, he actually looks uncertain. The warrior I've come to expect—the one always in control, always put-together, always unshakable—is gone. And I don't know what to do with the male standing in front of me, fumbling through his words like he doesn't know how to hold onto them.

"I was born into service," he says, his voice rough. "I was meant to die in service. My loyalty was to Prince Aelith. Only him."

I sneer, shaking my head. "Oh, fuck right off." I don't understand that kind of devotion, that level of self-sacrifice. I know I should respect it, should see this as some kind of cultural divide—

But it's so damn hard when it's my life he's talking about.

Kael exhales sharply, his nostrils flaring. "The moment I felt you on Terrafeara," he admits, "I fought my instinct every day not to find you. Not to claim you. Not to make you mine."

My dick should not stir at that. At the possessive gleam in his eyes. At the absolute conviction in his voice. He doesn't deserve my perfect cock showing any interest.

"I had to forcefully stop myself," he continues. "Neither my shame nor my promise to serve Prince Aelith would have allowed it."

I bark out a bitter laugh. "That's the whole 'my word is my bond' shit, right?"

Kael nods once.

"And your bond to me?" I snap. "That's worth jack shit?"

His expression darkens, his markings pulsing wildly. "Not anymore," he says, the words weighted.

My blood runs cold.

Because suddenly, I remember—

The bond.

His words before I passed out. He started the bond. He saved my life. Is that what it took?

My stomach clenches. "Because the process has started?"

"Yes," Kael confirms. "Saving your life was one stage. Another was absorbing your blood."

Jesus, fuck.

Just how many steps are there?

I swallow hard, my mouth dry. "And how many are there? What's the last one?"

Kael's expression shifts—serious, unreadable. He hesitates for just a second before he says, "Sharing a heartbeat."

I blink. "The fuck does that mean?"

"It is... a synchronisation," he says, as if that actually explains anything. "A way to align ourselves permanently."

I stare at him, waiting for something horrifying about how exactly we do that.

Like sex.

Because if it's sex, I swear to God—

"It doesn't involve mating," he says quickly, cutting off my impending breakdown.

I exhale. "Oh. Well. Good." I don't trust the relief rolling through me, because none of this should matter. None of this *does* matter. I force myself to meet his gaze. "I have to do the same?" I ask. "All three things?"

"Yes."

I hate the way something inside me yearns. The deep, painful ache in my chest that screams at me to give in. To take what's mine.

But I can't. Because he didn't want me. Not at first. Not when it mattered.

I straighten, locking my jaw. "No."

Kael stills.

"I don't want it," I say, the words like glass in my throat.

He watches me, silent.

I clench my fists, digging my nails into my palms just to keep my voice even. "I don't give a shit about fate or anything else," I tell him. "You don't deserve me."

Kael flinches like I just stabbed him in the gut. His markings go wild, flashing in chaotic bursts, his skin vibrating with unspoken emotion.

He has no words.

The pain in my chest nearly doubles me over, but I don't let it show. I inhale sharply. "Let's get moving."

His jaw ticks. "Son—"

I hold up a hand. *No.*

"We need to find the doctor," I say firmly. "We need to get back to Dathanor. Save Dawson." I force myself to swallow the lump in my throat. "And then we can go our separate ways."

Kael doesn't respond. But he doesn't need to. Because the look in his eyes? It says he heard every single word.

And it fucking destroyed him.

Good.

It should.

Even if it's destroying me too.

WITH THE DARKNESS DRAWING IN, IT'S ALMOST time to rest. We've been lucky so far—no beasties with too many teeth trying to take a bite out of us. But travelling at night? Yeah, that's a shit idea. Not to mention, I'm starving.

Neither of us ate after Kael's big soul-destroying reveal. Nausea had taken over, stealing my appetite right along with any shred of emotional stability I had left. We left fast.

And yes, I'm still in the stupid backpack contraption.

Talk about awkward.

The bitter silence between us has stretched on for kilometres, thick as the creeping dusk. "I think we need to stop," I say, my voice cutting through the quiet.

Kael's shoulders tense, just a fraction. Then he nods.

He scans the horizon, moving with that infuriating, measured control of his. Since his eyesight is way better than mine, I let him do his thing.

"There is a cave up ahead," he says. "It will offer you some shelter."

I clamp my mouth shut, noting his formality, before I say something snarky. Something like "I don't need protection." Because obviously, I do. Not just from the toothy nightmares lurking in the darkness but also from the cold.

The bite of the *ithran* frost is already nipping at my skin, its slow creep making my fingers and toes tingle. "Okay," I mutter. It's all I can manage without bitterness slipping in.

My stomach growls, loud enough to echo in the quiet. I pointedly ignore it. I have supplies in my pack. As soon as we stop, I'll force down whatever rations I've got without thinking too hard about what I'm eating.

Kael's voice jolts me. "I will find you fresh food when we make camp." His words are quiet. Simple. And yet something about them unsettles me.

Maybe it's the fact that he even cares whether I eat. Or maybe it's the fact that he's still trying—even after everything. He keeps walking, his pace still effortless, still unfairly smooth, even as the terrain turns into jagged, uneven ground. He isn't even breathless.

"I have my own food," I say.

His shoulders tense again. "I know," he says. "But

there are *rethog* nearby. You can keep your supplies for when there is no fresh food."

I hesitate. *Rethog*. They taste like chicken, and I haven't had one in ages. Back in Dathanor, we only get them when hunters bring them in, which has been happening less and less lately—what with the queen's lackeys closing down trade routes and cracking down on rebellion activity.

I sigh. "Fine." Too tired, too hungry, and too wrecked to argue.

Kael says nothing.

We settle in once we reach the cave—if you can even call it that. It's really more of a jagged overhang, barely deep enough to block the worst of the wind. Kael leaves to hunt, and I'm left alone with my thoughts. A fucking terrible place to be.

My mind drifts.

To Kael.

To how wrong I was about him.

I'd convinced myself he had a thing for Varek. That every lingering glance, every tense exchange had meant something. But it didn't.

It was never Varek. It was me.

I rub at my chest, irritation coiling tight in my gut. Am I just hurting myself more by pushing him away? Will I ever be able to forgive him?

I don't know.

And maybe worse—I don't know if I even feel

different since the bonding started. The bond is supposed to mean something, but I feel like... me.

Though, if I'm being honest with myself, I've always found Kael attractive. That was never the problem. The problem is—what now?

I know bonding effects are different depending on the species, but what should I even expect?

Before I can spiral further, Kael returns. His expression is... forlorn, like he's carrying some silent weight on his shoulders, but he doesn't let it stop him. He sets to work, skinning and preparing the *rethog* like nothing is wrong. Like he isn't unravelling right in front of me.

Kael tries. More than once. Small, hesitant attempts —a question here, a comment there—all of them careful, all of them deliberate.

"Does your wound still ache?"

I don't answer. I haven't complained about my wound. Not once. Does he know because he senses my pain?

"You are cold."

Nothing from me. And yes, I am cold. I'm also relieved that I'm out of the elements and the biting wind. The fire he's made is finally doing the trick of warming me up. It would do an even better job if I moved closer, but since he's there and I'm a petty bitch, I stay nearer to the shadows.

"The fever has not worsened." A quiet observation, not quite a question.

Still, I refuse to engage. But fuck, I had a fever? I suppose that happened when I was unconscious. Fun times.

I focus on the fire, watching the flames flicker and curl, casting his face in shifting light. He comes closer as he works on cooking the fresh meat. He's too close, but I won't ask him to move. I won't give him the satisfaction.

So I sit, silent and stiff, my arms curled around my knees. I can feel him watching me. Waiting. And then—

"Have you always been stubborn?"

It's a casual question with no heat or spite, but it's one I know is meant to prod at me. And goddammit, it works. My head snaps up, a glare locked and loaded, because excuse me?

His lips twitch. Just a little. Almost like he's relieved I took the bait.

I scowl harder. "You don't know me."

"I know enough."

I scoff. "Yeah? And what exactly do you think you know?"

He tilts his head, studying me, his eyes flickering gold with the firelight.

"I know you act like you don't care," he says evenly, "but you care too much."

Something in my chest twists. I hate that he said that. I hate that it's true. I shift, looking away. "You don't know shit."

Kael exhales, slow and measured. He pokes at the fire, adjusting the wood. The silence stretches again—heavy, but different now. And then, softly, "I wish I had done things differently."

It's not the first time he's apologised. But this time... this time, it feels different. Not just words. Not just duty. Something real.

I risk a glance at him.

His jaw is tight, his expression pained. Not just the usual unreadable stoicism. This looks like actual regret. I don't know what to do with that. I don't know if I even want to do *anything* with that.

So I shake my head. "Yeah, well. Too late."

His gaze flickers, like the words hit him somewhere deep. But he doesn't argue. He just nods. Somehow, that makes it worse.

He turns his attention back to the fire and the cooking *rethog*. I should look away, but I can't seem to find the will or the desire. I don't know if it's curiosity, exhaustion, or something deeper that keeps my gaze fixed on him. On the way his massive frame seems smaller somehow in the dim firelight. On the faint, pulse-like glow of his markings, flickering in a rhythm I can't quite track.

Kael doesn't seem to notice me at first, focussed on the food. But then his nostrils flare. A sharp inhale. And when he glances up, his eyes locking with mine, he stills. His surprise is obvious. I expect him to smirk, to make some arrogant remark about my staring. Instead, he clears his throat, a rare show of discomfort, and breaks eye contact first.

The moment is over too quickly.

"Eat." He passes me some of the cooked *rethog*, his fingers brushing against mine.

I swallow hard at the contact, my grip tightening around the cooked meat as if that will stop the traitorous shiver running through me.

His eyes flare. A barely there reaction, but I see it. Feel it.

My stomach twists, my thoughts a mess, but I remember my damn manners. "Thanks," I mutter.

Kael gives a small nod. No arrogance, no teasing. Just a nod.

We eat in silence for a while. The fire crackles, the scent of the cooked meat thick in the air, but I barely taste it. My mind keeps circling back to something else.

Energy manipulation.

The Glowranth can do it—I've seen a couple of the ones who joined the Riftborn cause use it. It's different from what I know of tech, different from magic too. Rawer. And now, with the bond partially formed, I can't help but wonder....

I clear my throat. "So. Your... abilities. The energy manipulation thing."

Kael pauses mid-bite, blinking. Then, to my surprise, he brightens. Not physically—though his markings do shift slightly, his bioluminescence flickering a little more vividly—but his whole presence changes. Like he wasn't expecting the question but is eager to answer.

Almost happy about it.

"It's... difficult to explain," he says, setting his food down. "We don't see energy the same way humans do. To us, it's a current, a force that can be shaped. We train from childhood to harness it, to use it in combat, in construction, in healing. It's...." He hesitates, searching for the right words.

I watch, fascinated despite myself. This is the most open I've ever seen him.

"It's a part of us," he continues. "Like breathing. We draw it from our bodies, from the world, and wield it."

I frown. "Like how?"

Kael lifts a hand, palm up. At first, nothing happens. Then a faint shimmer appears just above his skin, like heat distortion. It twists and shifts, slowly forming into a crackling sphere.

'My breath catches. It's not fire. Not electricity. Something between. The sphere pulses once, then vanishes in a flicker of energy.

I exhale, realising I'd been holding my breath.

Kael watches me carefully. Too carefully. Like he's gauging my reaction.

I try to keep my voice even. "And humans? If... if a human and a Glowranth... complete the bond, do they

—" I don't finish the question. But I don't have to. He understands.

Hope flares in his luminous eyes, so sudden and raw that my stomach bottoms out. I shouldn't have asked. I shouldn't have let him hope.

And fuck me, I shouldn't want to comfort him.

But I do.

I want to reach out, touch him, say something that makes that vulnerable look in his eyes hurt less.

I don't.

Can't.

Kael shifts, the light of the fire casting shadows across his sharp features. He exhales slowly, like he's choosing his words with care. "I don't know."

I blink. "What?"

"I don't know if you'd gain any of my abilities," he clarifies. His markings pulse faintly, a slow, steady rhythm. "There are no bonded Glowranth. Not in this lifetime, anyway."

I nod, knowing that fated mates, or having the ability to have one, wasn't possible for his species. "Until me and Dawson."

He hesitates, then says, "The ability to bond—the way it's meant to happen—stopped over seven generations ago."

"So, your species used to have fated mates?" I ask.

"Yes." Kael's voice is calm, but there's an undercurrent of something deeper. Resignation, maybe. "The old records—the Kezthran Archives—mention fated mates, but only amongst other Glowranth."

I tilt my head, absorbing that. "Not surprising, I guess. There's no recorded history of the rifts, right? No proof that other species ever got pulled into your world before now." Because that's something we'd know about, right?

He nods. "Exactly. All Glowranth can manipulate energy, so there was no way to tell what... exchange happened between mates back then." His voice turns contemplative. "Though it's said that bonded mates could communicate without words."

I sit with that for a moment, thinking. "Like telepathy?"

Kael inclines his head.

I nod, my mind drifting. "I've heard similar things. Existing interspecies mates sometimes develop... side effects. Shared dreams, extra senses, even minor and some major shifts in biology. Nothing like energy manipulation, though." I chew my lower lip. "Still, the whole mind-talking thing would be kind of cool."

Kael's mouth quirks at the corner. "You would like that?"

I huff. "No need to sound so amused."

His lips press together, amusement fading. "Bonded pairs could also sense emotions."

That gives me pause.

"Joy," he continues. "Pain."

I watch him closely. His jaw tightens. His nostrils flare. And then—a wince.

I narrow my eyes. "What?"

Kael exhales sharply through his nose, gaze flicking —just briefly—to my back. Where he saved me.

My stomach knots. I shift, feeling the tender pull of the healing wound. "You can feel that?"

His luminous eyes meet mine, glowing softly in the dim light. "I can feel all of it."

And he's not just talking about my back.

I suck in a breath, realisation slamming into me. My pain. My anger. My bitterness. He feels it. All of it.

I swallow hard, shifting uncomfortably. "And that means... what? That you'll always be able to sense me?"

Kael nods. His gaze is steady, but there's something raw underneath it.

How would that feel? To be known like that? To be seen without filters, without masks, without bullshit?

It should bother me. It *does* bother me. But at the same time... bloody hell, at least it would cut through the bullshit. At least I wouldn't have to guess what he's thinking.

Or what I'm thinking.

Kael's voice drops lower, rougher. "I would be yours. And you would be mine. I would never leave you."

Something inside me tightens. Because fuck, I don't know if I want that.

And I don't know if I don't.

Clearly sensing my confusion, he indicates towards my uneaten food. "Eat. Then it's time to rest."

I nod. He's right. It'll likely be tomorrow by the time we reach the doctor. I have a feeling I'll need my energy to be able to think and act fast so that when her mate spots us, I can talk him out of killing us.

It's easier to think about that confrontation than everything else Kael has shared with me. So, with a resigned sigh, I take a bite of the *rethog* and allow myself to enjoy the flavour. I totally don't think about Kael and how he provided for me or the longing glances he keeps sending my way.

If only he'd come to me when I'd first arrived, scared and so damn confused. But it's a pointless wish. I learned a long time ago that wishing is for children and fools.

And it's been a long time since I was either.

CHAPTER
EIGHT

THE TEMPERATURE'S DROPPED BY AT LEAST fifteen degrees, which wouldn't be so bad if I was dressed for a visit to Tasmania in winter. In fairness, I had no idea it would be so cold, especially since we're truly not that far away from dry heat.

I've given up all pretence of handling the cooler temperature and am full-on snuggling against Kael's back. While his armour is uncomfortable, it's warm from his body heat, and my teeth have somewhat diminished chattering.

"We're not far." Kael's voice is strained, whether from my discomfort or his own, since I'm clinging to him, I don't know. But he hasn't pushed me away or asked me not to strangle him. What he has done is picked up the pace, which seems like a hell of a feat since he was likely already going a good 40 kph.

Needless to say, I've never been in these parts before. The way to Iris's home is simply in my head, a descriptive route I committed to memory before she left Dathanor—something I promised I'd do so I could reach her if needed.

"A little higher and we'll camp." Kael jumps over a gap in the increasingly jagged rock, making my teeth rattle.

I grunt in answer. It's all I can manage.

The wind howls as the temperature plummets further, cutting through my clothes like icy daggers. The first flakes of snow swirl around us, lighter than back home, almost luminous as they catch the dim light. It's beautiful in a way, but I'm too busy focussing on not freaking out to appreciate it.

Kael moves effortlessly, muscles flexing beneath me as he scales the uneven terrain. I try not to look down, but a gust of wind makes me sway, and my stomach lurches. Definitely a mountain.

Shit.

"Hold on," he warns, his voice a steady anchor against the storm. "I will keep you safe." His sigh is soft, as are the words "Now and always" that follow, but I hear them all the same.

The words shouldn't mean so much, but they do. They settle into my bones, a promise I desperately want to believe in.

I bury my face against his shoulder, squeezing my

eyes shut as he lunges forwards, leaping onto the next ledge. His grip is sure, his body a force of nature as he clutches the rock face with one hand before swinging his other arm up to secure us.

I'm clinging to him so tightly, I'm probably cutting off his air supply. "Please don't let me die," I mutter.

Kael grunts, the sound almost amused. "You won't."

To distract myself, I start talking—nonsense, mostly. Stories about home, about Sydney's blistering summers, the scent of eucalyptus in the air, the chaotic energy of city life. I tell him about the beaches, the sand that burns your feet, the weird wildlife that could probably kill you just as easily as whatever's out here.

Kael hums in response, a low vibration beneath me. He's listening.

"You sure I'm not distracting you?" I ask after a moment, my voice tight with nerves.

Another grunt, this one more deliberate. "Your voice... helps. Keeps me focussed."

That startles me into silence, but only for a second. "Really?"

He exhales sharply, and it almost sounds like a laugh. "Yes."

That tiny, unexpected response warms something in my chest, pushing back against the cold.

Then it happens.

He reaches for the next ledge—a solid rock, or so it

seems. But the moment his fingers curl around the edge, it crumbles. I scream as we lurch downwards.

Kael reacts instantly. He twists midair, shoving off the wall to avoid the falling debris. The movement slams me tighter against him as the chunk of rock crashes down, striking his arm before shattering below.

He grunts, but he doesn't let go. His grip is iron, his body straining as he finds another hold and pulls us back up.

My heart is hammering so hard, I might pass out. "Kael! Are you okay?"

"I'm fine," he says, but his jaw is clenched. His breathing is heavier, controlled but rough.

I glance at his arm—no visible blood, but the way he flexes his fingers makes me suspicious. "That rock hit you pretty hard."

He doesn't respond right away, just keeps climbing. When he does speak, it's quiet. "It's nothing."

Bullshit. But what can I do? We're dangling off the side of a bloody mountain. So, I have no choice. I believe him.

The cold is relentless as we continue up. Not even being pressed against Kael's broad back does much to keep me warm anymore. The wind howls through the jagged rock formations, carrying flurries of snow that sting against my exposed skin. My toes are completely numb, and I'm starting to wonder if I'll ever feel them again.

"Iris didn't mention how fucking cold it would be up here," I grumble, my voice muffled against Kael's armour.

He doesn't respond immediately, just keeps moving with that same unwavering determination, but I don't miss the way his arms tighten slightly around my legs with every other pull up, keeping me secure as he climbs.

By the time we reach a clearing—a small, flat stretch of ground nestled against the cliffside—the temperature has dropped even further. The snow is coming down thicker, obscuring everything beyond a few metres. Kael slows and then stops. Without a word, he removes me from his back, setting me down before bundling me towards the cliff wall, away from the deadly edge. His grip is firm but careful, as if he's mindful of how frozen I probably am.

"Wait here," he orders.

A spike of panic lances through me. "What? Where the hell are you going?"

His glowing gaze meets mine. "I'll be back."

The snow swirls around us, making it nearly impossible to see. I can barely make out the tense set of his shoulders, the way he scans our surroundings like he's searching for something.

"Kael—"

Before I can protest further, he pulls something from the pack at his waist—a thin blanket-coat made from some kind of rough, insulated material. He wraps it around me, adjusting it carefully, making sure my neck is covered. It's light but surprisingly warm.

We're close. Closer than we've ever been. Well, face to chest, since he's so damn tall.

He dips his head lower, ensuring the blanket is tucked properly, and I catch the faint glow of his markings beneath the snow dusting his skin. The moment is almost tender. My heart leaps, my mouth suddenly dry, making me momentarily forget the brutal cold threatening to make my dick drop off.

Then his gaze snaps to mine.

Shit.

Right. He can feel what I'm feeling.

He hesitates, his breath visible between us in a thick cloud, and fuck if I don't wonder what it would be like to kiss him. To be his.

But then he steps back. The moment shatters. Immediately, the cold rushes in like a vengeful god.

"I won't be long," he says. And then he's gone, disappearing into the blinding snowfall.

I stare after him, my mind turning against me with every passing second. What if he doesn't come back? What if he loses his way? What if something happens to him?

Why does the thought of that squeeze at my heart so painfully?

I pull the coat tighter around myself, shifting my

frozen feet, trying to keep circulation going. The snow thickens, and I lose sight of the path Kael took. My pulse quickens. Then—movement. A towering shadow emerges from the storm.

For a split second, my panic spikes. But then I recognise the broad frame, the glowing eyes beneath the ice-caked ridges of his skin. Kael looks like a damn abominable snowman.

A laugh bubbles out of me, sharp and almost hysterical. "You look fucking ridiculous."

He stops, snow slipping from his shoulders, and stares at me. He *really* stares at me—deep, searching, like he's peeling back every layer of my soul.

And then he smiles. Not a smirk. Not a brief, amused exhale. A real, blinding, breathtaking smile.

My heart stutters.

"Come," he says. "I've found somewhere out of the storm."

He extends his hand. Three deep blue fingers, palm up. Waiting.

I hesitate for only a fraction of a second before I take it. His skin is cold, but the warmth beneath is unmistakable. He swallows hard, his throat bobbing, before he pulls me closer, wrapping an arm around me to shield me from the wind as he leads me forwards.

We stumble through the snow, Kael's massive frame breaking the worst of the storm's fury. Then I see it—a cave. Different from the last one, as it's properly out of the elements. It's small, barely big enough for four people if they squeezed together. But it's dry.

Relief crashes over me as I all but stumble inside. Kael follows, bending low to get through the entrance. His shoulders almost brush the narrow walls as he straightens inside, his markings casting an eerie, mesmerising glow against the stone.

I sag against the wall, exhausted. "I never want to see snow again."

Kael exhales a short, amused breath. "You say that now."

I roll my eyes. "No, I mean it. If I make it out of this alive, I'm retiring to a fucking desert."

He rumbles a low chuckle, and I realise something —I feel warmer already. The cave is dry, but that's about the only good thing I can say about it. The air is thick with cold, pressing in from all sides. I huddle deeper into my blanket-coat, but the chill has settled into my bones, and no amount of fabric is going to fix that.

Kael sits beside me, still dusted with snow. He exhales, a warm gust of air against the frigid space between us. "There's no wood for fire." His gaze flicks to me, assessing. "But I can warm you another way."

I blink, immediately suspicious. "Uh-huh."

He doesn't react, just continues, "Energy manipulation. I can transfer warmth through touch."

My brows lift. "Oh. All right, then." I pause. "Wait. You have to touch me?"

His glowing eyes remain steady. "Yes."

I narrow my gaze. "Uh-huh. And this isn't some elaborate excuse to get your hands on me?"

He jerks slightly, eyes widening, as if the thought had never even occurred to him. Then, just as quickly, his expression shifts—shock giving way to amusement.

He tilts his head. "Would it work if it was?"

I scoff, even as my eyes widen when he takes off his armour, revealing a light blue tunic. "That wasn't a no."

His lips twitch. "You're cold. I'm offering warmth. That's all."

"Mmm. Right." I rub my arms, shivering harder. My brain is still suspicious, but my body is desperate. Also, I'm starving. The faster I get warm, the faster I can focus on food.

I weigh my options. How do we do this without making it weird?

A few seconds pass, and I give up. *Screw it.* My fucks have all vacated the premises. With a sigh, I clamber over and plant myself directly on Kael's lap.

He stiffens. "What—"

I grab his hands, lift my shirt, and plop his palms onto my stomach. "Do your magic, Glowranth."

His breath hitches, and I don't miss the way his fingers twitch against my skin. He's warm—hot, actually—and I immediately sigh in relief.

Then he groans. Loudly.

Oh.

He cuts it off quickly, but I hear it. I feel it vibrate through his chest. Do I like that I affect him? Fuck yes. Does that make me a little bit of a bastard? Probably. But having someone want me so badly is... well, it soothes something raw inside me. Bruised ego? Check. Bruised heart? Maybe.

I pretend not to notice his reaction as I pull my bag close and start rummaging for food. His fingers flex against my abs, radiating heat, and it's almost impossible not to clench or flex. This is the first time anyone's been up close to my abs since I've had them, and I refuse to acknowledge how much I like the way his hands feel there.

Kael clears his throat, his voice slightly rough. "We should be able to leave at first light. If the storm eases."

"Mm," I hum, finding some dried meat and ration bars—at least that's what I convince myself they are. "And if it doesn't?"

"Then we wait."

I glance back at him. "You're worried about the Hendroy, aren't you?"

"He won't be easy to convince." His voice is quiet. "But if we approach in daylight, we have a better chance of avoiding a fight."

"Great," I mutter. "A chance." But we both know that even if the storm is still raging, we have to leave. Who knows what condition Dawson is in. If he's even still alive. I shove that thought aside, refusing to dwell on negative possibilities.

I tear into my food, chewing thoughtfully. Kael's still watching me, his hands moving slightly—either adjusting the energy transfer or just... touching me.

Kael watches me as I chew, his fingers still radiating warmth against my stomach. "Dawson needs to be saved. Prince Aelith...." He trails off, and I swallow my food, wondering what he really thinks of the prince I've been taught to distrust and who he's been trained to protect. "I understand why you and the Riftborn are wary and don't trust easily. But since Dawson, everything has changed for the prince."

The food in my stomach sours. From the moment Dawson touched Terrafeara, the prince, of all people—one of the royal heirs sworn to enslave Riftborn for their mother—was willing to turn his back on everything.

Kael, though... he didn't change. Not when *I* arrived. Not when the rift ripped me from everything I knew and threw me into this world, into a life I never asked for.

I swallow the bitter taste rising in my throat and push the food around in my palm, the warmth of Kael's hands still sinking into my skin. Why didn't he change? Give up everything?

He chose duty. He chose the prince. He chose to ignore me.

I exhale sharply. "Must be nice. Having someone flip

their entire world view for you. Drop their whole life, abandon everything they believed in, just because you exist." I let out a dry laugh, though it holds no humour. "I bet Dawson will be thrilled."

I wince, pleased Kael can't see my face. Dawson has done nothing wrong—hell, his life is at stake—but sometimes, the bitch in me is strong. Feeling scorned hurts like a motherfucker.

Kael doesn't speak for a moment. His fingers twitch slightly where they rest against my stomach, his touch still steady. When he finally speaks, his voice is quieter. "You think he doesn't deserve that devotion?"

I shift uncomfortably. "That's not what I—" I sigh, rubbing at my face with one hand. "It's not about Dawson. It's about... how fast everything changed for him." I let my hand drop back to my lap. "For me, it's been over two years. I fought for every scrap of trust, for every bit of ground I gained. I bled for it. And I still don't know where I stand half the time."

Kael's fingers flex against my skin again, and I angle myself so I can look back at him. A muscle jumps in his jaw, but he says nothing.

I huff a laugh, shaking my head. "Not that it matters. You made your choice a long time ago."

His gaze sharpens, locking onto mine. "And what choice was that?"

I raise a brow, like it should be obvious. "Duty. Loyalty. To him."

Something in his expression shifts. "Sonny—"

"No, it's fine," I say, waving a hand. "I get it. You have a job. And you're good at it." My lips curl into something wry. "But you don't get to act surprised when I point it out." It doesn't matter that he said he was wrong and he's sorry... right? Two fucking years he effectively abandoned me, deciding even before he met me that I wasn't worth... well, anything.

And fuck if I don't hate myself a little for not being able to let this go. But this is me. Warts and all. I absolutely have issues for days.

Kael exhales slowly. His hands are still on me, still warm, still steady, but I can feel the weight of something pressing down between us. A long moment passes. Then another. Finally, he speaks. "Do you truly believe I wouldn't turn my back on everything for you?"

The words hit me like a punch to the chest. I freeze, my breath catching, my pulse stuttering against my ribs.

Kael doesn't move. Doesn't break eye contact. He just watches me, like he's waiting for me to understand something I refuse to believe.

Do you truly believe I wouldn't turn my back on everything for you?

I don't know what to say.

I don't know what to think.

Except... "Is this only because the prince has found his mate? Do you feel like he'll give you permission now?"

Kael's eyes darken, something like frustration flickering across his face. His grip tightens—just slightly—where his hands rest against my skin, the heat of his touch pulsing through me. "I don't need his permission."

I scoff, looking away, focussing on the rough stone walls instead of the intensity in his gaze. "Don't you?"

He exhales sharply. "You think so little of me?"

I swallow hard, the words getting stuck in my throat. "I think...." I hesitate. "I think you've spent your whole life putting him first. That's what duty is, right? That's what you chose."

His fingers flex again, like he's resisting the urge to grip me tighter. "Duty is what I was born to do," he corrects. "But you—" He inhales, steadying himself. "You are what I choose."

Something inside me clenches, twists painfully. I shake my head, trying to laugh it off. "And yet I'm still here. Freezing my ass off in some cave, two years in, and you're only saying this now."

Kael leans in, just enough that his breath ghosts over my skin, sending a fresh wave of warmth through me. "Then let me prove it."

I stiffen. "How?"

His hands slide slightly, palms smoothing against my stomach with deliberate intent. His voice drops lower. "I will convince you every day as long as my heart beats if I need to."

My breath catches. The storm howls outside, snow hammering against the cave's entrance, but all I feel is him. The warmth of his hands. The steady weight of his presence. The undeniable promise in his words.

I wet my lips, my voice quieter now. "That's a long time."

His gaze doesn't waver. "Then I had best start now."

And before I can think, before I can stop myself, I lean into him just a little more. Just enough that the last sliver of space between us disappears.

Kael exhales, the sound ragged, before he buries his face against my neck. His breath is hot, a stark contrast to the cold still clinging to the edges of the cave. I should push him away, should question this, but I don't —I won't. I can't find the will to move, except to tilt my head, giving him more access.

His lips press against my throat, a slow, lingering kiss that sends a shudder down my spine. My fingers clench in the fabric of his tunic on his arms, gripping him as if he's the only thing anchoring me in this moment. His breath is uneven as he whispers something in Glowranthian, the deep timbre of his voice rolling over me like a caress. I don't understand the words, but my body does, reacting with a sharp, visceral need that sets me alight from the inside out.

Another kiss, this time on my jaw. Then one against my cheek, his lips dragging dangerously close to my mouth. My pulse is a frantic, thudding thing, matching the barely restrained tension humming between us.

I know what's coming next.

And fuck it all to hell, I want it.

I turn into him, meeting his lips with my own. It's just a brush, a fleeting press, but it sets me ablaze. I barely have time to process the second kiss, deeper now, before Kael moves, flipping me so I'm straddling him, my knees sinking into the cave floor.

I've barely opened my eyes when he's on me.

Kael kisses me like he's staking a claim, like this moment has been inevitable from the second we met. And maybe it has. Maybe I've been fighting a losing battle against something that was always meant to unravel me.

His lips press, part, take, and I let him. I let him consume, let him mould me to him, let him make me forget the cold, the storm, the war brewing outside this cave. Right now, there is only this—us.

His fingers tighten at my waist, his hands so large, they nearly span my back, pressing me flush against him. Heat radiates from his body, seeping into mine, melting every layer of resistance I still might have left. I grip his shoulders, nails digging into the hard muscle beneath his tunic as his lips move with a deliberate, aching slowness that undoes me.

He kisses me like he's learning me, like he's memorising every shift, every intake of breath, every tremor that passes through me. And fuck, my body responds to him in ways it never has before.

I've been kissed before. I've wanted before.

But this?

This is something different.

This is a slow-burning fire licking its way through my veins, a deep, consuming hunger that settles low in my stomach and spreads outwards. It's not just desire—it's rightness.

Kael groans low, a rumbling sound that sends a shiver down my spine. His hands slide up my back, pressing me even closer, as if he's trying to fuse us together. His mouth moves from mine, trailing back to my jaw, down the column of my throat, pressing open-mouthed kisses against the sensitive skin.

I gasp, tilting my head to give him more access, and he takes it without hesitation.

His breath is hot against my skin as he murmurs something else in Glowranthian, his voice rough, reverent. I still don't understand the words, but my body responds, and I push against him, trying to get closer.

The sound of his words rolls through me like a pulse, like a second heartbeat, a calling I don't fully comprehend but feel all the same. I fist a hand in his tunic, dragging him back to my mouth, and this time it's me who takes, me who pushes, me who loses myself in him.

Kael groans again, and fuck, I love that sound. Love

the way he reacts to me, like he's barely holding himself together.

One of his hands slides up my spine, tangling in the back of my hair as he deepens the kiss, his tongue sweeping into my mouth, claiming, teasing, coaxing. He's heat and strength and something else entirely— something mine.

A sharp, unshakable certainty settles in my chest.

It's never been like this. *No one* has ever felt like this.

And fuck, I think I'm lost.

Kael's lips slow against mine, turning soft, gentle. Another press, then another, before he draws back just enough for our breaths to mingle, our noses brushing. His hands remain on my waist, anchoring me, but he doesn't pull me back in.

I don't move either.

I don't want to move. Because fuck, I want him. Desperately. Fiercely. But not like this. Not here, in the cold, in a cave carved into the side of a mountain with a storm raging outside.

I think he senses the battle inside me, because instead of pressing for more, he exhales, slow and steady, his fingers tightening just briefly before he eases his grip. "Let's finish eating and then sleep," he says, his voice low and a little rough. "Tomorrow, we'll need to be alert."

I swallow, grateful for the out. "Okay," I surprisingly

manage, despite the lingering heat in my veins. "That's probably a good idea."

Kael watches me, something unreadable flickering in his glowing eyes. Then, before I can second-guess anything, he leans in and presses a small, sweet kiss to the corner of my mouth. Something in my chest— something uncertain and shaky—unravels at the touch.

"Okay," I repeat, this time more confidently.

He studies me for a beat longer, then nods in satisfaction before easing back. The space between us feels unnatural after all that heat, but I force myself to move, to refocus. I take stock of myself, running a hand down my arm, my chest.

Huh. I'm actually warm. I blink, then glance up at him. "I'm toasty."

Kael tilts his head, clearly unfamiliar with the word. "Toast...y?"

I huff a quiet laugh. "It means warm. Comfortable."

Something shifts in his expression—just a flicker of mischief—before he murmurs, "Then I will ensure you remain as warm as the sun that sets fire to the ocean's edge, forever wrapped in my embrace."

I blink. Then I stare. He meets my gaze steadily, like he has no idea he just said something straight out of a dramatic romance novel.

It takes a second for it to click. "Kael," I start slowly. "Just how often did you read those romance novels?"

His lips twitch. "They were helpful for learning English."

A chuckle bursts from me, sudden and real, breaking the tension that had coiled tight between us. Kael's smile is small but there, and I shake my head, shifting off his lap before I do something stupid—like drag him back down and kiss him senseless again.

We eat, his hand on the naked flesh of my back, talking about everything and nothing, the storm still howling outside but feeling a world away. And when it's time to settle in for the night, I don't hesitate to let Kael pull me against him, my back to his chest, his arms wrapped securely around me.

His warmth, his strength, the consistent rise and fall of his breathing—all of it eases me into sleep faster than I thought possible. And just before I drift off, one final thought settles in my chest.

For the first time in a long time, I feel safe.

CHAPTER
NINE

"WELL, SOMETHING ABOUT DAWSON'S ARRIVAL IS seriously messed up. And not just because of the whole fated mate thing."

Kael tilts his head, waiting.

We've been travelling for maybe two hours. The sun is rising, the storm has passed, and thankfully, after another hour of climbing almost vertically, we're at the top of the mountain. Snow glistens on the ground, and with each step Kael takes, his booted feet disappear. I'm even more grateful to be in his kinky backpack.

I shift slightly, trying to get comfortable. "I've been here, like, two years. Dawson? Barely a few days. But here's where it gets really strange." We've been discussing Dawson's arrival, and go me, I've managed to not get sulky even once with the whole "well, Prince

Aelith came straight for his mate, but you didn't, arse-hole" thing. Everything shifted last night. Okay, make that almost everything. I don't want to throw myself at Kael and fully commit just yet. "Dawson was pulled through the rift in Portugal."

Kael frowns. "You both sound similar."

"Yeah, we're both Aussies. But the weird part is that he wasn't the only one, was he?"

His brows lift slightly. "Jack."

I nod. "Jack from Queensland. Which is on the complete opposite side of the planet from Portugal. But if you put a ruler through the Earth—" I mimic drawing a straight line with my hand in front of his face. "—their locations are practically parallel." I exhale, thinking back to the discussion I'd barely had with Varek about this before I left. "No one's ever heard of something like this happening. Not that I know of. Ever."

Kael is silent, his fingers pressed against my ankle, but I can tell he's thinking. Finally, he nods. "True. I've met a lot of Riftborn over the years, and only one rift, in one area, has happened at the same time."

A fizz of excitement bubbles in my gut that I'm onto something. "I think that's what went wrong."

He blinks, looking over his shoulder. "Wrong?"

I nod. "He wasn't just pulled through a rift. He was pulled through the centre of the Earth to get here.

Maybe the rift got confused, maybe it was unstable, maybe something else messed with it—but whatever the case, he came through wrong." Jack's words filter into my brain about the possibility of someone being responsible for the rifts, but I keep my mouth shut.

Kael's jaw tightens. "Dawson's arrival wasn't natural."

"No," I say, wondering at his word "natural." Does he also think someone was responsible? Fuck, considering his position, what if he knows more? Knows the truth? I forge on carefully, saying, "And now something's happening to him. Something's wrong, and if we don't get him help soon—"

Kael doesn't let me finish that thought. His grip flexes slightly on my leg before smoothing out again.

"We'll get to the doctor," he says, voice full of certainty. "We'll save him."

I let out an unsteady breath. Dawson has to be our focus, but the lingering thoughts of the reasons behind the rifts remain. "Yeah."

We stay silent for a moment, the terrain changing gradually around us to something—

"Holy shit!"

Gone is the snow and rock. In its place, a landscape so familiar, my throat closes up. Green grass spreads like a dream, the rolling hills and rich earth stretching towards the horizon. The air is different here—softer, thick with the scent of damp soil and sun-warmed leaves. And in the distance, something that makes my heart stutter.

A windmill.

The blades turn slowly, lazily, against the pale *blue* sky, exactly like the ones I grew up watching in movies. The kind that dotted countrysides back on Earth, where the air held the faint, distant scent of wheat and cattle. My breath catches in my chest, my pulse hammering too fast.

"Put me down," I murmur, my voice shaky, my fingers tightening in Kael's tunic.

He hesitates, his grip on me firm, his warmth grounding. A muscle feathers in his jaw, but after a beat, he obeys, setting me carefully on my feet. The cold shock of missing his heat barely registers as I sway slightly, legs shaky beneath me.

Kael helps unstrap me, his hands sure and steady as I stare at the impossible sight before me.

Home. It looks like home.

A lump rises in my throat, my body caught between longing and the eerie wrongness of it all. This can't be real. It shouldn't be real. Something isn't right.

The wonder curdles into unease when Kael stiffens beside me. I feel it before I see it—the shift in the air, the way the world suddenly holds its breath. His eyes sharpen, darkening as he scans the horizon, his body moving subtly, positioning himself between me and whatever lurks unseen.

Every hair on my body rises.

"We're not alone," he says, voice quiet but edged with steel.

Dread lurches through me, cold and thick. My stomach knots painfully.

It has to be him. The Hendroy.

I swallow hard, forcing my feet to move forwards even as every instinct screams at me to run. My pulse roars in my ears, my breath sharp in my chest.

"I know you're here," I call out, trying to keep my voice steady, though it wavers just enough to betray me. "I come in peace."

Silence. A heavy, unnatural silence that presses against my skin. Something moves at the edges of my vision. A ripple in the air, a disturbance in the stillness.

I wet my lips, forcing myself to keep going. "Do you remember me?" My voice is too fast, too desperate, but I can't stop. "I know Iris. She liked me! Not like that. I'm into dudes. I'm just saying, she didn't hate me."

The wind changes. The air thickens.

Smoke.

It doesn't rise from the ground or spill from a fire—it manifests, curling and seething, thick and black, swirling in the shape of something enormous.

A figure emerges from the dark.

Monstrous.

Too tall, too broad, his presence warping the space around him. Shadow and substance bleeding together into something jagged, shifting. His limbs are too long, his body wrapped in an armour of dark, glistening ridges that flex and move like living metal. Spines curve along his arms, his back, his shoulders. His face—if it can even be called that—is a mask of shifting bone and blackened flesh, eyes burning red in the depths of his skull.

My stomach twists, my knees locking as every part of my brain screams, *Wrong, wrong, wrong.*

Kael moves. Not towards him but in front of me. Lethal, unyielding, his entire stance coiled and ready to strike. His blade is in his hand before I even register him drawing it, his muscles taut with the promise of violence. He doesn't speak. Doesn't challenge.

He just waits.

The Hendroy steps forwards, his presence like a void, sucking the air from my lungs. When he speaks, his voice is a thing of nightmares—low, distorted, vibrating with something ancient and terrible.

I don't understand the words. But I don't need to.

The intent is clear.

Glowranth are not welcome.

He must die.

My breath catches. My fingers tremble at my sides, my body screaming at me to move, but I can't. The air distorts around the Hendroy's hands, something jagged forming in his grasp—black, sharp, brimming with an energy that crackles and spits like living lightning.

I can't think.

Kael is a statue, unmoving, unwavering, his entire being a blade poised to strike. But I know the Hendroy will be faster.

My body moves before my brain catches up. I shove forwards, the words tearing from my throat in pure, unthinking desperation. "He's my mate!"

Time snaps.

Everything freezes.

The Hendroy halts, the deadly energy he wielded poised midair, humming with power, inches from unleashing hell.

My legs give out.

I hit the ground hard, pain ricocheting up my side, my lungs burning. Kael shouts something—distant, warped—but my ears ring too loudly to make sense of it.

Then a new voice slices through the chaos.

Sharp. Commanding.

"Enough!"

Iris.

A gasp claws up my throat, but I don't have time to do more than register her presence before the world tips.

And then—

Fuck it all to hell. Not again.

Darkness.

"—DOESN'T COME AROUND SOON, I'M GOING TO put your balls in a vice."

Iris's words pierce through the fog in my skull, dragging me towards consciousness like barbed wire snagging skin.

"He's awake."

Kael.

Terror crawls up my throat even as relief bounces around my chest. My body pulses with something raw, sharp-edged, emotions not entirely my own. My breath shudders out. My fingers twitch.

And then it slams into me.

Fear. Not mine.

Kael's.

It grips my lungs, coils tight in my ribs, a gut-deep panic that doesn't belong to me but pulses through my bloodstream as if it does. My stomach lurches. My hands clench. The unease grows, hot and suffocating, right alongside a searing anger.

I gasp.

The bond. Fuck.

The events play out behind my closed eyelids—Kael, the Hendroy, the sheer, inhuman terror of standing in front of him, of knowing Kael was about to die. And then my voice, my body moving before thought, throwing myself between them. The words I spat out: *He's my mate.*

I started the process.

And Kael knows it.

Knows I'm awake. Knows I can feel him. His worry mounts, rising in waves, crashing over me so fiercely that my own thoughts scatter. I need to move, to let him know I'm here, but my body still feels like lead, sluggish and wrung out.

Move, idiot.

I force my hand up, blindly reaching into the space beside me. Kael's fingers latch onto mine instantly, strong and grounding, his grip firm like he's afraid I'll disappear. A second later, his other hand brushes my hairline, fingers sifting through strands damp with sweat, sweeping them back with a gentleness that rattles me.

"You're okay," he murmurs, rough with relief. "You're okay."

I hum, a weak, croaking sound, but it's enough. His fingers tighten around mine before smoothing out again.

"Yeah," I rasp. "Alive, I think."

"You are." His voice is thick with something unspoken.

"I was about to beat the shit out of Henny," Iris grinds out, her voice sharp with fury.

A laugh—rough, choked—punches out of me. "Henny?"

"Not his real name, obviously," she mutters. "But that bastard deserves it for nearly killing you."

I pry my eyes open slowly, the light sending a stab of pain through my skull before it evens out. Blinking past the haze, I take them in. Kael, crouched beside me, fingers still tangled in my hair, his gaze burning with an intensity that makes my throat tight. And Iris, arms crossed, shoulders tense, her mouth pressed into a hard line.

Iris exhales sharply. "I'm sorry."

That yanks me out of my haze. I shift, trying to push myself up, but Kael's hand instantly presses against my chest, urging me to stay down.

I frown at her. "For what?"

She glances at Kael before looking back at me, her lips twisting. "You remember what happened?"

"Your... the Hendroy," I say, throat dry. "He... he was going to kill Kael. And I—" My breath hitches. "The bond."

She nods grimly. "You initiated it. Not fully, but enough that it stalled him. Enough that he knew."

A shiver rolls through me.

Iris sighs, rolling her shoulders. "My mate isn't like the rest of us. He's... something other, even for the Hendroy. He's built for destruction, for war. And he was made that way." Her expression darkens, guilt flickering across her features before she quickly shoves it down. "But you—" She exhales, shaking her head. "He was going to kill Kael. I don't think anything would have stopped him. Not even me."

A cold weight settles in my chest.

"Then why did he?"

Her gaze flicks to Kael's hand still resting against my chest, his other still in my hair, and something like understanding sharpens in her eyes. "Because of the bond." Her voice is soft now, edged with something like awe. "Because you claimed Kael, and you meant it."

A muscle feathers in Kael's jaw. His clawed fingers curl slightly in my hair, a quiet anchor, but he doesn't say anything.

Iris scoffs, shaking her head. "I don't know if this was wanted or not, but I swear to the gods, if you ever pull that reckless shit again, I will personally murder you."

I huff out a weak laugh. "Noted." Though, to be fair, how else was I meant to get a message to her?

Kael still hasn't stopped touching me. His fingers slide gently along my scalp, down to my temple, grounding.

It should feel weird. Too much.

But it doesn't.

It just feels... right.

"Let's get you up, and you can tell me what brought you here."

Just like that, my mind sharpens. Dawson. His life is hanging in the balance, and every second we waste is a second too long.

Kael must sense my urgency because he moves first, easily shifting me upright, his arm bracing my back as I push myself up. My body protests—hell, my soul protests—but I shove it all down.

Iris watches me carefully, and before she turns to lead us forwards, I ask, "Where's your mate?"

Her lips press together before she exhales. "Lurking."

I raise an eyebrow.

She rolls her eyes. "After you passed out, I ripped him a new one. Then I told him to make himself scarce before you woke up."

I glance around, gaze skimming over the green pastures and rolling hills. Scarce probably means he's standing just beyond sight—or in his woo-woo black smoke—watching us like a possessive demon-lurking arsehole. Because, well... that's exactly what he is.

As we follow her towards the house, I take in everything, and my mind short-circuits. Again.

This is not what I expected.

The vibrant green grass underfoot, the crisp blue sky above, the scattering of wildflowers that look like they belong in an English countryside and not on a goddamn alien planet. It's too... real. Too perfectly Earth-like.

I glance at Kael, but he's busy keeping a hand on my

lower back, steadying me as I try to take it all in. "How?" I breathe, eyes widening. "How the hell does this exist here?"

Iris's lips quirk. "What, never seen grass before?"

"Not like this," I say, still turning in a slow circle. "Well, not in years. Hell, Iris—this is literally something I've only ever seen on TV." It is simply perfect. And then I freeze, my eyes snapping towards the stone cottage ahead of us, and my brain breaks. My lips part. "Hold on. Is that Jude Law's cottage from that Christmas movie?"

She stops. Then, to my utter shock, her cheeks flush. She crosses her arms and mutters, "Maybe."

"Oh my God," I whisper, turning wide eyes on her. "This is the cottage from *The Holiday*."

Iris exhales through her nose, looking vaguely embarrassed. "Yeah. So?"

I blink at her. Then at the house. Then at her again. "Your mate built this?"

She nods, not meeting my gaze. "Created it for me."

I don't even know where to start with that. "Jesus. Okay, first, he's a terrifying, uhm"—I hold back from saying "demon"—"Hendroy who nearly murdered me, but his skill set apparently includes architecturally perfect recreations of romantic comedy film sets?"

Her mouth twitches. "Guess so."

My eyes goggle as I stare at the stone walls, the

charming little windows, the goddamn ivy crawling up the sides. "This is insane."

Iris clears her throat, her gaze flicking towards the door as if her mate might suddenly materialise. "*The Holiday* is one of my favourite movies," she admits, voice quieter now. "I always dreamed of living in a place like this."

I let out a slow, awestruck whistle. "Damn." I shake my head. "Impressive." The second the words leave my mouth, I feel it. A sharp pang, deep in my chest. Not mine. Kael's. I blink, confused for half a second before realisation dawns.

He's jealous.

A laugh nearly spills from me, but I swallow it back. He knows I felt it too. The way he tenses slightly beside me, the way his hand presses just a little firmer against my lower back. I rub at my chest absentmindedly, trying to smooth the feeling out.

It's funny. A little ridiculous, really. I could tease him about it.

But I don't.

Because I passed out. Because he had to watch me go down, helpless, probably wondering if I was going to wake up at all.

Instead, I just exhale softly, letting warmth pool through the bond, through us, and I let him feel it.

I'm here.

And how the hell I've done that or even know that's

possible is beyond me. I'm going by pure instinct here. I don't think he heard me as much as he sensed me.

Kael's fingers twitch against my spine. And then, finally, the tension in him eases.

I'm sore, but I'm coping. I don't know exactly what I was hit with or why I went down, but one of the things I've learned since being spliced through the rift is to not question everything. Some things just are, and survival depends on rolling with it.

Iris leads us inside, and the second I step into her cottage, I almost forget the soreness pulling at my muscles.

It's perfect.

Warm and inviting, with wooden beams across the ceiling, a stone fireplace that crackles with soft orange light, and a couch so plush, I could sink into it for days. The air smells like fresh wood and something lightly floral. And then there's the kitchen—a rustic dream, with dark oak cabinets, gleaming brass fixtures, and a sink that looks like it belongs in a period drama.

But all of that pales in comparison to what Iris hands me.

A glass of water.

A *real* glass—smooth and solid in my grip, not some cheap, repurposed scrap metal.

The water inside is crystal clear, beads of condensation trailing down the sides like something out of a goddamn commercial. I stare for half a second before instinct kicks in. I bring it to my lips and take a gulp—then another, and another, until I drain the entire thing.

The cold rushes through me, fresh and impossibly crisp. It tastes pure, none of the metallic tang I've grown used to on Terrafeara. It's clean, smooth, almost silky against my tongue, quenching a thirst I hadn't even realised I had.

Pre-Terrafeara me wouldn't recognise this moment—me, standing here, damn near orgasming over water. I lower the empty glass, inhaling deeply as the coolness settles in my chest.

Iris watches me with an arched brow. "Thirsty?"

"You have no idea," I mutter, voice rough.

She smirks but doesn't comment further. Instead, she crosses her arms and nods towards Kael. "All right. Spill. What the hell brought you here?"

Kael glances at me, checking in. I give him a slight nod, still clutching my glass, and he shifts slightly, facing Iris. "It's about Dawson," he says, his voice steady but edged with something tight. "The new human."

Iris nods, indicating that she's listening.

Kael continues. "He's been here a few days, but something's... wrong."

He hesitates, and I can feel the frustration in him—the need to explain this in a way that makes sense when none of it does.

She waits, her expression sharp with focus.

Kael exhales. "He wasn't just pulled through a rift.

He was pulled through the centre of the Earth to get here."

Iris blinks. "Excuse me?"

He presses on. "Jack—another human—was pulled through from Australia. And we're sure it was at the same time, the same rift. Dawson came through in Portugal. Opposite sides of the world. If you put a ruler straight through the Earth—" He mimics the motion, just as I had earlier. "—their locations practically line up."

Her brows knit together, but her eyes gleam with something thoughtful.

Kael carries on. "Whatever happened to Dawson, it wasn't natural. And now, something's happening to him." His words catch slightly, his jaw tightening.

I take over.

"He was unconscious for hours," I say, gripping my glass a little tighter. "When he was found, his body temperature was low. Too low. Then he woke up—seemed fine—but out of nowhere, he fitted." I swallow hard. "He stopped breathing."

Iris stiffens. "As in had a seizure?"

I bob my head. "Yes. He had a pulse but no breath. I gave him CPR, and he started breathing again. It didn't make sense. It still doesn't." I meet her gaze, my stomach twisting. "We don't know what's wrong. We're at a loss and need your help."

Iris doesn't answer immediately. Instead, she stands.

I track her movements as she goes to a cabinet, opening it with quick, precise hands. She starts gathering supplies—bundles of herbs, small vials filled with liquid, things I don't recognise but I suppose must be important.

"So, let me get this straight," she says, not looking up. "This guy wasn't just pulled through a rift. He got slingshotted through the core of the Earth?"

Kael nods once as I wince, saying, "It's just a theory at this point."

Iris snorts, shaking her head. "Jesus. No wonder he's fucked up."

I almost laugh. Almost. Instead, I watch as she keeps working, pulling more items from her stores. And despite everything—the pain, the exhaustion, the way my body still doesn't quite feel like my own—relief unfurls in my chest.

Because she's already moving. Already helping. Already calling, "Hen—" Iris barely gets the second syllable of his name out before her mate appears.

One second, the space near the doorway is empty. The next, he's there.

I jump. Hard. Nearly dropping my empty glass.

Kael doesn't jump. But he does turn to steel, his entire body locking down in a way that makes my own muscles tense in response. He doesn't reach for his blade, but I can feel how much he wants to.

I can't blame him.

The Hendroy—*Henny*—stands like something conjured from the deepest, most primeval parts of existence. Shadows coil around his massive form, his eyes gleaming with something unreadable and deeply unsettling.

If he had eyebrows, I'm pretty sure they'd be furrowed into a scowl.

Iris, completely unfazed, just sighs and turns to him. "I need to go to Dathanor."

Henny does not like this.

His stare sharpens, his entire presence seeming to vibrate with displeasure. And yet neither of them speak. They just... look at each other.

It lasts long enough for the hairs on my arms to rise. I shift uncomfortably, glancing back and forth as something icy and silent passes between them.

Oh. Oh hell.

They're talking. Not out loud, but in that eerie, telepathic, I'm-so-bonded-to-you-I-don't-even-need-words way. My pulse stumbles, my stomach lurching as the realisation lands with a weight I wasn't ready for.

Because I started my side of the bond with Kael.

I swallow hard, my heart jumping—not quite in panic, but in the stark awareness that my life is already irrevocably changed.

Before I can spiral too much, Kael shifts closer. Then, to my surprise, he comforts me.

He leans in, his breath warm against my ear as he

murmurs, "You are not alone in this." His voice is low, deep, and threaded with something so steady that my entire body reacts before my mind catches up. A shiver —a delicious one—runs down my spine.

Damn.

I can't wait to get on a proper bed with this man. This Glowranth who's promised to be mine. Somehow, I hold back my amusement at myself. Apparently, I'm a fickle bitch.

Iris interrupts before I can do anything about it. "All right, I'm ready."

I blink. "Shit, already?"

I know we have to go. I know Dawson's life is hanging in the balance. But damn, I'd really been hoping for food. And maybe five glorious minutes in an actual bed.

Iris watches my expression shift, and then she laughs. "Oh, don't worry," she says, her grin knowing. "We're not walking."

"What do you mean?" I narrow my eyes.

She gestures vaguely towards Henny. "Why would we trek when my Henny can transport us there in the blink of an eye?"

Kael goes rigid. More rigid than before. I glance at him, then at Henny, who just stares at us. And not in a friendly way. More like he's picturing our bodies splattered against a rock and wondering whether it would be inconvenient to clean up.

"Right," I say, exhaling sharply. "That's... great. I love interdimensional smoke vortex travel."

Kael does not love it. At all. He looks at me. Looks at Iris. Looks at Henny, who hasn't moved an inch but still somehow feels closer. "This is a bad idea," he mutters.

Iris waves a hand. "Relax. You'll be fine."

Kael does not relax. Neither do I, honestly. But eventually, we agree, because what other choice do we have?

Henny lifts one massive hand. Smoke swirls around us, thick and curling, swallowing everything in an instant.

As the world distorts, I barely get the chance to say, "If we die, I'm haunting you, Iris," before the ground vanishes beneath my feet.

The shift from swirling smoke to solid ground is so abrupt that I stumble forwards, catching myself just in time. We're inside Dathanor's headquarters, not the main township.

Smart. No need to terrify the masses with Henny's looming, shadow-drenched presence. That being said, the weapons trained on us aren't great.

My hands fly up instinctively. "It's me, Sonny! I've brought Iris!"

The mist fully clears just as Varek races through the door. His gaze locks onto me, his frown deep and assessing—but then, just as quickly, it eases. A smile forms, relief flashing in his sharp eyes.

"Sonny," he greets me, and that single word carries more weight than I expected.

I grin. "Told you I'd make it."

Varek lets out a short laugh, shaking his head. "That you did."

We're still grinning at each other when his gaze flicks past me, landing on Henny.

To most, Varek looks completely calm. Unruffled. But I know better. The tension in his jaw, the subtle way his stance shifts, weight distributing evenly, his body ready despite his relaxed posture—he's anxious.

Because everyone knows the Hendroy's reputation.

Varek doesn't step closer—because he knows that would be stupid. Instead, he inclines his head in something between diplomacy and self-preservation. "Thank you for coming."

Henny doesn't respond. Just stares.

Varek moves on quickly. "We relocated Dawson to a medical room on the west side of Dathanor."

I nod, understanding immediately. That area isn't for residents. It's cordoned off. Secure. Likely hiding the prince away as much as possible—though let's be real, everyone knows he's here.

Shit. Has Aelith been throwing his title around? I want to ask. I won't, though, not with Henny and Kael here. Instead, I cut straight to what matters. "What's his status?"

Iris speaks before Varek can. "Explain while we walk. I want to see him."

No argument there.

We move, falling into step with Varek leading us. I stay at Iris's side, Kael a silent shadow behind me. Henny lingers just beyond that, and even with all the space around us, everyone gives him a wide berth.

Varek doesn't comment, keeping his voice level as he starts explaining. "He was conscious once, but not for long," he says. "His body isn't stabilising. We put him on a drip."

I nod. "Good thing we've scavenged enough human buildings to stock some medical supplies."

"It's helped," Varek agrees. "But his vitals keep fluctuating. He should be dead."

Something in my stomach twists. "But he's not."

"No." Varek glances at me. "Not yet."

The unease in his voice needles at me, but I keep my focus forwards as we step outside. The air is fresh. Familiar. It smells like home.

The blue sky and green grass back at Iris's place were glorious, but this—this is real. Not conjured. Not built from the dreams of a woman who wanted to live in a Christmas movie.

Dathanor is mine. And I belong here. Something I can't believe I'm actually admitting to myself, but here I am.

The walk is short, our route avoiding prying eyes.

But when we arrive at the west gate, the guards let us through immediately. I catch the way their gazes widen slightly when they see me. And damn it, is it bad that I want to stick my chest out a little?

Because fuck yeah, I made this happen. Admittedly, Kael may have done the grunt work, but I managed to not get us killed by Henny. It's a definite win.

The moment Varek silently opens the door to the medical bay, my self-praise screeches to a halt. My gaze lands on Dawson, and my stomach plummets. *What the fuck?* He's pale—so pale, his skin looks almost translucent. His usual warmth, the deep bronze of his complexion, is gone.

"We were only gone three days," I whisper, my voice wobbly.

A sharp movement pulls my attention. The prince. Prince Aelith looks—*fuck*. He looks haggard. Barely half the Glowranth he was when we left. The sharp lines of his face seem more pronounced, his posture wrong, like he's not just exhausted but drained.

Kael's worry slams into me. It's visceral. Deep. Shakes my very core, and it propels him forwards. He doesn't hesitate, moving straight to his prince's side.

I watch the exchange, the way Kael's hands press to Aelith's shoulders, steadying him, offering whatever comfort he can. Aelith exhales sharply, and though he doesn't speak, I feel the weight of what passes between them. My chest tightens.

Iris, meanwhile, rushes straight to Dawson, her movements quick and certain.

A sound rumbles low in the room.

The prince.

A warning.

Kael turns sharply. "No." The word is a command, his voice edged with steel, and Aelith stills, though tension vibrates through his body. Then, suddenly—

Black mist billows into the room. Thick. Blinding.

I curse, instinctively reaching for Kael, but before I can so much as move, Iris's voice cuts through the haze. "Henny, knock it off!"

Silence.

Then the mist vanishes just as suddenly as it came, revealing an irritated Iris and a stone-faced Henny near the door, dark energy still curling faintly around his fingers.

Iris exhales sharply. "I need space. Room."

"No," Aelith says immediately, his voice hoarse but firm.

She turns to him fully, her eyes searching, really looking. Then she says, "You're his fated." It's not a question. Kael stiffens beside Aelith. Iris lifts a brow. "But it's not a fully formed bond yet?"

A beat. Then Aelith answers, voice tight. "No."

She nods, gaze shifting, calculating. "Fine. You can stay. Everyone else, out."

Tension crackles through the room. The mist stirs again, thickening.

Iris sighs and turns to Henny. "Fine," she says softly, frustration curling at the edges of her words. "Stay. But disappear."

Henny legit goes *poof*. One second, he's there. A hulking, ominous presence. The next—gone.

I gape at the now-empty space. Will there ever be a time when I get used to this weird, monstrous shit? No. Probably not.

I move towards the door, Kael at my side—until Aelith speaks again.

"Kael. Stay."

Kael hesitates. His shoulders tense. He's torn.

I glance at him, catching the war on his face, the conflict in his stance. His concern for Aelith is palpable. And so, before I think too hard about it, I offer him a small smile. A reassuring nod. And I send comfort to him through our bond.

His breath stutters. His gaze flicks to me. Then he swallows, and I feel his gratitude ripple through the growing tether between us.

The door closes behind me. And fuck—

Why does it hurt? It shouldn't hurt like this. Right?

A shadow moves in front of me, blocking my view of the small window in the door. Varek. His massive frame looms, his presence solid. His expression? Not good.

"Sonny," he says, voice low. "What the fuck have you

done?" Concern laces his features, sharp and unre-lenting.

I grimace. "You make it sound like I burned down a village."

He doesn't even blink.

"*Frigth drigth*, Sonny," he mutters, dragging a hand down his face. "Three days. Three days you're out of my sight, and you what? Tell me what I'm sensing isn't true." His eyes bore into me. Waiting. Demanding.

I swallow. And suddenly, I really, *really* wish I'd got a full night's sleep before dealing with this shit.

CHAPTER
TEN

Varek had sensed something before Kael and I left in search of Iris. His woo-woo ways had tipped him off to the possibility of a bond forming, but when I confirmed that the mating ritual—or whatever the hell it's called—had started, he'd been concerned.

He didn't say why.

And now, nearly twenty-four hours later, his concern is becoming more obvious. Maybe because, after completing one of the three bond stages, I haven't seen Kael since. Not once.

Not when I swung by the medical room before turning in for the night—only to be refused entry. Talk about a kick in the nuts.

Not when I woke up this morning, chest aching like a bruise I couldn't press my fingers to.

Not even when I stomped my foot in the privacy of my quarters, fuming like some jilted lover.

Which, technically, I'm not, because nothing has been sealed.

But still. I feel it. The hollowness where Kael should be. The pull of the bond, frayed at the edges, stretching thinner and thinner the longer we stay apart. And yes, I know poor Dawson is gravely ill. I know Kael is loyal to Prince Aelith. I get it.

But what about me? What about the connection we started?

Kael had whispered sweet words when we were alone, when there were no distractions beyond our survival. But now? Now he's back to being Aelith's lapdog.

My fingers twitch at the thought, curling into a fist before I shake them out. I need to move. To hit something. To do something before this frustration eats me alive. Which is why I'm currently stalking towards the training grounds, hellbent on hacking at one of the mannequins—made of some weird material that won't dull my blade, won't splinter beneath my daggers.

Maybe it'll make me feel better. Or maybe I just need to stop thinking about Kael for five damn minutes.

The training grounds are alive with movement, the air thick with the sounds of combat—grunts, shouts, the unmistakable clash of steel and other, stranger weapons.

The space itself is an open-air compound, cordoned off by towering stone slabs that serve as both a barrier and a tactical advantage. Some fighters use them for cover, others for vertical manoeuvring, leaping unnaturally high with the help of enhanced limbs or their species' abilities. The ground beneath my boots is a mix of packed dirt and sections of smooth, reinforced alloy —areas designed for heavier combat that could shatter stone or kick up debris dangerous enough to blind.

To my right, a Xelthari swings twin crescent blades, their shimmering edges slicing through the air with whistle-sharp precision. Their four arms make it an impossible dance to track, each limb a blur as they carve patterns in the air. Their scaled skin shimmers with each movement, as if drawing power from their own exertion.

Nearby, another Riftborn tests a weapon that looks like a fusion of a staff and a long-range rifle, the energy core in its centre glowing faintly. He's sparring with someone wielding an orbital whip—a segmented weapon that snakes around its target before snapping closed like a wild dog trap.

The scents here are familiar—sweat, dirt, the metallic tang of weapons being tested and recalibrated. But layered beneath is something distinctly other—the faint crackle of energy in the air, an ozone-like sharpness that prickles against my skin.

I nod at a few rebels as I pass, exchanging brief

greetings with some of the fighters I've trained with before. But there's tension in the air beyond just the usual combat energy.

Taliah, a lean, dark-skinned female Frigthor with short silver-streaked hair, is wiping down the edge of her glaive when I reach her. She lifts a brow in greeting. "You hear?"

I pause, already reaching for my sword belt. "Hear what?"

She tilts her head towards a group gathered near one of the equipment stations. Their voices are low but urgent, shoulders tense.

"The Queen's Guard hit one of our communication networks. Dismantled it."

I exhale sharply, running a hand through my hair. That explains the frantic energy, the increased numbers here today. I glance at the others, catching snippets of conversation.

"—lost the relay completely—"

"—no transmissions since last night—"

"—Varek's going to have to make a move—"

My jaw tightens. That's a direct hit against us. We rely on those networks to track movements, keep our supply lines steady, and maintain any kind of upper hand. And if the Queen's Guard is actively tearing them down, they're gearing up for something.

Which is why Varek wants Aelith on our side so badly.

I file the information away and roll my shoulders, refocussing on why I came here.

I head towards the training dummies—life-sized constructs made of reinforced fibres and adaptive plating, designed to withstand relentless strikes without falling apart. The one I choose is humanoid-shaped, lined with impact sensors that flash when a strike lands.

I grip my dagger, flipping it once before shifting into stance.

Breathe in.

Move.

My first strike is quick, my dagger slashing across the dummy's midsection before I twist into a second strike, aiming higher, slicing upwards in a brutal arc. The clang of metal against reinforced plating echoes in my ears, and I feel the vibration through my arm.

My footwork is precise, honed from hours of practice. I move fast, light on my feet, slipping into the close-quarters combat that suits my smaller frame. I may be shorter and leaner than most here, but my muscles are defined, built for speed and efficiency. Where others rely on brute force, I focus on technique —slipping past defences, striking in quick, and what I hope are devastating, bursts.

Heat builds in my limbs, sweat slicking my skin as I lose myself in the rhythm of the fight.

Jab. Slice. Pivot.

A feint, followed by a deep slash—my dagger

catching the dummy's "neck" in a brutal finishing move.

I exhale, stretching my arms and neck, before reaching for the hem of my shirt and pulling it over my head. The cool air hits my skin, but it does little to chase away the heat burning beneath. I toss my shirt onto a nearby bench, stretching briefly before resetting my stance—only to hear a sharp snort of laughter behind me.

"Should've known the royal guard had a type."

I still, my grip tightening on my dagger before I turn. Zeyv.

Of course it's Zeyv.

His species—something between reptilian and humanoid—gives him an unsettling, scaled appearance. His elongated pupils gleam in the midday light, forked tongue flicking briefly as he smirks.

I don't bother to hide my irritation. "And what exactly is that supposed to mean?"

His grin widens, showing serrated teeth. "Small. Pretty. Obedient."

A few of the others nearby pause in their training, sensing the tension.

I arch a brow. "You clearly don't know shit about me if you think obedient is anywhere on the list."

Zeyv shrugs his thick shoulders. "Not what I heard. Word is, you've been getting real cosy with the prince's pet."

Gossip travels fast. Too fast. And it's clear that despite Varek's efforts to keep the prince's presence quiet, the community knows.

I exhale sharply, forcing my stance to stay relaxed. If I react too quickly, I lose.

Zeyv circles me slowly, watching. "Didn't think a Riftborn would be so quick to roll over and become some royal lapdog."

And fuck if I didn't think the same thing earlier about Kael. *Ouch*. Talk about having my words thrown back in my face. My blood boils, but I keep my face blank. Because I know exactly what Zeyv is trying to do.

And fuck him. I'm not giving him the satisfaction.

The tension thickens like a brewing storm, the air practically vibrating with it. Around us, a few more fighters pause in their training, turning just enough to catch the exchange without making it obvious they're paying attention. Some pretend to stretch, others busy themselves with adjusting weapons, but I see the sideways glances, the subtle shifts of weight.

Zeyv circles me like a predator sizing up prey, but I don't move, just watch him with a bored expression. I've dealt with enough arrogant pricks to know exactly how to handle one.

"Roll over?" I repeat, tilting my head slightly. "Interesting choice of words. You spend a lot of time imagining me on my back, Zeyv?"

The low murmur of interest from our audience is

immediate. A few let out short, surprised huffs—half amusement, half intrigue.

Zeyv's smirk twists, his forked tongue flicking briefly. His species—whatever the hell it actually is—doesn't blush per se, but the darkening of his scales at his throat makes it clear my words landed. "I wouldn't touch you if I was starving and you were the last scrap of meat left in a dying dimension," he sneers.

I place a hand over my chest in mock devastation. "You wound me." Then I glance at his stance, the way his muscles coil, the irritation leaking through his usually cocky posture. "Wait—you are starving, aren't you?" I add, my tone dripping with false realisation. "For attention, I mean. And what, you thought I'd be an easy target? You really don't know me at all."

His pupils slit further, his tail flicking behind him in agitation.

Yeah, I hit a nerve.

"I know you," he snaps, stepping closer. "Varek's little project. The runt he scooped up and decided to play favourites with."

Ah. There it is.

I cross my arms over my chest, tapping a finger against my bicep. "Ohhh, this is about Varek. You're still salty he didn't take you under his wing?"

"I don't need anyone to carry me," Zeyv growls.

I hum. "Right. Because you're a big, strong, independent lizard-man who definitely isn't still crying over the fact that Varek didn't see whatever potential you think you have."

More murmurs from the gathered group. Some smirk behind their hands, others shift slightly—torn between amusement and the growing likelihood that this is about to get physical.

Zeyv's claws flex at his sides.

And there it is.

The truth of it all.

It's not just that Varek has always had a soft spot for me—it's that he didn't have one for Zeyv. The jealousy oozes off him like oil.

"You think you're special?" he hisses. "You think because you can swing a blade and piss off the right people, you matter?"

I let out an exaggerated gasp. "Me? Piss people off? That can't be right."

A couple of chuckles ripple through the crowd, which only seems to fuel Zeyv's frustration. He steps into my space, the heat of his breath hitting my face, his scaled fingers curling into fists. I don't back up. I just tilt my head up to look him dead in the eye, my stance loose but ready.

"Careful," I say, voice low, my blade still warm in my grip. "If you want to dance, I don't lead, Zeyv. I finish."

His eyes flick to the dagger in my hand, then back to my face.

Oh, he wants to. Every instinct in his oversized,

overcompensating body is screaming at him to take a swing.

But here's the thing. Zeyv's strong. He's fast. But he's predictable.

And he knows it.

He also knows that if he starts a fight with me here and loses? It'll never go away.

He hesitates, nostrils flaring, the tension crackling between us like a live wire. And then, just as I see the decision form in his narrowed eyes—

"Zeyv."

The voice that cuts through the thick air is frigid. Commanding. I don't need to turn to know who it is.

Varek.

And judging by the silence that falls over the training grounds, I'm not the only one who just got a chill down my spine.

Varek stands like an immovable wall, arms crossed, gaze sharp as it sweeps over the gathered Riftborn. But it's not him who steals my breath—it's Kael. He's right beside Varek, silent and brooding, his dark eyes locked on me.

Goddamn.

I eat him up with my eyes, noting the tension in his jaw, the way his shoulders are stiff, the slight crease on his forehead. He looks tired—and hella pissed off. My stomach swoops, heat licking at my skin because I can feel it, that barely contained rage simmering beneath his composed surface.

I straighten slightly, rolling my shoulders. What the hell is his problem? Is he pissed at me?

Varek speaks, but Kael stays silent, a sentinel of barely leashed fury. "Zeyv." His voice is like the crack of a whip, sharp and cold.

Zeyv doesn't flinch, doesn't cower like some would in the face of that tone. Instead, he lifts his chin and says, "Just trying to help. Wanted to spar with Sonny." His forked tongue flicks briefly, but his eyes remain on me.

I smile, slow and sharp. "Is that what we're calling it?"

Varek shifts his attention to me, assessing, no doubt weighing whether this is a terrible idea. Eventually, his lips press into a flat line, and he gives a single nod. "Fine. But if you get yourself killed"—he looks at Zeyv—"don't say I didn't warn you."

Kael looks ready to explode.

His fingers twitch at his sides, his entire body rigid. He doesn't speak, but his emotions roll through me like a wave—frustration, worry, anger. I send him a thread of calm, something quiet and steady.

I feel the way it hits him. The way he sucks in a breath like he wasn't expecting it. Then I grin, stepping back and gesturing to Zeyv. "Go ahead, lizard dick. Let's see what you got."

Zeyv smirks, rolling his shoulders as he steps forwards. "Hope you can keep up, human."

"Oh, I'll do more than that."

The moment Varek gives the go-ahead, Zeyv lunges.

I barely twist out of the way, my boots skidding against the worn ground. He's fast, I'll give him that, but I knew he'd go for brute strength first—probably hoping to end this quickly. Too bad for him, I don't play like that.

I move swiftly, ducking and weaving, using my size to my advantage. He's got reach, sure, but I'm small, and more importantly, I'm smart. I anticipate the next strike before it happens, shifting my weight just enough to let him miss, feeling the rush of air as his fist cuts through empty space.

The gathered crowd watches in silence, the intensity in the air thick enough to choke on.

I land the first solid hit, a sharp elbow to his ribs that earns a grunt. But Zeyv doesn't back down—he drives forwards, forcing me to dodge and pivot.

I feel Kael's gaze on me, burning. The weight of it distracts me for a second too long—and Zeyv takes advantage. Pain bursts across my side as he slams a heavy hit into my ribs. "Fuck," I gasp, stumbling back a step, even as another hit comes. I jerk my head back as his fist grazes my jaw and lip, enough to have it splitting, but thank Christ not enough to break my jaw.

A snarl cuts through the air—Kael's. Varek moves

fast, a hand snapping out to grip Kael's arm, stopping him from charging forwards.

"He's fine," Varek says, but his voice is low, almost a warning.

I don't look at Kael—I can't afford to—but I feel his frustration, feel the heat of it even from a few metres away. Instead, I wipe my mouth, dragging my forearm across my lips, and exhale sharply. "Not bad."

Zeyv grins. "Not done."

Good.

Neither am I.

I launch forwards before he can fully reset, going low this time. He expects me to meet him head-on, but instead, I slide beneath his reach, twisting at the last second and bringing my blade around in a controlled arc—just enough to press the cool metal against the underside of his chin.

Zeyv freezes. The crowd goes utterly silent. His throat bobs, jaw clenched tight.

I shift just enough to meet his wide, stunned gaze, panting. "Yield."

For a moment, he doesn't move. His pride is screaming at him to keep going, to win, but the cold bite of my dagger is enough of a reminder that if this had been real, he'd be bleeding out already.

He exhales sharply. Then, finally—reluctantly—he nods. "Yield."

I pull back and step away, dragging in a breath. The

moment my blade is no longer at his throat, Zeyv hesitates, then flicks a glance to Varek—and maybe Kael—before shifting his attention back to me.

I offer him my hand. His gaze moves between it and my face, something unreadable in his expression. For a second, I think he's going to refuse. Then, with a stiff nod, he clasps my hand, his grip firm but brief as I help pull him to his feet.

But even as he stands, something lingers in his eyes —something I don't trust. And when he turns, walking towards the small group of his friends that hover at the edge of the training grounds, I feel it. That prickle down my spine.

I roll my shoulders, shoving the feeling down as I turn—

Varek is right there.

But Kael?

Kael is not.

Disappointment slams into me.

Varek's presence beside me is solid, grounding as I grab my shirt and we make our way across the training grounds. The early haze of adrenaline is gone now, leaving only the sting in my ribs and a weird hollow ache I can't shake. Probably because the one person I want nearby isn't.

"Any word on Dawson?" I ask, breath still a little ragged.

Varek sighs. "Still unconscious. Iris has been

running tests and keeping him stable. It doesn't look great, but he hasn't got worse."

I slow slightly. "So... we're in limbo."

He nods grimly. "Exactly that."

I chew my cheek, trying not to let the disappointment sink too deep. "He's strong," I offer, even though I barely know him. "He's got that whole golden retriever optimism thing going for him."

"Let's hope it's enough," Varek mutters, voice low as he steers me towards the path leading around the main square. "I told Kael to take a walk."

My head snaps towards him. "Why?"

He gives me a sideways glance, one brow raised. "Because he was about to follow Zeyv out the gates."

Oh.

"Ah," I say, wiping my face with my shirt and feeling the stickiness of blood and sweat. A quick glance down tells me exactly what Kael saw before he left—my split lip, the smear on my jaw, a developing bruise at my ribs. No wonder he nearly combusted.

"I thought you'd want to avoid any extra explosions in the middle of training," Varek adds drily.

"Good call," I mutter, finally pulling the shirt all the way over my head with a grimace. "I must look like shit."

"You look like someone who fought and won." His tone is even, but he slows his pace. "Still, next time, maybe don't antagonize a guy who outweighs you by a hundred kilos and hates authority."

"I didn't antagonize him," I say, but Varek just lifts a brow. "Okay, I may have poked the bear. Lightly. With sarcasm."

He snorts. "You and your sarcasm are going to get us all killed."

We walk in silence for a few moments. The distant clang of metal on metal rings out again behind us, other Riftborn continuing their drills. The air smells of sweat, scorched rock, and the earthy scent of something unidentifiable cooking from the main cave system.

"You knew there'd be unrest when Kael and the prince came," I say quietly. "No shit people are twitchy."

Varek hums, not denying it.

"But you want them here," I continue. "You want to see if there's any way to... change things. The system. The repression of Riftborn, the control the queen has over everyone."

His lack of response is all the confirmation I need.

I shrug. "Can't say I blame you. If there's a chance to end this shit, even if it's a long shot, it's worth exploring."

Varek finally sighs. "It is. But if Dawson doesn't make it...." He trails off, tension creeping into his shoulders. "If the prince loses him before the bond fully forms, there'll be no incentive for him to stay. No connection. No reason for Kael to stay either."

I stop, my stomach twisting. "And without them...."

He nods once. "We'll lose more than an ally. We'll lose hope."

The word hits hard. Hope feels in short supply these days.

We round the edge of a building, the wind picking up slightly, fluttering the hem of my sweat-damp shirt. Varek stops.

Kael stands at the edge of the clearing, his massive form half in shadow, half lit by the afternoon light filtering through the canopy. His shoulders are squared, but there's tension in the slope of them. His arms are crossed tight over his chest, and he stares off towards the outer boundary wall like he's considering sprinting right through it.

Varek nods towards him. "Go to him."

He doesn't need to tell me twice.

Kael doesn't touch me at first, but his emotions brush against mine—thick, concerned, coiled tight like a cord stretched to breaking. I feel him in my chest, not just in my thoughts, and I instinctively reach out, sending him the pulse of reassurance I've come to understand how to give.

"I'm okay," I say softly, watching the way his jaw clenches before relaxing a fraction.

Without a word, I take the lead, guiding him through the winding corridors of the settlement towards my quarters. We attract attention. I feel it—eyes tracking us, whispers beginning before we've even passed. It's gonna spread faster than a bushfire tearing through dry outback scrub.

Still, I walk a little taller. With Kael's presence behind me, somehow I don't feel ashamed or embarrassed. The gossip doesn't sting. I've never had time for bullshit, and damn straight I have a backbone of steel.

My door creaks open, and Kael pauses just inside the entryway, his luminous eyes taking in the room. His gaze lingers on the copper-like pipework webbing the walls, a remnant from the original structure this space once belonged to. Warmth hums through the pipes, one of the few luxuries in Dathanor.

Without a word, he eases me back, step by step, onto the bed. I sit, watching him scan the room like he's assessing for threats. His expression softens when he finds the smoothed-out stone that I use for a washbasin, and I remain silent as he takes a cloth, wets it, and wrings it out before returning to kneel in front of me.

The cloth is cool against my skin as he dabs gently at the cut on my cheek. I flinch. He stills instantly.

"Sorry," he murmurs.

"S'okay," I mumble. "Just a little prick."

He huffs. "Zeyv is more than a prick."

I grin through the sting. "So you know *that* word."

His eyes narrow, but his lips twitch. "We have a word that means the same." He says something I can't begin to pronounce. It rolls off his tongue like a curse wrapped in velvet. "It translates to... 'vile-born waste of a clutch.'"

I bark out a laugh. "Bit dramatic, but I'll take it."

He finishes wiping my face, then runs his thumb gently under my eye where I feel a bruise forming. His touch lingers, featherlight, before he leans in and presses a kiss to my cheek.

The tenderness in it sucker punches me. It's soft, careful. A wordless apology. A balm to the aching space between us. He kisses me again—this time on my mouth. A warm, firm press. Nothing demanding. Just confirmation that he still wants this. Still wants me.

But does he want me enough?

He pulls back and frowns slightly. "What's wrong?"

I sigh, letting my eyes flutter shut. "Varek gave me an update on Dawson."

Kael straightens, just a little. "He's still not well."

I nod. "What about Aelith? He looked...." I trail off, unsure of how much to say.

His silence stretches. "He's not good," he finally says. "He's... not fully himself."

There's something off in his tone, a hesitation that makes my stomach clench. "What aren't you telling me?"

Kael hesitates. "He's been pushing his energy into Dawson."

My head jerks up. "Wait—what?"

He settles beside me on the bed. "I didn't realise at

first, but now it's clear. He's transferring his own energy... his life force. It's keeping Dawson alive."

"That's... that's insane." I stare at him. "Is that a Glowranth thing?"

He nods despite his frown. "Apparently. It can only be possible between fated mates. I don't know much, but I don't think it's a conscious act. It's... instinct. Compulsion. Aelith's body is doing it because Dawson is slipping away."

I feel sick. "Does Aelith know?"

Kael shakes his head. "He wasn't aware at first, not fully. He was just... willing Dawson to live."

"Does anyone else know this can happen?" I run a shaky hand through my hair.

"No. Not even the old texts speak of it clearly."

"So, Dawson might be alive right now because Aelith's body is... sacrificing itself?" I whisper.

Kael reaches for me, takes my hand. "It's not like that."

"It sounds like that," I snap, panic spiralling. "What if... what if I steal your energy? Your life force? What if bonding with me kills you?"

He squeezes my hand tightly. "You won't."

"You don't know that."

"I don't," he admits. "But I don't think that's how it works. What's happening between Aelith and Dawson —it's because Dawson hasn't completed the bond. More stages would help anchor him."

I shake my head. "But Dawson can't agree to that. He's unconscious."

Kael's voice lowers. "Sometimes stages complete unintentionally. You and I are proof of that."

"So, he's better off alive with stages in place," I whisper, "than dead."

"Yes."

"And Aelith?"

"He's ignoring Iris. And Aeroth. Won't listen to anyone." He leans back, frustration and sorrow written all over his face. "He just wants Dawson to live."

"That... surprises me," I admit. "Didn't think he had it in him."

Kael smiles faintly. "Aelith is not as he always seems."

I rub my chest and simply nod at his words. My thoughts are spinning, my emotions ricocheting off every corner of my mind, and Kael must feel it all. "It's a lot."

He nods. "Too much."

"I thought maybe we'd have time," I say softly. "Time to figure things out. But you're being pulled away again."

"I have to go," he says, pain flickering in his eyes. "He's still my prince, my charge. That hasn't changed."

The words slice into me. But I knew it. I always knew it. "You can't stand guard twenty-four-seven."

"Varek's posted two guards for extra protection," he admits. "But still...."

"I get it," I say. "He's not safe here."

"No."

"I hate this," I mutter. "But... will you come to me? Tonight?"

He looks at me, long and hard, and I know he feels the ache inside me. "Yes," he whispers. "I will."

Relief loosens something within me, even if it's temporary.

He stands, ready to go. I rise with him, and he leans in and kisses me—quick and soft. But it's not enough. Not even close. So I grab his shoulders, and before he can stop me, I climb him like the Glowranth-shaped tree he is.

His arms instinctively go around me as I wrap my legs around his waist, pressing my mouth to his. He sinks into the kiss, and so do I, mouth fierce and possessive and filled with everything I haven't been able to say. My heart, my breath, my whole damn soul is in this kiss.

When he finally pulls away, we're both wrecked, breathing heavily and wishing he could stay. He lowers me gently to the floor and whispers goodbye, and I watch him walk away, feeling the hollow ache inside me expand with every step he takes.

"Fuck," I murmur to the empty room.

I'm so screwed.

CHAPTER
ELEVEN

THE CANTEEN'S BUZZING, LOUDER THAN I'D LIKE. Chatter bounces off the stone walls, plates clatter, and the smell of a stew that's probably 80 percent eyeballs clings to the air like an overly affectionate ex.

I've tucked myself in the far corner, away from the noise, away from the questions I don't want to answer. I'm hunched over my tray, idly picking at my food. It's decent, thanks to Decca and Molsi—my favourite snarky kitchen duo—but my appetite's halfway to hell, and I don't have it in me to track it down.

I promised them I'd catch up properly soon. Just not today.

Today, I want time to sprint by so I can see Kael. Which... yeah. I've officially become that guy. The needy one. The one who stares at doors like a forlorn puppy and makes up imaginary scenarios where his stoic maybe-boyfriend sweeps in dramatically.

Tragic.

I sigh and scrape the last of my food into my mouth, chewing without tasting. I'm about to take my tray up when a voice pipes up behind me.

"Sonny?"

I turn to see Jack approaching, his Akubra still somehow pristine, like it's immune to the grime of Terrafeara. He's got Solan with him—still a walking tank of calm menace—and trailing beside them is the kid I saw a few days ago, with a mop of sandy-brown hair and a grin that's way too wide for this cursed world.

My heart does a weird lurch.

"You must be Jamie," I say, nodding to the kid.

"Yep!" he chirps. "You're the guy who went off with the Glowranth guard to find the human doctor, right?"

"That's me," I say, a little startled. "News travels fast."

"People talk," Jamie says, shrugging like a mini adult. "Also, everyone's been on edge about the prince being here. My uncle won't shut up about it."

Jack rolls his eyes. "You love it, don't lie."

Jamie just grins wider. "Only a bit."

Next to him is someone I haven't met yet, but I clock them instantly as the fourth member of their small group. Calythra.

The kid gestures to him. "This is Caly. He's my other best friend."

Caly nods at me, ethereal as all hell. His skin's so pale, it makes paper jealous, and his eyes—big and bright blue—don't seem to blink nearly enough. "Sonny, g'day, nice to meet ya," he says, and—what the hell—it's in a perfect Aussie accent.

I blink. "Wait. Did you just—"

"Yep," Jamie says, trying (and failing) to whisper. "He can mimic voices. Accents. Sometimes even languages if he hears enough."

Caly smirks. "Crikey, mate. You all right?" he says, now full Steve Irwin.

I choke on my laugh. "You're terrifying."

"Flattering," he replies.

Jack laughs, then jerks his head towards the exit. "Wanna take a walk? Got something I want to ask you about. Been thinking on it since you left."

I eye him. "Sure." I glance at Jamie and Caly. "You two good?"

"Going to get food," Jamie says. "Caly says the tentacle pie's decent today."

"Good luck with that." I dump my tray and follow Jack and Solan out of the canteen, the din behind us fading into the background.

Away from the bodies and chatter, the air's cooler, clearer. It's good to breathe, even if the tension's already coiling in my chest. Jack's quiet for a beat, Solan a few steps behind us, his presence a constant thrum of protection.

People step aside when they see him. Not just because he's a Pyronox—built like a stone wall and just as expressive—but because this Pyronox used to be an enforcer. One of the queen's.

The gossip's out. No one dares say anything directly, but I've heard the whispers. Still, I get it. He did what he had to do to survive. Hell, who here hasn't?

After a moment, Jack breaks the silence. "What you said before you left—it stuck with me."

I glance at him sideways. "You mean the rift stuff?"

He nods. "The idea that Dawson came through wrong. Through the Earth."

"Following the same course as you," I say, remembering the mental line I'd drawn through the planet.

"Yeah," Jack says. "But what if it wasn't an accident?"

That gets my full attention. I stop walking. It's very similar to what he said just before I left a few days ago.

He faces me. "I know it sounds nuts, but what if someone's interfering with the rifts? Guiding them. Controlling them."

A chill races up my spine. Not from the air. From something colder. Deeper.

"You said it," he goes on. "No two people have ever come through at the same time in different places. Not until me and Dawson. That can't be some sort of natural phenomenon."

"Do you really think someone brought you both here?" I ask quietly. "All of us here?"

"I think someone—or something—wants people here. Specific people. And not just human people either."

I exhale slowly, thinking about all the different species that make up the Riftborn. "And why would they want a twelve-year-old?" I ask, my mind immediately going to Jamie.

Jack glances back towards the canteen, towards his nephew. His face softens. "I don't know. But I'll protect him with everything I have."

"You're not alone in that," I say. Instinct guides me, as well as the need to protect an innocent. I'm barely cut out for this dimension, so a preteen will need all the help they can get.

He looks at me. "That's why I came to you."

We walk in silence for a few more moments. My mind is already racing with possibilities. If someone's pulling the strings on the rifts—well, we're in deeper shit than we thought.

"Have you spoken to Varek?" I ask.

Jack shakes his head. "I know you said we can trust him."

"You can," I say immediately. There's not a sliver of

hesitation. "Without question—it's something I believe. Trusting Varek has kept me alive."

Behind us, Solan finally speaks, his deep voice cutting through the hush of evening like a warm blade. "We believe you. But there are others here who don't. The Riftborn factions... they're uneasy."

"More than uneasy," Jack adds. "A few of them flat-out don't like the way Varek's running things."

"No shit," I mutter, rolling my eyes and immediately picturing Zeyv's smug face and his merry band of dick-heads. I thumb towards the training compound. "That lot? They'd rather take the 'stab first, question never' approach."

Solan's lips twitch, and Jack raises an eyebrow.

"It's not really about Varek himself," I explain. "He's strong. Ruthless when he has to be—believe me, I've seen it—but he's also diplomatic. He listens. He weighs consequences. That freaks some people out. Especially the species who are used to power being all about domination."

"So, they see his negotiation as weakness," Solan says.

"Exactly."

Jack frowns, nodding slowly. "That's... dangerous."

"You're not wrong." I sigh, glancing towards the main camp, where the glow of lights bounces off the cavelike walls. "There's a growing group who think we should just declare war. No more negotiation. No more discussion. Just... burn it all to the ground."

"Including the queen," Jack says.

"Including every Glowranth," I say quietly, and the thought leaves me cold. My stomach knots tight thinking of Kael. Of his quiet voice. His steady hands. His kisses.

"I'm sure you've seen the others," I add. "Apart from Kael and Prince Aelith, there are a few Glowranth who've joined us over time. Quietly. Carefully."

Jack nods. "We've seen them. They don't get treated well."

"Nope," I say, mouth twisting. "And I've done jack shit to prevent that." I shake my head, annoyed at myself. "I need to do better. I *will* do better."

Solan studies me for a beat, then says, "Tomorrow. Come with us. When we speak with Varek."

"I'll set it up," I promise. It's the right thing to do. "He won't ask what it's about. I'll make sure of it."

They nod, and we pause at the junction where the canteen glows in the distance. Jamie's still in there, probably talking Caly's head off about dragons or space or the way food here jiggles without warning. Or maybe I'm projecting the sorts of things I was into when I was a preteen.

"Go get food," I say with a small smile. "I'll catch Varek now."

We part ways, and I head towards Varek's quarters, slipping through the quieter back path where fewer people linger. I pass one of Zeyv's loyal followers—a thin, long-limbed dickwad with perpetually greasy hair and something unpleasant always smeared on his clothes.

He sneers at me.

I offer him the most mature, diplomatic response I can muster.

Middle finger up, baby.

He snarls but keeps walking. Wise move.

I shake my head, thoughts already spiralling back to Jack's theory. The implications. It's not even about Rift-born equality anymore. Not *just* about that. If someone's playing puppet master with the rifts—choosing who ends up in Terrafeara—that changes everything.

How long have they been doing it? Why me? Why Dawson? Why Jack? Why a twelve-year-old boy? The questions feel heavier with every step I take.

And then Kael.

I've thought about telling him. Hell, I almost did when we were travelling to find Iris. But I hesitated. Now, though… things are different.

He's my mate.

He would tell me if he knew anything… *wouldn't he?*

SLEEP KEEPS DRAGGING ME UNDER. EACH TIME I blink, it feels harder to open my eyes. I'm in bed, the covers tangled around my legs, the pillow soft beneath my cheek, and still I try to stay awake. Kael said he'd be here. He promised.

But the night's grown heavy, stretching on and on, and there's still no sign of him.

My chest aches. Not just with disappointment but with something sharp, something that feels dangerously close to heartbreak. I roll onto my back, staring at the ceiling. I want to believe he'll come. I need to believe it.

And then—a knock.

I jolt upright. It's soft, hesitant. But it's him. I know it's him.

I'm at the door in seconds, fingers fumbling with the lock. When I pull it open, Kael stands there like a shadow, all towering height and luminous eyes, his markings dim and his expression carved with exhaustion.

He looks wrecked, but he's here.

Still, I don't throw myself at him. I step aside, gentle. "Come in."

He hesitates, just for a breath, then steps inside. I close the door and turn, already reaching for him. "What's wrong?"

His jaw clenches. "It's Aelith. He won't stop giving to Dawson."

Giving. My stomach tightens. "You mean...?"

"He's disappearing," Kael says, voice low, barely a whisper. "I had to sedate him. Iris helped."

My mouth drops open. "You drugged your prince?"

"It was for his own good."

I nod quickly. "Of course. It's okay. You did what you had to." But guilt is rolling off him, thick and oppressive. I step closer. "You shouldn't be alone with that in your head."

He shakes his head. "I shouldn't be here."

"Why?" My gut tightens. My heart aches for him— but I'm still me. Still deflecting, still grasping for something solid when the air between us turns heavy with everything unsaid.

He glances at me, and something fractures in his gaze, a quiet shattering that almost makes me look away. "Because I feel guilty," he says, voice barely above a whisper, like guilt itself is sacred and should only be spoken of in a hush.

"About what?" My voice is steady, but inside, I already know.

"You," he breathes. "That I get to have you. That our bond strengthens, becomes something undeniable… while his fades into pain. While he suffers."

His words are a blade—sharp, precise, and unshakably kind. I raise an eyebrow, trying to hide the sudden ache swelling in my chest. "You wanna martyr yourself now? What, next you'll tell me you're off to live in a hovel and write poetry about forbidden love?"

A faint puff of air escapes him. Not quite a laugh—but almost. A moment of warmth in the ruin. "I just—"

"Kael." His name is a tether. I cut through the spiral before he can drown in it. "Sit down. Rest."

He hesitates, caught in the limbo between guilt and surrender.

"Do you care for me?" I ask. The question lands heavily in the space between us.

His answer is immediate—like it's been waiting, coiled and urgent. "More than anything."

I press, softer but no less firm. "More than anyone?"

He flinches like the truth hurts him to admit, like it's a betrayal even though it's the only thing that's ever felt right. Then he nods—agonising, but certain. "Yes."

That's all I need.

I guide him towards the bed, my touch light. He lets me strip him, piece by piece, not helping, just allowing. Trusting. The size difference between us is... notable. He's all breadth and height, solid muscle, his skin that deep, dark blue that gleams faintly in the dim light. His bioluminescent markings pulse gently along the ridges of his arms and sides, hypnotic.

He sits, waiting. Still. Like I might change my mind.

"You okay with this?" I murmur, my hands at the waistband of his trousers.

He nods, breathless. "I want you."

That's enough.

I reveal him slowly, my breath hitching as I take in

the sheer size of him. He's... glorious. Sculpted and overwhelming. But I can take it. I want to. I encourage him to lie back, then reach for my own clothes, letting them fall to the floor until I'm bared to him.

His gaze devours me, reverent and hungry.

"Good," I whisper, a smirk playing at my lips. "I was worried you might be missing a cock."

He growls low, a sound that vibrates through me, and I can't help but grin.

"I mean," I add, climbing onto the bed beside him, "it wouldn't have been a dealbreaker. But this is a hell of a bonus."

Kael lies back at my urging, the lines of tension still coiled tight in his frame. But he's watching me now—no masks, no royal duties, no distance—just open, vulnerable need. His markings glow softly in the dimness of the room, like a quiet storm beneath his skin, each flicker synced with the cadence of his breath.

I straddle his thighs gently, still in awe of the sheer scale of him beneath me. My hands explore his torso first—his chest, broad and firm beneath my fingers, rising and falling with a rhythm that speeds with every stroke. His skin is warm and smooth, slightly slick in a way that's foreign but not unpleasant, and the subtle pulse of energy beneath his surface makes every touch feel alive.

"You okay?" I ask, my voice soft. "You can rest if you need to. We don't have to—"

"No." His voice is a low, gravelly thrum, and his hand comes to rest lightly against my hip. "I want this. I want you." His eyes blaze with honesty. "All of it."

The way he says it—like I'm not just something he wants but something sacred—nearly undoes me. I smile, slow and sure, before leaning down to press a kiss to the curve of his collarbone. "Okay, then," I whisper against his skin.

I explore him slowly, reverently, mapping out every inch with my fingers and mouth. The ridges of muscle that line his abdomen twitch beneath my touch, his glowing lines flaring brighter every time I kiss along them. The taste of him is different, too—clean and faintly mineral, like mountain air after rain—and something about that feels right. Other, yes, but also his.

Kael's hands fist in the sheets, his chest arching slightly as I continue down, my lips pressing against the delicate trail of light that runs from beneath his ribs to the edge of his hip. The groan that escapes him is raw, primal, and I feel it echo all the way down to the soles of my feet.

"You're beautiful," I murmur, tracing the flare of light along his side. "It's ridiculous."

His breath hitches. "You... mean that?"

"Kael," I say, meeting his gaze, "you're like a walking, glowing wet dream. You know how long I held out thinking I hated you?"

A small, stunned laugh breaks from him, and it's like watching thunder soften into sunlight.

"I thought I didn't deserve to be seen," he admits. "Not after I abandoned you."

"You do," I say, firm now, the gut punches I've previously experienced nowhere in sight. "Every piece of you."

When I finally reach for him, he shudders. His cock is long and thick, a darker shade than the rest of his skin, the tip already slick with a pale, faintly glowing fluid. The difference in anatomy should freak me the fuck out—but it doesn't. Not with the way he looks at me, not with how his body trembles under mine.

I stroke him slowly, curiously, watching his head fall back and the markings across his chest shimmer in response. His hands grip the sheets again, his breath coming in ragged gasps now.

"I—" He tries to speak, but his words melt into another groan.

"I've got you," I whisper, leaning down to kiss the centre of his chest, where his heartbeat thunders under my lips. I swear I can feel the bond tugging at me again —not painful, not overwhelming, but real. A tether. A promise.

Kael reaches for me, pulling me up with surprising gentleness. "Come here," he murmurs, his voice thick with emotion and want. "Let me touch you."

I let him. I want him to.

And wrapped up in heat and hunger and something dangerously close to love, I realise I would give this man, this Glowranth, everything. Even the pieces of myself I thought were long gone.

Kael cups my face like I'm made of something sacred, and there's an admiration in his gaze that nearly undoes me. His hands—broad, strong, careful—trail down my neck and over my chest, fingertips brushing over the lines of my collarbone, the curve of my pecs. He studies each shift of my breath, each flicker of my muscles like I'm a text he's only just learned to read.

"You are...," he breathes, almost to himself. "Bright. Alive. I never knew what it meant to want something so much and fear it all at once."

His fingers skim my abdomen, and I shudder. I guide his hand lower, letting him touch the hard, aching evidence of how much I want him. He swallows thickly, his expression raw as he strokes me slowly, carefully, like he's terrified he might break me. But I'm the one breaking apart under his touch.

"You feel...," he whispers, shaking his head, like there are no words in his language—or any—for this.

"You're doing good," I manage to say, half breathless, half undone. "Too good. If you keep that up, I'm gonna embarrass myself in about three seconds."

Kael grins softly. "Embarrass? You would not."

I huff a breath, catching his wrist and pulling his hand gently away before I go off like a firecracker. I shift lower, eyes locking onto the thick length between his legs—impossibly flushed, glistening at the tip.

"Can I...?" I glance up at him. "Use my mouth?"

Kael blinks. "Mouth?"

I pause. "You don't do that?"

His ears tint a shade darker. He shakes his head. "No. The Glowranth do not. It's... not our way."

"You've never...?" I sit up a little straighter, blinking. "You've never had this done to you?"

"No," he admits softly. "Royal guards are meant to remain chaste until they leave their service after at least three decades. Focussed. We're trained to protect our mark, not to seek pleasure."

His confession hits me like a bolt of lightning. "You've never—" I blink, leaning back slightly to study his face. "Wait. You're actually a... virgin?"

Kael frowns, that familiar furrow pulling between his glowing brows. "I do not know that word."

I blow out a slow breath. Apparently the romances he read weren't full of blushing virgins. Got it. "You've never been with anyone? Never had sex?"

A pause. Then, softly, "No. The royal guard are sworn to chastity while serving. Focus. Discipline. My body has always belonged to my duty. Until now."

I stare. My brain goes offline for a second. "But before we left, you said"—I mimic his low, flirty voice "—'For what it's worth, you were right about one thing.' You were teasing me."

His markings flare. Not just glowing—they ripple in a cascade of soft bioluminescent pulses. His embarrassment brushes against me like a wave, all through the bond.

"I said it because of you," he murmurs. "I had never said anything like it before. But... I remembered your words. The way you spoke of me. Of my body. Of... what we might do." His voice dips to a rumble. "I wanted to be part of that. I wanted to try. For you."

I'm speechless for a long moment. Then, gently, I say, "You flirted for the first time in your life... and nailed it?"

He shifts awkwardly. "I was... compelled."

My heart damn near breaks. "Kael."

I reach for him again, letting my fingers trail down the hard planes of his chest, over the ridges of his abdomen, lower still. He doesn't flinch—he leans in. His body hums beneath my touch, his breath hitching every time I graze a sensitive spot.

"Do you trust me?" I whisper.

His answer is immediate. "With everything."

"Then let me take care of you."

He gives the faintest nod. It's all I need.

I move slowly, letting him feel every moment. My hands explore the deep blue of his skin, learning his shape, the places where he tenses and the places where he shudders. His body isn't like any I've touched before

—larger, denser, other—but it's his, and I want every inch of it.

Kael's head tips back slightly, his eyes fluttering shut, his lips parted as if he's barely breathing. He's never done this. Never felt this way. And now, here he is —laid bare, letting me lead.

"You feel amazing," I murmur, voice thick with awe, every word trembling with the weight of how much I mean it.

Kael's eyes flutter open, their glow softer now, almost shy. Vulnerable in a way that knocks the breath out of me. "So do you," he murmurs, and there's a reverence in his tone that goes straight to my chest.

His hand lifts, tentative at first—like he's afraid I might disappear if he touches me too roughly. But then his clawlike fingers graze my chest, slow and searching, mapping the curve of my ribs, the dip of my waist. His touch is warm, a little unsure but achingly intentional, as if he's learning me by sensation alone.

When his hand finally wraps around my cock, I suck in a sharp breath, my hips jolting before I can stop them. His grip is gentle, almost hesitant, but the effect is devastating. Pleasure crackles through me, sharp and sudden, chasing up my spine. Each stroke is slow and deliberate, his glowing gaze fixed on me like he's memorising every gasp, every hitch in my breath, every twitch beneath his palm.

I'm already too close. Embarrassingly close. My thighs tremble with the effort to hold back.

"I—fuck, Kael. That's—yeah. Just like—" My words break off in a gasp as I press my forehead into the crook of his neck, desperate to ground myself. "Okay, I have to slow down, or I'm gonna—fuck." I arch back.

Kael's lips curl, smug and pleased, and of course the bastard loves it. He's proud of every unravelling second.

I huff out a shaky laugh and lean in to kiss along his jaw, open-mouthed and slow. His skin tastes faintly of minerals, like the first drops of rain hitting sun-warmed stone—strange and addictive and uniquely him. My tongue flicks out, chasing the flavour as I trail lower, kissing down his throat, his chest, then lower still.

When I nudge his thighs apart, he goes rigid—nervous—but I pause, resting a hand on his stomach. I glance up, giving him the space to stop me. "This okay?"

His eyes meet mine, glowing like wildfire in the dark. His breath catches, and then he nods—tiny, breathless. "Yes. I want it. I want... you."

My chest aches with how much I want him too. I press a kiss to his inner thigh, soft and adoring, and the bond between us pulses—thick with heat, with promise, with the unbearable sweetness of anticipation. His skin is warm beneath my lips, trembling.

And then I move lower.

"I trust you," he says.

And bloody hell—I trust him too.

That thought floods me the moment I take him into my mouth, and something inside clicks. Not just metaphorically. It's tangible. Real. Like a jigsaw piece sliding into place, locking in a part of the bond.

I feel it everywhere.

Him.

In my chest. In my breath. In the frantic rhythm of my heart that now pulses in time with his. Deeper than pleasure. Deeper than desire. I feel *him*.

Kael groans above me, hands fisting the sheets, glowing markings flickering in wild, frantic bursts across his arms and chest like stars caught in a storm. His hips stutter, control fraying at the edges, and I hold him steady, grounding him—not just with touch but with everything I am as I suck him deeply.

There's nothing cautious or uncertain in him anymore.

Only need.

Only me.

He whispers something unrecognisable in Glowranthian, voice wrecked and full of devotion I don't need to understand to feel. It wraps around me like a promise as I lick up the length of him, my grip firm and gently stroking the part of him I can't cram into my mouth.

Maybe one day I'll take all of him—bury him so deep, he forgets his own name. But it's been a long time since I deep-throated anyone. And never someone Kael's size.

Still, I'm greedy. I want to feel the stretch, the ache, the weight of him on my tongue like a promise. I wrap my lips around the thick head and sink down slowly, inch by inch, letting my spit slick his length as I work him deeper.

He groans—low and ragged, like it's dragging out of his chest against his will—and fuck, it's addictive. His hips twitch, but he doesn't thrust. Not yet. He's holding back for me. Letting me have this.

I moan around him, the vibration pulling another sharp breath from Kael. My fingers dig into his thighs as I bob faster now, sucking him in with messy, wet sounds, spit pooling at the corners of my mouth. He tastes like heat and salt and something wild, something fucking delicious.

His claws scrape the air beside me, his body trembling with restraint, but I can feel it—how close he is to losing control. And bloody hell, I want that. I want him wrecked, undone, roaring my name as he fucks my throat like he owns it.

And maybe, just maybe... he does.

When he finally spills, it's sudden—hot and overwhelming. I pull back just slightly, lips still wrapped around the head of his cock as thick pulses of cum flood my mouth. I try to swallow, but there's so much. It spills past my lips, warm and viscous, dripping down my chin and onto my hand.

Fuck.

His taste hits me hard—like warm cinnamon chased with the earthy sweetness of summer rain. It clings to my tongue, and I savour it, like I could memorise the exact flavour of him, burn it into my senses. I let the luminous fluid trail down my fingers, watching it glisten in the low light, slow and syrupy, and for a moment, I'm just... mesmerised.

I give him two slow, firm strokes, feeling the way his body twitches with every aftershock, before something tightens deep inside me—my breath hitching, muscles coiling. That tension, sharp and sudden, takes me by surprise.

And just like that, I'm gone.

Holy fuck.

My orgasm shoots through me, so fast and unexpected that I shudder and jolt. It's like a live wire lit up my spine, sizzling through every nerve as I cry out—louder than I mean to. My hand clenches around him instinctively, milking the last of him as my thighs twitch and my vision whites out at the edges.

I barely manage a breath before collapsing against his thigh, chest heaving, skin flushed and slick.

Jesus. I just short-circuited.

Kael's whole body is taut, trembling beneath mine. His chest rises and falls rapidly, like he's struggling to catch up with himself—like the world tilted beneath him, and he's only just feeling the shift.

I wipe the corner of my mouth, eyes locked on him, and I swear... I feel it.

My lips are swollen, my chest heaving. I barely manage to crawl up his body before collapsing against him, my cheek pressed to his shoulder, the wild thrum of our shared heartbeat pounding in my ears.

I'm breathless. Wrecked. Floating in a way I never expected.

"How?" I whisper, half dazed.

Kael's body shudders again. I feel it against mine—every tremble of relief, every shiver of bliss, every ripple of emotion breaking beneath his skin. "I... don't know."

But I do.

It pulses through me—warm and certain.

Our hearts.

They're beating as one.

I press a hand to his chest, then to mine. Same rhythm. Same tempo. I glance up at him, eyes wide. "Wait. You said sex wasn't part of the bonding."

Kael lets out a sound—half laugh, half groan. "It's not. I swear. At least... not from anything I've ever read or heard."

I frown, thinking it through. Then it hits me. "Trust," I say softly. "That's what was missing."

His arms tighten around me. "Yes."

"For both of us," I murmur. "That was it."

The weight of what we've just done settles in slowly

—not heavy, but solid. Real. And I know, beyond doubt, there's only one part of the bond left to complete.

My thoughts drift, not to that, but to what comes next. To tomorrow.

To Varek.

To Jack. And Solan. And the theory that keeps swirling through my mind about the rifts and what—or who—might be behind them.

I lift my head, pressing a kiss to Kael's shoulder. "There's a meeting tomorrow. With Varek. Jack and Solan asked me to be there. I want you to come with me."

He studies me for a long beat, searching. "You want me there... as your guard?"

"No." I shake my head, meeting his eyes. "I want you there as mine."

He doesn't answer immediately, but I feel it. That soft, low yes that ripples through our bond. And with it... the terrifying, wonderful realisation that this is just the beginning.

But also...

Holy fucking shitballs—*luminous spunk!* If unicorns were real, would their cum be just like this, but maybe with sparkles?

Something I can consider another time when I'm not so close to passing out.

CHAPTER
TWELVE

By the time I wake fully, Kael is long gone. Not that he left without thoroughly kissing me and promising to join me for my meeting with Varek. And when I say kissing, I mean the kind that haunts your dreams and makes your body buzz long after you've stumbled back into sleep.

Now, though, I'm floating somewhere between sleepy bliss and semi-functional. There's a warmth under my skin that isn't just from the blanket—or even last night's activities. No, this is all Kael. The bond is pulsing, soft but steady, like a low-frequency hum in my bones. It's... nice. Comforting. Kind of addictive.

The morning haze doesn't lift as I make my way to the canteen, still in that postorgasmic dream state where every bit of food smells like heaven and gravity feels optional. I drift through the door and head straight for the back, where I know Decca and Molsi will be stationed like two dragons guarding their culinary hoard.

"Look who's got the walk of the thoroughly fucked," Decca calls the moment I appear.

I blink at her. "You do realise there are delicate, innocent ears in here?"

Molsi snorts. "Delicate where? You think Fringt's innocence is still intact after he tried to cook with that expired root rot last week?"

"Fringt tried to what?" I cringe. "Why didn't I hear about that?"

"Because you've been too busy playing Glowranth snugglepuff," Decca says, flicking her four-fingered hands at me like I'm smoke in her kitchen.

I slide onto a stool at the far counter and swipe a crusty roll from the tray. "Snugglepuff, really?"

"Your glow tells me all I need to know," Molsi mutters, then gives me a once-over. "Plus, it's the eyes. All soft and smug. And don't think I can't feel the Kael-vibes radiating off you. It's like being stalked by warm thunder."

I groan and let my head drop dramatically to the table. "I hate how emotionally perceptive you two are."

"No, you don't," Decca replies. "You love us. And you're gonna love us even more once we fill you in."

I lift my head, one brow raised. "Oh?"

Decca and Molsi exchange a look, then lean in with matching grins.

"Zeyv's causing trouble," Molsi says, voice low. "More than usual."

"Apparently," Decca adds, "he's still reeling after yesterday."

I can't help the grin that forms. Kicking his arse was pretty awesome.

Decca rolls her eyes. "Yes, he's not happy about that, but he's focussing on complaints about the royal Glowranth and guard being here."

I sigh, not surprised but wishing Zeyv would wind his neck in. "How much of a dick is he being?"

"He's not standing up and talking shit in public," Molsi says. "Yet. But there's rumbling. It's not just the usual passive-aggressive stink-eye either. They're spreading the idea that Varek's gone soft. That he's giving the enemy a foothold."

I huff. "Typical Zeyv bullshit. Varek can be diplomatic and terrifying. Just because he's not decapitating people every Tuesday doesn't mean he's losing his edge."

Decca slides a plate towards me stacked with smoked meat slices and roasted gukle weed. "You might want to tell the camp that. Because a few folks are listening to Zeyv."

I chew that over. Figuratively and literally. The *gukle* are crispy on the outside and buttery in the middle—

how the hell do these two make everything taste like a hug? Okay, maybe that's just my postorgasmic state talking. They've served several more-than-questionable meals.

It's too early for a camp-wide PR campaign, though, when it comes to making it clear that Varek is the dog's bollocks. And honestly, I've got bigger fish to fry.

Jack. Solan. Their theory.

Someone pulling the strings on the rifts. Deliberately? I've barely scratched the surface of what that could mean, and the implications are spinning around my skull like chaos on a carousel.

I exhale slowly and glance at the small satchel I brought with me. "I'm going to be late," I mumble, grabbing two rolls and an extra slice of meat. "If you see Kael before I do, feed him."

Molsi raises a brow. "You're waiting on him now?"

"Obviously," I say, loading up a cloth with the food. "He needs looking after. Plus, I might be a little obsessed. Or stupid. Or both."

Decca smirks. "Both."

"Gee, thanks."

I'm halfway to the door when I pause, glance over my shoulder, and grin. "But seriously—Fringt tried to cook what?"

Molsi groans. "Don't ask. Just know it involved tentacles and nearly melted a pot."

I let out a strangled laugh and wave them off,

heading towards Varek's war room over at the bowling alley.

Kael's presence flickers in the back of my mind—distant but there, like a heartbeat echoing in my own chest. Strong. Reassuring. God help me, I'm really starting to like this Glowranth thing. And yes, I've already considered what it'll feel like to start touching myself when I'm alone just to see if he reacts while he's on duty.

Life might be chaotic, but I fully intend to have some fun with it.

The journey from the canteen to the bowling alley passes in a blur of shifting stone and the low thrum of life in the settlement. I keep my head down, barely nodding at the handful of Riftborn who cross my path, my mind spinning with everything Decca and Molsi told me.

But as I near the edge of the training quarter, Jack and Solan fall into step beside me like it was planned.

"Morning," Jack says, eyes bright despite the tension behind them.

"You look well-rested," Solan adds, a hint of a smile tugging at the corners of his lips. He might be a Pyronox enforcer-turned-rebel, but his humour still catches me off-guard.

"Not sure if it counts as rest when half of it involved a giant, glowing guard and a mattress that didn't survive," I reply, grinning.

Jack barks a laugh, and Solan chuckles low in his throat. "Noted."

Together, we slip through the entrance of the bowling alley. Inside, the repurposed lanes are quiet for once. No distant sound of pins being scattered from the one almost-intact lane, no shouted commands from trainers or the grunts of sparring. Just an eerie stillness that sinks into my bones.

Varek is already waiting.

He sits at the head of the oversized table at the back of the room, the one built from salvaged doors and reinforced panels. Shanae is beside him, ever stoic, her stance protective but calm. Her dark gaze flicks over me with a sharp once-over that doesn't feel unkind.

Kael is already here, and my chest flutters. The moment our eyes meet, a warmth spreads through me, low and deep. My pulse skips, then steadies under his gaze. He looks tired—hell, more than tired—but the flicker of relief in his eyes when he sees me nearly drops me to my knees.

I want to run to him, to wrap my arms around his solid frame and bury my face against his chest. Instead, I manage a small smile, one I know he feels through our bond.

Varek gestures for us to sit.

The table's surface is covered with maps, printouts, and a smattering of reports. There's no one else here. No hunting party, no officers, no gawkers. That alone is telling. Varek took my request seriously. He took *me* seriously.

"Thank you for coming," Varek says, voice calm, deliberate. "Let's get started."

We sit, Kael sliding into the seat beside me. His knee bumps mine, a silent reassurance. I glance towards Shanae, who gives me the barest nod. Then I exhale and look at Jack.

Time to talk about what we know—and what it could mean for all of us.

Jack clears his throat as we all settle around the table, his fingers drumming lightly on the scratched surface. "Thanks for giving us the time," he says, gaze flicking between Varek, Shanae, and Kael. "What we want to talk about might sound far-fetched at first, but... we've seen too much to ignore it."

Varek leans forwards, those silver eyes glowing faintly. "Go on."

Solan takes over, his voice measured. "We've been tracking rift patterns after what you shared. And what we've found—what Sonny uncovered before he left—it suggests there's a possibility these rifts aren't natural. That they're being... manipulated. Created."

Kael visibly stiffens. His reaction isn't the disbelief I expect. It's deeper. Sharper. Like something old and painful has just cracked open. I feel it ripple through the bond like a shadow I wasn't ready for.

I glance at him, frowning. "You don't doubt it."

He doesn't speak right away. His jaw clenches, and his eyes meet mine, stormy and raw. There's guilt there. Thick. Heavy. "I do not," he says at last.

I tilt my head, wondering at his emotions.

His throat works like the words are fighting him. "If someone brought you here—deliberately—*because* you're my mate...." His voice trails off, but the bond pulses with everything he can't say.

"You're wondering what that makes you," I murmur. "That I was here for over two years, and you didn't come."

Kael flinches. His emotions surge, too tangled to separate—shame, self-loathing, fear. He swallows hard, the weight of it choking him. I reach for him, not physically, but through the bond. Letting him feel the steadiness inside me. The forgiveness I've already given. It settles him. Not completely, but enough.

Solan gives a small, knowing nod. "Then maybe the real question is why now. Why are the bonds beginning again? Why all of a sudden are mates being drawn together after so long in this dimension? And why are they pulling together different species to do so?"

Shanae, quiet until now, studies us both. Her gaze sharpens. "You bonded?"

I nod, heat creeping up my neck. Kael shifts beside me like he's preparing for backlash. Like he still expects to be punished for something he never understood.

"It's not complete," I say quickly. "But yeah... the bond's started."

Shanae doesn't comment, but the look she gives us is full of questions. The room shifts, a new kind of awareness settling in.

"But not every Riftborn has bonded," I say, grounding us again. "Not all of us have someone. Right?"

"Yet," Jack says firmly. "That's what I keep coming back to. What if they're here? What if they just haven't found each other yet? Like you. Or more likely, the humans have yet to be pulled into the rift yet."

Solan folds his arms. "It would make sense. The bonding doesn't just link two people—it changes them. Strengthens them. I'm stronger with Jack. Physically. Mentally. Energetically."

Shanae nods slowly. "Same with me and Ril. It's like we balance each other out, but more than that, I have their special skill set, and they are definitely stronger since we completed our bond."

Varek hums thoughtfully. "Which brings us back to the rifts. We know that humans are the common denominator, since every single human here that we know of has bonded. And if your presence catalyses bonding that hasn't happened in generations, it does sound like more than happy coincidence or simply fate."

Kael shifts beside me. "But why would someone control the rifts? What would they gain?"

Jack leans forwards. "That's what we want to find out. If someone is manipulating the rifts, choosing who gets pulled through and when... they're playing God... or fate maybe. And if they have a goal or an angle? We need to know what it is."

I glance around the table, the gravity of it all settling like lead in my chest. "This isn't just about our freedom anymore," I murmur. "Or equality. It's about control. About power. And about who's behind it."

Varek's expression hardens with a slow nod. "We need more information. Proof. But you're right. If this theory is true, then everything we thought we knew about the rifts... about it being a natural phenomenon... was wrong."

Kael stays quiet beside me, but his hand brushes mine beneath the table. I don't say anything. I just hold it.

The meeting stretches on, the weight of revelations growing heavier with every passing minute. As Jack, Solan, and Varek dive deeper into their theories about the rifts—about the possibility that they're not natural phenomena but intentionally created—I notice Kael stills beside me.

At first, it's subtle. A shift in his posture, a tension in his jaw. But I feel it through our bond, like a current humming under my skin. His disbelief spikes, not just as an intellectual reaction but emotionally—like he's been dreading this exact conversation.

Jack leans forwards, his voice urgent. "If someone's behind the rifts—if they're being controlled—then we're talking about targeted abductions, not accidents."

Solan nods solemnly. "And based on what we know about fated bonds, maybe there's a reason. Maybe humans are being brought here to restore what was lost. That or to provide the current rulers with more power."

"Or maybe it's nothing to do with the rulers or strengthening their forces. Maybe it's someone pulling the strings to overpower and weaken them. To change society," Shanae adds, her brow pulled down in thought.

What's clear is we have no idea of the purpose or who's behind it. It could be a million different things or explanations.

"Hell, maybe we're wrong and—what was it that you called it, Varek? A nexus, right?" Jack prods.

Varek's nod is slow, his gaze assessing. "Yes. I said Terrafeara, this dimension, is the centre, the nexus. A hive pulling threads from countless worlds into one chaotic web."

"Well, it *could* just be that, but still the questions remain. The *why* and the *how* remain the same," Jack says.

Varek listens, eyes narrowed, but when I glance at Kael, I catch something flicker in his expression. A ripple of guilt. And then... shame.

He doesn't speak. He doesn't fidget. But his

emotions speak volumes. I don't call him out. Not here. Not now. Not with all eyes on us.

Instead, I gently nudge reassurance his way through our bond, offering comfort. I don't know what he's hiding—or if he's just processing something—but I trust he'll tell me when he's ready.

Varek leans back, fingers steepled. "If these rifts are being manipulated, it changes everything. Not just for us."

Shanae's voice cuts through. "But for the worlds people are being torn from."

I wince. I have no idea what was left behind when I came here. Something I need to talk to Jack about. But based on Shanae and the other humans here, we've all said the same: There've been no news reports of "monsters" roaming Earth, no abductions reported, no discussions about new slivers of world popping up.

So either there are some pretty phenomenal hush jobs from our respective governments, or something else is going on that we'll never know.

Jack nods, grim. "We need to find out who—or what —is behind it. And what they want."

Varek adds, "And we need to prepare for what it'll mean when others find out. This isn't just a Riftborn issue. This could shift the balance of every alliance we've made."

Shanae studies Kael and me, her gaze lingering. "And now that you're bonded and it's almost complete... you're already at the centre of that shift. As far as we're aware, you're the first home species, the first Glowranth to have bonded with their fated mate."

The table falls into a heavy silence, but it's broken—abruptly and quietly—by Jack.

"When we find out who's behind the rifts," he says, voice measured but firm, "my mission is going to be about finding a way back."

The silence deepens, thickening. My heart stutters.

Back?

Home?

I swallow hard, vision clouding for a second as the images flash unbidden—my old bed with a spring mattress that squeaked if I shifted too fast, eating green curry on the couch while watching trash TV, and blue sky so vivid and endless, it made your chest ache.

But then... Kael.

My gaze shifts to him instinctively. My chest tightens. Could I leave him? Would I even survive it? Not seeing him for almost a day had made my skin itch and my soul twist in on itself.

"I won't leave Solan," Jack continues, cutting through my spiralling thoughts. "But Jamie... he's still a kid. He deserves a future where he's not dodging blade tips and plants that want to kill him, where his life isn't someone else's rebellion." He turns to Varek, and there's steel in his voice now. "I don't give a shit what anyone thinks about what Jamie's 'role' could be. He's not a soldier. Not a pawn. If there's a way to get him home... we'll take it."

It hits the table like a thunderclap. Even Varek looks taken aback, his luminous eyes narrowing slightly—not in judgment but consideration. The mood shifts. Heavy. Complex. Real. And the possibilities stretch out like a chasm in my chest.

Kael's hand beneath the table is gentle, grounding when he squeezes lightly. He doesn't speak, but the unease still ripples under his skin, through our bond.

I squeeze back. Whatever he's not saying, we'll get there.

As the group disperses from the meeting table, it's clear there's no solid plan yet. No grand solution. No dramatic declarations. Just a mess of questions, tension, and theories that are way too big to untangle in one sitting.

Varek moves off with Shanae to speak in hushed tones about the rift a few days ago—the same day Kael came here. As far as I'm aware, whoever came through the rift has yet to be found. Jack and Solan glance at each other before quietly stepping back towards the exit, giving me and Kael a moment.

Kael stays silent beside me, but his emotions aren't quiet. Not even close.

The flicker of unease he tried to hide during the meeting has thickened, curling around us like fog. I feel it thrum through our bond—a mix of wariness, shame, and something more elusive... dread?

I place a hand gently on his arm. "Walk with me?"

He nods, but his jaw's tight. We step out of the meeting room and into the corridor that cuts through the old bowling alley's back. The moment the door shuts behind us, I slow to a stop and turn to face him.

"You were holding something back."

Kael doesn't pretend otherwise. He looks away, his shoulders tense. "I felt something. When they talked about the rifts. The theories. It wasn't just disbelief—it was recognition."

I study him. "You've heard something before?"

"There are whispers in the guard," he says slowly, carefully. "Not facts. Not anything anyone speaks about openly. But I've picked up fragments... suspicions."

"About the queen?"

His mouth is a grim line. "There's speculation that Queen Serresta has found a way to influence the rifts. To decide who gets pulled through. That she's... curating Riftborn for their abilities. For what they can offer Terrafeara—or her rule."

I stare at him, breath caught. "And you didn't say anything in there because...?"

"I don't have proof," he says, finally meeting my gaze. "And I'm not sure how much I believe it. I have enough knowledge of the queen to believe if she can gain power, she would absolutely tear through dimensions. But pull fated mates together?" He shakes his head. "Fated mates are strong. For her, dangerously so. She would not encourage any pairings here whose strength would rival her own or could potentially break the system."

I press my palm flat to his chest, feeling the faint echo of my own heartbeat in him. "Okay. I kind of understand why you wouldn't want to share more theories, and I trust your decision."

Kael's eyes soften, but the tension doesn't leave him.

"I also felt something else in there," I add, a little quieter now. "Like you were ashamed."

He doesn't answer immediately. He steps in closer, his voice barely above a whisper. "You were the only human who didn't have a bond. I did that to you. For two years, I left you alone, because my duty to the prince came first."

"But you felt me," I say, hearing the raw edge of emotion in my own voice. "The second I arrived."

We've been over this more than once, and I hope one day it all becomes a distant hurt. Hell, not even that. Not even a small blip in our memories. I'm all for focussing on the future, which actually surprises me even as I think it. As let's be honest, since being in Terrafeara, I've been living in the moment, grateful when I wake up in the morning.

My expectations have been pretty low.

He nods, grief flashing through his luminous eyes. "I felt you. And I turned away."

It doesn't hurt the way it used to. Not now, not after everything. But it still aches.

I wrap my arms around his waist, resting my head against his chest. "It doesn't matter now. You're here. *We're* here."

His arms come around me, firm and sure. "I won't let anything pull you from me again," he says.

Jack's words about finding a way home flitter in the corner of my mind. I shut it down. That discussion will only lead to more hurt and uncertainty. I want neither in my life.

We stand like that for a long minute. Just the two of us, in this weird in-between place—caught between questions and conspiracy, the past and whatever the hell's coming. Eventually, I pull back and smile, just a little. "I didn't know I could feel someone this deeply. Even without words."

He brushes his thumb under my jaw. "It's more than bond. It's you."

Goddamn him and his Glowranth poetry. Who'd have thought a badass royal guard would have it in him?

And goddamn me for already being half in love.

CHAPTER
THIRTEEN

THE CORRIDORS TO THE WESTERN WING ARE quieter than I expected. Kael walks beside me, his stride purposeful. I don't need the bond to feel how reluctant he is to leave me again. It flows from him in waves. Still, he says nothing, his lips pressed in a thin line, jaw set like stone. That Glowranth soldier control on full display.

I almost hate how hot it makes him.

Almost.

The closer we get, the more tension coils in my gut. I can already feel the weight of it pressing through the walls of the facility. The heavy pulse of grief. Hope. Determination.

And fear.

Kael opens the door first. The medical bay is dimly lit, shadows playing along the far wall where Iris crouches beside the bed. Dawson hasn't moved. Still pale. Still far too still. If not for the slight rise and fall of his chest, I might have thought we were too late.

Prince Aelith sits in a chair, unmoving, regal despite the exhaustion carved into his face. His luminous eyes are duller now, the once-fierce glow softened to something hollow. He doesn't look at us. Kael immediately steps closer to his prince, then pauses.

Iris looks up, offers me a nod. "Good to see you."

I nod, swallowing past the lump in my throat. "How is he?"

"Stable," she says. "For now. But Aelith's not helping his own case. He keeps trying to give more. I had to sedate him again this morning."

I glance at Kael, who doesn't flinch. Of course he already knows. I suspect he was the one who gave permission.

"You should rest," Kael says quietly to the prince, but Aelith doesn't respond.

The room buzzes with unspoken things. What's happening to Dawson. What it might mean. What Kael told me in confidence just yesterday.

Iris rises, brushing her hands on her trousers. "Dawson had another seizure early this morning. Brief, but intense. I managed to stabilise him, but we're running out of time."

"Is Aelith still... feeding him?" I ask, trying to keep my voice level.

"Not while sedated or it's still in his system," she says. "But when he's fully comprehensive and the drugs have worn off, I doubt I can stop him."

Kael places a hand on Aelith's shoulder. Something wordless passes between them, and though the prince doesn't lift his gaze, his hand reaches up to cover Kael's.

I look away. It's not jealousy. Not exactly. But it's something.

"I have to stay," Kael says to me, voice low.

I nod. I knew it was coming.

He steps back towards me, pausing close enough that I can feel the heat of him. His hand finds mine briefly. Discreetly. "Tonight?"

"Tonight," I promise.

He doesn't kiss me. Not here. But the look he gives me before he turns back to Aelith is enough to keep me going.

Just.

I let myself linger at Dawson's bedside for a moment, watching the slow rise and fall of his chest. His hands look too small against the sterile white sheet. He looks young. Too young to be dying.

I glance at Iris. She's already back at her post, monitoring something on the screen. "Tell me the moment anything changes," I say.

She nods without looking up, and I leave quietly. The door clicks shut behind me, and the ache in my chest doesn't ease. It only grows.

As I step back into the hall, I don't leave immediately. I linger, leaning against the wall just outside the door, waiting for the tightness in my lungs to relax. It doesn't.

Has Kael even told Aelith about me?

I'm not sure why the question hits so hard, but it does. The way the prince didn't even glance at me—like I was just another Riftborn come to hover. Like I wasn't... bonded. Not to him, obviously. But to Kael.

His personal guard.

Would Kael risk telling him?

The logical part of my brain says no. Of course not. Not yet. Not when the prince is teetering on the edge of burning himself out. Why give him something else to carry?

But the irrational part? The piece of me that's already cracking from the weight of not being enough for my mother, for myself, for Kael during the early days... that part whispers that maybe I'm still something to hide.

The door creaks open behind me. I jolt upright, turning just as Iris slips out, gently pulling the door shut behind her.

She raises an eyebrow. "You didn't leave."

"I was about to," I lie.

She doesn't call me on it. Instead, she rubs at the back of her neck. "He's holding on. Dawson, I mean.

But... whatever's happening in there, it's pulling on all of us. Aelith's getting reckless."

"I know," I say. "Kael told me."

We fall into silence. Her gaze flicks back towards the door.

I shift, uncomfortable. "Your mate... he's here?"

A smile twitches at the corner of her mouth, but it doesn't reach her eyes. "He never really left."

That doesn't help my creeping unease. "I can't see him."

"No one does unless he wants it." Her tone is casual, but I don't miss the way her fingers twitch slightly, like she's reminding herself to stay relaxed. "He's always watching. Protective as hell. He was hovering while you were out, y'know. Not in a creepy way. Well... okay, maybe a little creepy."

"Creepy's generous," I mutter. "More like pants-shitting terrifying."

She snorts. "He likes you."

I blink. "That was him liking me?"

"Well, he didn't impale you, so yeah. That's Hendroy for 'I tolerate your presence.'"

My skin prickles. "Comforting."

"You get used to it," she says, then pauses, tilting her head slightly, studying me. "You okay?"

I open my mouth to say yes. What comes out is "I think something's... shifting."

Her brows lift.

"In me," I clarify. "I've been feeling things. Kael. Even from a distance. And now... I don't know. It's like something's... humming. Inside me. Warm, buzzing."

Understanding floods her expression. "Energy manipulation."

I nod slowly.

"Transference between bonded mates. It's a lot, I know. But you'll get used to it. Obviously, each fated pair is different, but as long as you take it easy and lean on your mate, you'll be just fine."

While I appreciate her confidence in me, I'm not so sure. For one, I'm not the most patient guy in the world —Earth or Terrafeara. But I've felt... sharper today. More attuned. And yeah, I haven't flung lightning bolts from my fingers or anything—not that I think Glowranth can actually do that—but I swear I could've lit a sconce just by touching it earlier.

"Is it dangerous?" I ask. "For humans," I clarify.

"No," she says. "Not unless you try to use whatever skills may have been transferred without understanding them. Kael should train you."

Right. Kael.

The bond pulses faintly, warm and steady. Even if he hasn't told the prince yet, I can feel him. And I know he feels me. That's something.

I exhale, bracing myself to move again. "I should get back. Varek wanted a word." Which is an absolute lie, but I also want to speak to him without outsiders present. And yeah, it sounds shitty calling a fellow Aussie or even my mate that, but I've put my trust in both Varek and Shanae for over two years of my life. I want to know what they're really thinking and if they have a plan.

She nods. "Come back later. Dawson's not out of the woods, but... it's good he has people fighting for him."

"Yeah," I say, voice a little rough. "He's got us."

I just hope he survives this. If not, I have no idea what that will mean for me and Kael. And obviously, I *want* Dawson to survive. That goes without saying. But yeah, selfish or not, I'm thinking about myself too.

IT STARTS WITH A TINGLE.

Not the sexy kind, unfortunately.

More like the pins-and-needles buzz of a limb that's been asleep too long, crawling under my skin, moving in strange, rhythmic pulses. It begins in my palms. Spreads to my forearms. I rub them, thinking maybe I'm imagining it. That maybe I just slept weird or need to hydrate.

Spoiler: I'm not imagining anything either.

Since Varek wasn't available to chat, I caught up on some of my community chores—joyous tasks like restocking rations, clearing the dried creeper vines from the main water pipe entrance, and arguing with

Decca about the definition of "edible." Standard Tuesday stuff.

Not that I know what day of the week it is in human terms.

But I'm very much awake.

And still tingling.

I'm back in my quarters, sitting cross-legged on the floor like I'm about to meditate—which is hilarious considering I have the focus of a magpie on a caffeine high. I stare at my palms, flexing them slowly.

It's still there. That fizzing buzz of energy.

Curiosity gets the better of me.

I concentrate, like Kael described in one of our hushed, half-asleep conversations last night. Open myself to it. Picture the hum of connection, like a thread running from me to something... more.

At first, nothing. Then the space in front of me wobbles.

I blink. Lean forwards.

The air folds.

A ripple spreads like heat above asphalt, distorting everything it touches. My breath hitches. The ripple builds, spiralling into a tiny vortex the size of a grapefruit—right in front of me. It's not a portal. Not quite. More like a pocket of unsteady space, warping the edges of my vision. My chair near the wall creaks, then slides three inches to the left, as if nudged by an invisible hand. Comics I've scavenged lift and flutter into the air. My shelf groans.

"Shitshitshit—"

I swipe at the ripple like that'll help. It burps in protest, expands to the size of a beach ball, and pops with a sound like a deep, wet hiccup.

Books go flying. The natural lights in the walls flicker wildly. The floor shudders beneath me. One of the storage crates in the corner topples with a dramatic clatter.

I freeze.

And then the ceiling creaks ominously.

"*Sonny!*"

The door slams open, and Kael storms in, eyes wild, his bioluminescent markings blazing like lightning beneath his skin. He takes one look at the room—the floating books, the warped air, the bent metal ladder I use to hang my clothes on—and zeroes in on me, sitting wide-eyed on the floor like I'm summoning a demon.

"Hi," I squeak.

Kael doesn't smile. He crosses the room in two strides, drops to his knees in front of me, and grips my shoulders. "Are you hurt?"

"No?" I offer weakly. "Just... spatially challenged."

His eyes flick across my face, down my arms. "What did you do?"

I glance at my palm. "Energy manipulation?"

"You folded the room," he says, like I just admitted to shifting tectonic plates.

"Unintentionally!"

He exhales hard, forehead bumping against mine. "You scared me."

"I scared *me.*"

He cups my cheek, grounding me, the heat of his skin steadying the last of the chaotic energy. "Next time you want to bend the fabric of reality," he mutters, "call me first."

"Deal," I breathe. My heartbeat slows. The air settles. No more wibbly-wobbly timey-wimey bullshit. Just Kael. And my very slightly imploded bedroom.

Next time, I'm starting with something safer. Like lifting a spoon.

But also, what the fuck? If I can do this, an untrained, completely-making-shit-up-as-I-go human, what the hell can Glowranth really do? The ones here in Dathanor? They keep it low-key. Use their abilities for small shit. Lights. Precision. Warming or cooling things, mostly. I've never seen any of them do anything like... *that.*

That has to mean something.

If energy can bend a room, manipulate the very space around us, then deliberately tearing through dimensions isn't just a theory—it's a possibility. With strength and intent.

And holy shit, this is huge.

"Are you sure you're not hurt?"

"No," I say, my voice still high-pitched with leftover adrenaline.

Kael closes the distance, hands on my face, scanning me. He pulls me close, pressing his lips to my forehead before we move off the floor and to my bed.

While Kael is calming down—and I'm pretty sure inhaling my scent—my brain is whirling. I'm hyper-aware of just how deep we're in this now. Seriously, if I can do this, then we're standing on the edge of something massive.

And someone—*somewhere*—knows it.

Kael's breathing has finally evened out, the wild panic that chased him into my room now settled into a slow, steady thrum. His hand is still curled lightly around the back of my neck, clawed finger brushing gently over the column like he needs to feel I'm here. Real. Whole.

"I've been thinking," I begin, voice cautious. "If I can do that—whatever the hell that was—just by messing around... untrained, unprepared..."

Kael hums low in his throat. His heartbeat stutters slightly, like he already knows where I'm going.

"... then what can you really do? What can the *Glowranth* really do?"

A flicker of guilt flashes across his face—and brushes against my chest through the bond, cool and ashamed. He doesn't meet my gaze right away.

"It is... possible," he says slowly, each word like a stone laid with care. "What you did today? That kind of manipulation? It's within reach. I can only theorise it would be especially possible for bonded pairs."

"So... what, you're saying tearing through dimensions, rifting space—whatever brought me here—that's definitely possible for a Glowranth?"

Kael nods. Hesitantly. "It would take strength. Purpose. Deep intent. But yes, it's within the scope of power. For some."

My mind spins. "Some. Like... who? The queen?"

He pauses. That tells me everything before he even opens his mouth. "She is powerful," he admits. "But not the strongest."

"What?"

"She is... strategic. Cunning. And yes, gifted in energy manipulation. But the strength you speak of— the ability to bend reality, to pull from worlds, to shape —" He pauses, his emotions stuttering as he thinks something over.

"What is it?"

"I don't know for certain since I only have stories to go from, but that would require a Glowranth born of royal blood and them being bonded to a fated mate. A complete bond."

I stare at him. "So... fated mates are really... what? The ultimate weapon?"

His jaw tightens. "Not a weapon. But a force. The

joining strengthens both—amplifies. Our energy entwines. And the royal bloodline is... different."

"I've seen it," I say. "Your markings. Aelith's. Yours are darker, his brighter. But it's not just pigment, is it?"

Kael's shoulders rise and fall in a deep sigh. "No. Our markings carry lineage, power, history. And when one of us bonds... I think the abilities we've trained all our lives become something else entirely. It's more than power. It's legacy."

The word settles like stone in my stomach.

"And that's why you didn't come for me," I say, piecing it together aloud. "Because if you did... if you claimed me, and our bond took hold...."

"I would become a threat," Kael finishes, voice low. "Not just to the crown. To the entire queendom."

His regret slams into me, a wave of sadness edged with something that feels a lot like self-loathing. I reach out instinctively, my fingers curling around his.

"Kael...."

"I wanted to," he says. "From the moment I felt you arrive. I felt it. The pull. The instinct. Every day I fought it. Because the moment I came for you—"

"You'd be choosing treason."

He nods once. "Yes."

I swallow thickly, heart thudding. "So, if it wasn't you... if it wasn't Aelith... then who has that kind of strength? Who could've opened two rifts at once? Who could've pulled from across the world—and through the centre of the Earth?"

Kael's expression darkens, shadows gathering in the hollow of his gaze. "That," he says, "is the question I fear the answer to most."

He doesn't say anything more. His silence is telling. Not thoughtful. *Careful.*

I shift closer on the bed, knees drawn up, watching the tension return to his shoulders. Not panic this time. Not guilt. Something else.

Fear.

"You know something," I say quietly. "Don't you?"

His luminous eyes flick to mine—uneasy, calculating. "I know... stories," he says finally. "Old ones. Not in the records. Not shared anymore. But I remember them from when I was a child. Before the prince. Before I became part of the guard."

"Stories?" I repeat, my voice sharper than I mean it to be. "Kael, we're talking about rift theory turning into real possibility, and you've got stories in your back pocket?"

"They were forbidden," he says tightly. "Tales whispered by my father, who had them whispered to him by his father. Meant to frighten us. Or humble us."

I blink at him. "Okay, you're gonna need to be more specific before I combust again and turn the walls to Jell-O."

His lips twitch—but he doesn't smile.

"There was once a Glowranth," he says, voice low, as though the walls themselves might be listening. "A royal heir. Long before the reign of Queen Serresta. Before the queendom unified the outer dominions. His name was erased from our histories. But in whispers, they called him the Shardwalker."

I straighten, heart thumping. "That sounds... not terrifying at all."

Kael ignores me. "He was the most powerful of our kind. Fated to one not from our world but another. He found a way to bring his mate here. When they bonded, it is said the rift between their dimensions... broke. Permanently. Reality bent for them. Rules—changed. And they didn't use that power wisely."

I inhale slowly. "Let me guess. War? Chaos? Death?"

He nods grimly. "They brought destruction. Not just to our kind but to others. They are the reason fate stepped in and prevented any more true bonds from forming for the Glowranth. Our species dwindled. Fragments of worlds collapsed. What was left of the rift— their rift—was sealed by the council of that time and buried so deep, it no longer appeared in royal records. Only the oldest bloodlines whisper the old stories."

"And your family is one of them.... You don't think they're just stories made to frighten you," I murmur.

Kael doesn't deny it.

"I think what we're seeing now... it may be something like that. Not the same, but similar. Someone with power—maybe even a bonded pair—has reopened that kind of wound."

I suck in a sharp breath. "So, you're saying you're pretty certain there's someone out there who can do this... and we don't know who. Or why. Someone who could have even been here *before* all the recent rifts started?" As far as I'm aware, the rifts have been more regular over the past few years, but they span a couple of decades at most.

"I'm saying I need to find out," Kael says.

The weight of his words settles between us.

"You'd have to leave," I say slowly. "To find answers."

He nods. "Yes."

"With everything going on—with Aelith, Dawson—"

"I'd have to go," he says again, firmer. "But not without you."

My stomach flips. I don't know if it's fear or excitement or both. "You'd take me with you?"

"I won't leave you," he says, no hesitation this time. "And you've already proven you're stronger than anyone gives you credit for—including yourself."

I exhale slowly, already thinking of Varek. Of the community. Of what they'd say if I took off now.

But then I meet Kael's eyes. That same intense glow that always cuts straight through me.

"And if this is real," I murmur, "if someone's been

slicing worlds open like oranges and it's not the queen striving for more power...?"

His expression hardens, but not with anger. With resolve.

"If it's not her," he says slowly, "then the unknown feels riskier."

True. But still, whoever did this brought me to Kael. Jack and Solan together. I tell him as much, adding, "They could be all about the love—an interdimensional Cupid who shoots lightning bolts rather than arrows."

Am I grasping here, searching for the good? Absolutely, but with so much uncertainty, what else is a loved-up bloke meant to do?

Kael's jaw works, but he doesn't argue. Doesn't need to. He knows I'm reaching for hope—no matter how ridiculous it sounds. But he also knows I'm not wrong. Someone brought us here. Maybe it was chaos. Maybe it was cruelty. Or maybe, somehow, it was something else.

His fingers brush against mine again, hesitant at first, before they thread through with a quiet certainty. His grip is firm. Solid. Like he's silently saying, *I don't know what we're walking into, but I'm with you.*

The silence holds—not awkward but charged. Something between us settling. Strengthening. Maybe it's delusion. Maybe it's madness. But maybe, just maybe, it's fate doing its weird, messy, terrifying thing.

"We need to sleep on it," I say eventually, my voice

quieter than I intended. "We need to think. You need rest. We both do."

He doesn't move, doesn't speak, just watches me.

I sigh and give his hand a gentle squeeze. "I'm not saying no to leaving. I'm just saying... fuck it all to hell."

Kael lets out a soft exhale—equal parts amusement and exhaustion. "That's fair."

I lean forwards, brushing my forehead to his. "We don't even know what we're facing."

"No," he agrees. "But we won't face it apart."

I swallow hard against the lump in my throat. Bloody hell, I wish I could bottle that kind of certainty and drink it by the litre. "Okay," I whisper.

He tugs off the heavier layers of his armour and places them in a neat pile by the door. I throw off my outer tunic and collapse back onto the mattress with all the grace of a sacked potato.

Kael joins me, curling close behind. Not sexual. Just solid.

Secure.

Safe.

His arm slides around my waist, and I sigh into the pillow, my muscles uncoiling one by one. "Sleep," he murmurs, already half under.

My lips curl into a small, stupid smile. "Only if you promise not to go all broody and noble on me tomorrow."

A pause. Then, soft and low: "No promises."

CHAPTER
FOURTEEN

"I NEED YOUR BLOOD."

Since this isn't the most romantic way I can ask to finalise our fated bond—nor perhaps the best way for Kael to be woken up—when he startles awake and stares at me like I've said the sky is falling, I offer him the sweetest smile I can manage and press my lips to his.

"Morning," I start again, gentler this time. "I hope you slept well. When you're awake properly, I think we should complete our bond."

Do I add more confidence than I'm feeling? Absolutely. I'm nothing if not great at laying on the bullshit. Though I know it's also pointless—bravado, that is—since my emotions are there for Kael's viewing pleasure. The tangled mess of anticipation, longing, nerves, and that tiny speck of fear? Yeah, he's probably feeling all of it.

But Kael's reaction isn't what I expect.

His brow furrows, tension creeping into his shoulders as he props himself on one elbow. He doesn't speak at first, just watches me like I've asked for a limb, not a drop of blood. That bond, still unfinished, shimmers between us—aching.

"You're... worried?" I ask.

His silence confirms it.

I sit back on my heels, heart thudding a little harder. "I figured it was the next step. Right? We've already done the energy exchange. The emotional merge is—" I gesture between us. "—well, clearly a thing."

Kael rubs his hand over his face. "I want to. You know I do."

"But?"

His luminous eyes meet mine, stormy. "After what we talked about yesterday.... If someone's manipulating rifts, using bonds or pulling power—this could make us a bigger target. We don't know what finishing this will do."

I blink. "We're already bonded, Kael. We've done everything but this last part. And sure, maybe it makes us glow brighter in the dark, but we can't leave this thing unfinished. That's not how fate works. Or... movies. Or romance novels."

His lips twitch faintly.

Despite the smile, I mean it. I'm not forcing this on him. If he's not ready—if he's scared—it has to be a choice.

Before he can answer, there's a sudden, sharp pounding on my door. Urgent. Loud.

Kael's already on his feet, warrior instincts snapping into place. He tugs on his pants with swift efficiency, hand already reaching for the knife on the table. I scramble up, too, dragging on my shirt.

"Sonny!" Shanae's voice. Firm. Pressing.

Kael yanks the door open.

"It's Dawson. The prince. You're needed. Now."

No more explanation is needed. Every drop of blood in my body rushes to my feet and head simultaneously. Adrenaline explodes through me, and Kael doesn't hesitate. He sweeps me off my feet, bridal style, like it's the most natural thing in the world.

"Seriously?" I mutter as he bolts through the corridor.

"It's faster," he replies, and that's all I get before he's a blur, his boots pounding the ground as we race towards the medical wing. And for once, I don't argue. Because something's wrong. That much is obvious.

The corridors fly past in a rush of cold air and flickering lights, my heart hammering in time with each of Kael's strides. When we burst into the medical wing, the tension hits me like a wall. The room is too quiet.

Prince Aelith lies on the bed—unmoving. Unconscious. Not just resting or sedated like before. His skin, usually glowing faintly with that royal bioluminescence, is dim. Shadowed. Wrong.

Iris is already here, flitting between monitoring devices and handwritten notes, her face drawn tight with concern. The swirling black mist in the corner confirms her mate is here, too, lurking like some watchful, angry guardian spirit.

Kael sets me down with care but is instantly at Aelith's side.

"What happened?" he demands—calm, steady, but I can feel the storm beneath his voice.

Iris doesn't flinch. "His sedation wore off sometime during the night. I spoke to him briefly before I turned in. He seemed... lucid. Determined. I left him under guard and checked back an hour later. He was unconscious."

"Foul play?" I blurt, heart in my throat. "The guards?"

She shakes her head. "They're loyal. Varek chose them himself. I stayed up most of the night in the next room, checking in every hour. No one came in. No alarms were triggered. And Henny would have known."

I eye the prince again, swallowing hard. "Then... what?"

"He gave too much," Iris says quietly. "He's stable—for now. His vitals are... borderline. But his Glowranth energy is low. Dangerously so."

Kael's jaw clenches. "How low?"

"Too low," she replies. "I've never seen anything like it. Not in Glowranth, not in any species. It's like... he burned himself out."

Before Kael can respond, the door swings open and Varek enters. He looks like hell. His clothing is rumpled, his usually immaculate hair a little dishevelled, and his expression is a thundercloud. Shanae follows him, offering me a quick nod of acknowledgment, her sharp eyes flicking between Iris and the prince.

Varek's luminous gaze meets Kael's. "How bad?"

Kael steps back from the prince's bed. "Worse than before."

Iris answers with a clipped nod, "He needs intervention. Something bigger than anything we have here."

Varek runs a hand down his face, exhaling sharply. "There was a flare-up overnight. Rumblings of revolt. The usual suspects." His gaze flicks to me, then to Kael. "But this? This is bad."

"What's the plan?" I ask, pulse still racing. "We can't keep him like this." *We can't let him die.*

"There are two options," Varek says. "Neither of them good."

Shanae steps forwards. "The first—taking them both to the palace."

Kael's head jerks towards her. "You can't be serious."

"It might be the only chance we have," she says.

"The Glowranth palace has technology. Resources. Archives. If there's anything—anything at all—that could help, it would be there."

"They'd kill him on sight for desertion," Kael growls. "And they wouldn't spare Dawson either. They'd use this as justification for a purge." He glances at me, and I know he's thinking about me, about us. Our own bond and the threat we pose.

"Not if we go with him," Varek says.

"You mean… escort them?" I ask, trying to keep up. "Like a diplomatic mission?"

"Something like that. If we show up on their doorstep with a Riftborn envoy and the royal guard— Kael—they might pause long enough to listen."

"Or they'll see it as a direct attack," Iris mutters, "and we'll all be dead before we hit the front steps." She huffs out a breath, and her mate's mist pulses around her.

So, she'd plan to go too? I suppose someone would need to check on Dawson. But still… this all seems crazy and is getting out of hand. Right?

Shanae shakes her head and faces Varek. "Do you honestly think leaving Dathanor right now is wise?"

The room falls into a heavy silence, and I wonder just how bad things are getting with Zeyv. To be honest, the dickwad has just been looking for an excuse. I hate to think it, let alone say it, but maybe Varek needs to go all Nyxerian on his arse. While I don't know a lot about

Varek's species, I know enough to understand he's deadly and not to be challenged unless you generally are all that.

"What's the other option?" I ask finally.

"There's a library?" Kael questions.

Varek bobs his head while I just glance between them in confusion.

"There's a library that predates the queen's reign. It's hidden, only known to a few. I've only heard rumours, but if it exists and tells us more about fated mates...."

"It could hold what we need," Varek finishes.

"But we'd have to find it first," Shanae adds. "And time's not exactly our friend."

I look at the prince—at his still, quiet form. Then at Dawson, equally still on the neighbouring bed. My gaze meets Kael's. "We can't lose them."

His hand finds mine. "We won't."

Varek nods. "We'll split our forces. I'll keep order here. Iris, you'll stay with both patients. Shanae, prepare the diplomatic documentation just in case. Kael, Sonny —you'll find that library."

My heart jumps. "Us?"

"You're bonded," Varek says. "Glowranth and human. If the old stories are true, you might be the key to opening its gates."

What fucking gates? What old stories? Does he mean how Glowranth used to have fated mates, but their ability stopped centuries or however long ago?

And what happened to simply going to the queen for help? Not that I necessarily think that's an awesome idea, but still....

Kael's thumb brushes over my knuckles.

"So, we go?" I ask him quietly.

He nods, resolve hardening in his jaw. "We go."

I wince. My courage wavers. There's also the other "thing" we need to search for. The whole "who's responsible and has the power to be creating these rifts in the first place" thing. I look at Kael, wishing he could hear me.

Should we tell them what we discussed last night? Would that complicate shit even further?

But he just looks at me, curiosity in his eyes. Yeah, he can feel my emotions, but we need the whole shebang. Which leads us back to the blood exchange he was reluctant to—

"Henny will take you." Iris's words cleave clean through the swirl of questions spinning through my head.

Kael stiffens beside me. I blink at her. "Henny will—he'll what now?"

She lifts her chin, unshaken. "He can get you there faster than anyone else. Quietly. Safely."

I flick my gaze towards the corner, where the black mist is already coalescing like a living shadow. Henny's presence curls at the edges of the room, cool and terrifying in its stillness. Right. Because nothing says low-key and not alarming to my nervous system like being zipped through space via an eldritch cloud demon with a personality kink for vengeance.

Okay, I tagged that bit on, but he's got the whole *grr-argh* thing going for him.

I open my mouth, shut it again, then offer what I think is a very reasonable question: "How do we get back?"

Henny doesn't reply—shocker since he's not fully formed and doesn't currently have a mouth—and Iris lets out a breath like she's been holding it since forever. "He'll leave a mark on you," she explains. "A tether. When you're ready, he can follow it back."

"Follow it?" I repeat, heart stammering.

"It's like a scent," Kael adds quietly, his grip tightening slightly around my fingers. "A memory encoded into energy. He'll find us."

"And what exactly is there? And where is *there* exactly? A hidden library no one can find unless they're bonded? That sounds... mystical. Is this woo-woo magic or actual science? Or both? Because if you're expecting me to wave my hand and chant incantations, I have bad news."

"I don't know what you'll find," Varek says, surprisingly calm. "I only know the stories. That the library holds ancient records, knowledge lost to most of Terrafeara. It's protected by something only a fully mated pair can pass."

Yeah, sounds like woo-woo shit to me.

"Protected how?" I ask, then eyeball Kael. He never mentioned any of this shit yesterday.

He shrugs, his confusion pulsing through our bond. It makes me feel mildly better.

But back to my question. I glance around, but no one answers. Of course no one answers.

I rub my forehead, heat prickling at my nape. "You're asking us to go into some secret, possibly cursed, ancient maze-library—that might be a crock of shit and not actually real—and hope we find a book that says 'how to save your maybe-dying friends and prevent reality from ripping itself apart for dummies'?"

Varek doesn't even blink. "Yes."

Kael murmurs, "I will keep you safe."

I look at him, my fated, my pain in the arse, the man who literally glows in the dark and somehow still manages to make my stomach flutter with one look.

Yeah. I believe Kael. But does he really believe all this shit? I know he mentioned something similar, which I suppose gives Varek's words credit, but this is all a lot of what-ifs. Admittedly, I regularly jump in with both feet and without a plan, and this is a sort of plan. Kinda. Or as close to a plan as I can expect to get.

And don't even get me started on why Varek would have such information in the first place. The big fucker is full of secrets. Arsehole.

I glance again at the prince, lying silent. At Dawson,

still unmoving. At Varek, who looks like he hasn't slept in a week, and Shanae, standing like a sentinel, trying not to show how worried she is.

And then there's Kael—watching me, the weight of so many unspoken things behind his eyes.

I breathe out slowly. "Okay," I say. "Let's get packed and weaponed up. Let your creepy demon-mist boyfriend zap us to a mystery ruin in the middle of nowhere so we can flirt with ancient doom and maybe save the world."

Kael's smile is soft. "You make it sound so poetic."

"Shut up and kiss me, Kael."

He does. And I don't give a rat's ass that everyone is watching.

And just like that, we're committed.

To the bond.

To the search.

To saving them both.

Whatever it takes.

But first... I'll need a little taste, which makes me sound all vampire-ish. I would make an awesome Spike, a thought that I absolutely keep to myself as I give Varek an up-nod and tug Kael out of the room with me, hollering, "We'll be back soon!"

"BLUE BLOOD MEANS SOMETHING SUPER different on Earth." I wrinkle my nose. Am I also disappointed in myself that I'm not like Spike at all? Not even a little? Maybe, but the blue blood that pools at Kael's wrist is absolutely not doing it for me.

Not to get me wrong—if it were red, human blood, without a doubt I'd react the same. Still, I need to do it. Plus, Kael surprised the shit out of me by immediately getting on board. Apparently, if we're entering the heart of the queendom, I need kick-arse powers, and he needs to be at optimum strength.

Our romance game is not at all strong, but hey, I'm trying here.

I scrunch my nose again, my eyes seeking out Kael's when I see his lips twitch. "You're enjoying this," I mutter.

He tilts his head slightly, the faintest smile tugging at the corner of his mouth. "Your face is very… expressive."

I huff. "I'm about to suck your blood and bond our souls for eternity, but sure, let's mock my eyebrows."

Kael shifts closer, his knees brushing mine as he holds out his arm, the blood still glistening at his wrist, bright and unnatural. "It only takes a taste," he says, voice soft. "You don't have to—"

"I want to." And I do. It hits me then—not just the necessity of it, but the weight, the meaning. The commitment. My heart skips. "Okay," I whisper, then bend forwards and press my lips to the wound.

It tastes... not like copper. Not like anything I've ever tasted before. There's a strange effervescence to it, like the edge of lightning before a storm, a kind of fizz and hum that dances across my tongue and zings straight through me.

I blink.

Kael gasps.

Everything shifts.

The moment the blood hits my system, something changes—fast and deep—like a door blown open inside me. My spine arches involuntarily, light bursting through my chest, wild and electrifying. The bond slams home with a force that's impossible to deny, like the final lock sliding into place on something ancient and unbreakable.

And then—

He's there. Not physically, though his body is still pressed close. He's in my mind. Not as thoughts, not as words, but as... presence.

Pressure.

Warmth.

"Let me in."

It's not a command. It's a request. A feather-soft nudge in my mind that curls around the edges of me like a tide, patient, quiet, steady.

And I know what to do.

I let him in.

Emotion explodes between us like a supernova. Love. Longing. Relief so thick, it nearly drowns me. And underneath it, a hunger. A need. Bright, molten, alive. I feel him shudder. His hands tremble against my waist. I grip his shoulders, anchoring us both.

"Holy shit," I breathe, chest heaving.

He presses his forehead to mine, eyes glowing bright with a thousand feelings I can barely parse.

"You feel it too." His voice slides through my thoughts like silk, rich and reverent.

I nod. "Yeah. Kael, I... this is... fuck." Words fail me. For once, language doesn't cut it. It's all too much and not enough, like my body's too small to hold this.

I kiss him. Because what else can I do?

His mouth meets mine in a collision of relief and fire. Our breath mingles. Our bond pulses. I feel every flicker of emotion echoing through him—his awe, his disbelief, his joy—as though it's my own.

His hands are everywhere—gliding, gripping, trembling like he can't believe I'm real. And I feel the same, overwhelmed by the sheer rightness of him. The glow of our bond is blinding now, threaded through every touch, every gasp. It's not just lust—it's everything.

I kiss him again, deeper this time, letting the hunger speak for me. His mouth opens under mine, and our tongues tangle, slick and hot, matching the frantic rhythm of our hearts. We move like we've done this a thousand times in dreams and are finally awake. My fingers dive into his hair, tugging gently. He groans, a low, broken sound that vibrates straight through me.

Clothes are ripped away in clumsy, eager pulls. I don't even know whose hands do what—his or mine—it doesn't matter. All that matters is skin. Contact. Now.

My thighs straddle his hips, and his hands come to rest at my waist, steadying me like he's afraid I'll disappear. "Let me ride you," I whisper, but it's not a request. It's a promise.

Kael exhales a shaky breath, his lips parting in awe as I rise over him. His precum glows faintly—celestial, wild, *other*. He's beautiful. Almost too much to look at.

He stops me with a gentle touch to my thigh, voice barely a whisper. "Wait. Let me…. I want to do this right."

His hand dips between us, slick with his glow-in-the-dark precum he must've grabbed without me noticing. Fuck me, his dick is a gift that just keeps on giving. He coats himself in long, deliberate strokes, every movement precise—almost practiced.

"Do you need help?" I ask, breath catching as he reaches lower, fingers circling my rim with startling confidence.

Kael meets my gaze, flushed and fierce. "No. I've got this. Remember, I've read a *lot* of romance novels."

And bloody hell, it shows.

He preps me slowly, thoroughly—two fingers sliding

inside with care that borders on worship, curling just enough to make my hips twitch. The claw-shaped curve hits my prostate with such perfect precision, it's almost too much. He watches every reaction like it's gospel, adjusting, deepening, learning me with an intensity that might just unravel me.

His other hand never stops moving, stroking himself in time with the rhythm he builds inside me. His breath is ragged now but controlled. Focussed.

"You're doing perfect," I manage to gasp, gripping his wrist. "Kael, I... please—"

The moment his fingers slip free, slick and trembling, I don't wait. I *need* him. I take him in hand, position us, and brace myself. He hisses as I lower myself slowly. Inch by thick, pulsing inch.

The stretch burns, delicious and overwhelming, and Kael watches me with eyes like suns, wide and reverent.

"You're...," he starts, but the words die on his tongue. His hands shake on my hips.

"I know," I murmur, voice trembling, breathless. "I feel it too."

He gasps as I finally sink all the way down, and I swear I see stars—real ones, not metaphorical, like I've just been launched into low orbit. There's a beat of stunned silence between us. My mouth hangs open. His hands are gripping my hips like he's afraid I might disappear—or implode.

I glance down, half expecting to see the outline of

his cock pressing *through* my stomach like I've just walked into an animated monster porn feature. "Kael," I pant, "are you sure you're not part divine creature or something?"

His only answer is a wrecked groan that vibrates through his chest.

"Because I swear to God, I can *feel* you in my lungs."

He laughs—breathy, stunned—and then growls, "Then don't stop riding me until I'm all the way in your *head*."

My laugh turns into a moan, and I start to move, every inch of him lighting up nerves I didn't even know I had.

Fucking my own monster? Turns out, it's not just hot as hell. It's holy.

I lean over him, my mouth pressing against his neck, the tension between us electric, unbearable.

We move. Slow at first, measured, like the build-up of a storm. Each rise and fall sends tremors through us both. His fingers dig into my skin, grounding me, worshipping me. Every motion sends more of him against that spot inside me, and I cry out, my voice ragged, guttural.

"You're perfect," Kael grits, his hands now guiding me harder, faster.

Our bond hums—an unrelenting current of ecstasy and emotion—and soon we're past words, past reason. There's only sensation: the sound of skin meeting skin, the shuddering gasps, the heat, the slick slide of bodies made for each other.

I ride the edge of it, my hands braced against his chest, my head thrown back. He meets every thrust from below, matching my rhythm, his breath raspy, worshipful.

"I'm not going to last," he growls, and the tension in his body, the ecstasy of his emotions tells me he's close.

"Then don't," I whisper, leaning down, kissing him hard when he angles his face for me. "Let go. With me."

And when he does, it's like the world shatters around us—light, heat, love, and hunger exploding in a blinding surge that leaves us trembling and undone. For a heartbeat, the rest of the world falls away.

Then another.

And another.

We stay this way—breathless, entangled, our bodies still joined, our bond humming like a pulse beneath our skin. His fingers trace slow, reverent circles along my back. My forehead rests against his, our breaths mingling in the quiet aftermath.

Nothing exists outside this moment. No missions. No chaos. Just us.

But reality is a persistent little bastard. It snaps back like a rubber band, fast and rude. The cold air brushes sweat-damp skin. Somewhere in the distance, people are counting on us.

Kael pulls back slightly, his chest heaving. His hand lingers on my cheek like he's not quite ready to let go.

I exhale, dragging a hand through my hair. "So. That happened."

"You are radiant," Kael murmurs, like he can't quite believe it.

I flush. "Right, well, now that I've been filled with your magical lightning juice or whatever it is—"

Kael chokes on a laugh.

"—we should probably go see if I've gained any superpowers. Like heat vision. Or the ability to eviscerate someone with sarcasm."

"You already had that," Kael says drily, brushing a thumb along my cheek.

"True."

We stand together. Our bond thrums steady and alive between us, a lifeline tethering us to something far bigger than ourselves. And even with everything waiting outside this door—danger, politics, a possibly dying prince—I know this: We're not alone anymore.

Not ever again.

The cum still in my arse is a pretty spectacular reminder too. Am I sticky? Yep. But fuck if I don't like it. And from the way Kael watched his cum leak from me when I bent over to get dressed, he's fully on board with my desire to keep him inside me for as long as possible.

I knew he was a kinky fucker.

The thought guides me as we strap on our weapons.

Kael is a walking weapon himself, his full armour fitted like a second skin—dark metallic plating contoured to his broad form, layered for both movement and defence. Flashes of burnt orange gleam at the joints and edges, pulsing faintly like coals in a dying fire. The jagged symbols etched across his chest plate are like scars—emblems of rank, of battles fought, of victories claimed.

He slips his helm into place under his arm, not putting it on just yet, and the way his muscles move beneath the thick armour is enough to make my knees forget how to function.

I, on the other hand, am in leather pants that might be the best trade I've ever made—scavenged from a recent haul and bartered for with some rare glassware I found months ago. They hug just right. Supple, dark, tough as hell, and lined with heat-reactive fabric that keeps me from freezing my ass off in the Terrafearan climate shifts. The dagger harness Varek gave me sits snug against my ribs and thighs—four blades total, one at each hip, two sheathed along my back. Functional and badass.

But still, I feel a bit like I'm playing dress-up compared to Kael's royal guard battle couture.

I tug my shirt down, self-conscious. "Kinda wish I had a gun."

Kael glances at me, amusement glittering in his eyes. "You'd shoot your foot."

"I would not." I pause. "Okay, yeah. I would."

"I will protect your feet," he says solemnly.

I snort. "My hero."

But the next moment happens so fast, I barely register it until I'm pinned.

Kael steps forwards, crowding into my space, his armour clinking softly as he backs me into the nearest wall. His large hands find my waist, gripping with just enough force to make my breath stutter. Then, in one smooth motion, he lifts me—just hauls me up the wall like I weigh nothing—and my thighs grip around his hips instinctively, our faces level now, our chests brushing with every breath.

"Kael—"

He kisses me.

No warning. No hesitation. Just raw, molten heat crashing into me.

It's not soft. It's not sweet. It's possessive and consuming and so fucking intense that for a second, I forget where we are or what's coming. His mouth moves against mine like he's memorising me—like this kiss is the anchor before we dive headfirst into something that could kill us.

His hands grip tighter, pulling me impossibly closer, like he's trying to fuse us together. My fingers find the edges of his armour and clutch tight, and he groans into my mouth like I've hit some pressure point that unravels him.

Every nerve ending in my body lights up like a star gone supernova.

I don't remember closing my eyes, but when I open them, his are already on me—glowing faintly, his nostrils flaring, his bioluminescent markings pulsing in rhythm with the bond thrumming between us.

"That," I whisper, breathless, my lips still brushing his, "was not from a Mills & Boon novel." For real, I don't recall any books from Mum's collection being cock-dripping levels of hot like this.

Kael's smile is slow, wicked. "Good." And then he lowers me gently to the ground—though his fingers linger just a moment longer as he reaches my butt and rubs his fingers against my crease. "Let's go save them," he says.

And damn it, I'd follow him anywhere. Even to a place I have no desire to visit, let alone to somewhere that might not actually exist. But as he grips my hand and tugs lightly, I follow willingly, trying to ignore my hardening cock.

Where he goes, I go.

CHAPTER
FIFTEEN

WE'RE JUST ABOUT TO REACH THE GATE THAT separates our community compound from the main HQ outpost—the one where Varek and Henny are waiting —when I feel it. A shift. A crack in the air that doesn't belong.

I stop short. Kael halts beside me, his head turning towards me in quiet question.

"What is it?" His voice brushes through my mind, even and low.

"It's too quiet," I send back, my mental voice less certain.

I look ahead. The gate that leads to the main court-yard should be open. It's never closed during daylight hours. But now it is—shut tight with the thick security glass that's reinforced against everything from the elements to minor explosions. And behind it, partially obscured, stands a Stirgule.

The glow of his green skin casts an eerie reflection on the glass. He's armed. Intent clear.

Kael's posture shifts immediately, weight centring. I feel his readiness ripple through the bond like a silent hum.

A sound scrapes behind us, and I turn, stomach clenching.

Zeyv.

Of course it's fucking Zeyv.

He's flanked by five others—both male and female, all different species. I recognise most of them. One is a human, and my gut twists with disappointment. We're so few, and to see one of my own standing with them?

Three more bodies appear beyond the gate, shadows becoming solid. That's ten in total.

Ten to two. Because undoubtedly that's what this is. There's no misunderstanding here.

And yet I don't feel fear.

Kael stands beside me like a living weapon, every inch of him taut and battle-hardened. I reach for my dagger but don't draw it yet.

"What the fuck do you think you're doing?" I demand, voice slicing through the tension like a whip crack.

Zeyv's grin is all sharp teeth, but it doesn't reach his eyes. It's the kind of smile that wants to see someone bleed. "I'll give you one chance to leave, Sonny," he says, which honestly surprises me. "You can walk. We're after him." He jerks his chin towards Kael.

I let out a low laugh, full of bitter sarcasm. "Oh, how generous of you. Really stretching that big heart of yours today, huh, Zeyv?"

"Careful," Kael warns me silently. *"They're unstable. And armed."*

Unstable? I barely hold back my snort. That doesn't cover the half of it.

"I have no quarrel with you," Kael says aloud, stepping forwards half a pace, his hands still at his sides. "Let us pass. I don't wish to fight."

Zeyv sneers. "Too late for diplomacy, Glowranth. You're a symbol of everything that's wrong here. Both you and the prince here in our home? What's next? The queen herself knocking on our doors?" He spits near Kael's boots. "You're a threat," he continues. "And once you're dead, we'll take out your prince next. Varek can't protect everyone. And don't think we'll spare your human toy either, if he makes the mistake of staying."

My jaw tightens. I feel Kael's fury spike—barely held back by sheer force of will. But me? Oh, I'm done playing nice.

I step forwards, dagger drawn now, my eyes locked on Zeyv. "Then come and try," I say. "Let's see if you survive the attempt."

His expression hardens, his sneer twisting into something far uglier. And then—chaos.

They surge forwards, weapons raised, the corridor narrowing with the weight of bodies and intent. Kael's arm swings up, intercepting the first blow aimed at me with the flat of his forearm. The impact rattles through his armour, but he doesn't flinch. He moves like liquid vengeance—controlled, precise, devastating.

His gauntlet glows, power thrumming beneath the surface as he drives his fist into one attacker's chest, sending them flying back into the wall with a crack that echoes down the corridor.

It's hot. Ridiculously hot. But I don't have time to be distracted.

Another comes at me fast, with a curved blade that whistles through the air. I dodge, barely, the steel grazing my shoulder. Pain sears through me, hot and wet. It's not deep, but it's enough.

Right. No more Mr Nice Guy.

I lash out, my foot connecting with their knee, and when they stagger, I slam the hilt of my dagger into their jaw. They crumple. Another takes their place.

There are too many.

Kael's fighting off three at once. His power crackles with each movement, light and heat pulsing from his palms as he uses his energy to throw them back, knocking weapons from hands and bodies into walls.

And fuck, he's beautiful like this. Focussed. Fierce. Lethal.

Distracting as hell.

But I push through it. Varek's voice echoes in my mind, sharp, relentless. *You're not the strongest. So don't try to be. Be smart. Be quick. Be unpredictable.*

I duck low, sliding between two combatants, and jab my dagger into the back of a knee. They scream, collapse. I roll away, using my momentum to dodge another attacker's slash, and come up swinging with the pommel of my dagger. It's not pretty, but it's effective. That's Varek's training—no frills, all grit.

I fight dirty. I use elbows, knees, teeth if I have to. My small size lets me slip through gaps, lets me strike where it hurts.

I'm covered in sweat and blood, and I don't even know which is mine anymore. A dagger flashes towards me. I twist, raising my arm too late—

—but the blade stops short. Hovers.

Glowing.

What the—

It's me. My energy. Instinctive, raw, wild. The dagger vibrates, caught in the shimmer of gold-blue light emanating from my palm.

"Sonny!" Kael's voice hits my mind, sharp with warning but also awe.

I don't have time to think. I push. The dagger flings back towards its wielder, knocking them off balance.

I exhale hard. "Okay. That's new."

"Stay focussed," Kael growls, slamming his opponent against the wall with bone-crunching force. "But yes. That was... impressive."

Another attacker lunges at Kael's back. I fling my hand towards them, the energy responding to my panic —arcing across the space like a whip and slamming into them mid-leap. They drop like a stone.

I blink. "Holy shit."

Kael sends another sprawling with a kick that makes the walls shake. His eyes flash to mine, blazing. "We'll talk later."

Yeah. We will.

But first, we survive this.

The corridor's still filled with enemies—I'm pretty sure more have joined Zeyv's ranks—but something's shifted. Zeyv's eyes narrow, uncertainty flickering.

He should be scared. He really, *really* should.

But that's when the rest of his little gang crashes in from the outside. Three more—armed and clearly ready for blood—burst through the exterior gate. It swings open wide enough to flood the corridor with harsh daylight.

We're boxed in.

Zeyv makes his move, darting forwards with a twisted smile. And this time, I don't hold back. He's strong—but I took him down once. I strike with brutal precision, low and fast, darting between bodies, slicing his thigh, cutting shallow across his ribs.

He roars and throws a punch I barely duck. I spin, drive my elbow into his gut, but he grabs me, slamming me into the wall.

Kael bellows my name, his fury tangible through the bond while Zeyv throws something. I don't know what it is until it's midair.

It's a weapon. Sharp. Spinning.

Headed straight for Kael.

Time slows.

Kael's occupied, his back turned as he wrestles a female attacker with claws and too many teeth. He won't see it.

But I do.

I don't think. I move.

I fling my hand forwards, energy surging before I've even formed a thought. It crackles out of me, a shimmering arc that blasts the weapon off course. It slams into the wall and embeds deep in the plaster.

Zeyv's eyes go wide.

Kael turns, eyes blazing. Then he turns back to Zeyv.

Kael moves like a force of nature. His body blurs, energy whipping around him like a storm. He hits Zeyv so hard, the air is knocked from the corridor. Zeyv stumbles, but Kael's not done.

One blow. Two. A third that sends Zeyv crumpling to the ground.

I stagger to my feet, blood dripping from my arm, heart thundering. Zeyv gurgles, trying to rise. Kael's blade flashes, and it's over.

Zeyv is still.

We breathe. We bleed. We survive.

Bodies litter the corridor, steam rising from sliced flesh and scorched clothing. My chest heaves, adrenaline buzzing like a hive under my skin. Kael's shoulder brushes mine as he straightens, blood and energy residue staining his armour.

We won—but it doesn't feel like a victory. Not when we're surrounded by the carnage of our own people. Riftborn. Rebels. Residents.

Footsteps echo beyond the far corridor. A door swings open. Gasps ring out.

Shit.

More residents filter into the hallway, faces pale and eyes wide. Some look horrified, others angry. More than a few are watching Kael like he's a fucking threat all over again.

No. Not today.

I step forwards, planting myself in front of him. "Back off," I snap, voice louder than I expect. "We were attacked. This"—I gesture to the bodies, to the mess—"was not our doing. Zeyv and his crew ambushed us."

There's murmuring, shifting, uncertain glances. Most know what a fuckhead Zeyv is. Was. No doubt whatever Varek got caught up in last night with Zeyv has reached the gossip mill too.

"Someone get Varek," I add, heart still hammering.

The doors at the end of the hall slam open before anyone can move. Varek storms in like a tidal wave wrapped in fury.

For most, it's the first time they see it—the full terrifying presence of our leader. His skin gleams in the light like a living oil slick, every muscle coiled with restrained violence. The silver of his eyes glows brighter than ever. His horns curve like weapons themselves, casting long shadows behind him. Massive. Lethal.

The crowd recoils, even without a word from him. They feel it. The weight of him. The threat he holds in check.

His gaze snaps to the corpses, the still forms. To Zeyv's body. Then to me. To Kael.

"What happened?"

"Zeyv tried to kill Kael," I say, voice steady now. "He didn't act alone. They were waiting."

Kael stays silent at my side, every muscle locked, ready.

Varek's gaze darkens as he surveys the scene. "Anyone else involved still breathing?"

One of Zeyv's group moans faintly, twitching at the edge of the carnage. Another stirs with what looks to be a broken leg from its odd angle, whimpering.

Varek doesn't even flinch. "Detain them. Now."

Enforcers appear out of the shadows like summoned wraiths, stepping around the stunned onlookers and moving in without a word.

Varek doesn't have to raise his voice. With one sweeping glare and a flex of his enormous form, he commands immediate attention. The Riftborn who'd joined us after the fight fall silent. Even the vocal ones hesitate, eyes flicking from the bodies on the floor to the blood-slicked walls and then to Kael and me.

"Disband," Varek orders, voice low and lethal. "This ends now."

A few mutter as they back away, clearly expecting answers, maybe even justice—or vengeance—but no one dares push it. Especially not with Varek radiating wrath and authority in equal measure.

"The bodies," he instructs Shanae, who appears by his side without a sound, "remove them. The wounded... get them treated under guard. No exceptions."

Translation: He believes us. Which... duh. Like we were going to start a brawl right before heading off to potentially save the two most politically inconvenient people in the realm.

"We don't have time for this," he mutters, mostly to himself.

I snort. "No shit, Sherlock."

Varek's brow lifts slightly. "Sher-lock?"

"Forget it," I sigh. "Earth thing. Brilliant, moody

detective with a god complex and no concept of personal space."

Kael tilts his head slightly, curious, but I wave it off. Only then do I actually get a good look at him. Kael is covered in blood. Not just any blood—like, a rainbow mess of other-species blood, thick and drying across the metal sheen of his armour. Most of it isn't his, thank fuck, but I can see a few shallow cuts on his arm and neck, glowing faintly blue at the edges.

"Shit," I breathe, reaching out without thinking. "You're a mess."

His gaze flicks over me like a scan. "You're hurt."

"I'm fine." I shrug, even though I'm not entirely sure if that's adrenaline talking or if I've gone into some next-level shock state. "Feels like nothing."

"It will ache later," Kael says, stepping closer. His hand comes up slowly, fingertips brushing the edge of the gash on my upper arm. "I can heal this."

"You can what now?"

He doesn't smile, but his eyes soften. "Energy manipulation, remember? It can be used to speed minor healing."

My eyes widen. "You mean I've been walking around with thigh chafing from your kinky bondage like a chump, and you could've magicked it away?"

"It requires focus," he says with a tiny smirk. "And permission."

"Permission granted. Full clearance. Heal away."

He lifts his hand again, but I hold up mine to stop him.

"Wait."

His brow furrows.

"Maybe not all of it." I point to the worst of the cuts on my arm. "I kinda want a scar. You know... to look fierce. Wounded warrior vibes. A little edge. Very 'don't mess with me or I'll channel my Glowranth boyfriend and energy-blast your face off.'"

Kael blinks. "That is... specific."

"You love that about me."

"I do."

Holy fuck. Did he...? Did I...? I swallow hard. The way he says it—quiet, sure—sends a warmth through my chest that I'm definitely blaming on residual battle adrenaline.

"Fine," I add, trying not to blush. "Heal everything except the sexy battle souvenir."

He leans in, pressing a gentle kiss to the uninjured edge of my shoulder before lifting his palm.

"And then we get cleaned up," I murmur. "Because if we show up at the queendom like this, they're going to think we just murdered a small army."

Kael doesn't reply, but the glint in his eye tells me he's already planning just how intimidating he wants us to look. Because hell, why not let the queendom know we're not fucking around? You know, if we do run into anyone and our stealth plans go flying out the window.

And let's face it, with the way our lives have been going since the moment we met, it's not exactly like subtlety is our strong suit. We've crashed through caves, scaled mountains, fought ambushes, and bonded in a blaze of bioluminescent glory. Sneaking in quiet-like? Not really our brand. So if shit goes sideways—and it probably will—we may as well look like the bloody storm rolling in.

Kael hums beside me, like he's reading that thought loud and clear through the bond. "We will be seen," he says, adjusting the last strap of his armour.

"Yeah," I say with a huff of a laugh. "And they're gonna shit themselves when they see us."

His hand brushes mine. "That's the goal."

Bloody hell help whoever stands in our way.

CHAPTER
SIXTEEN

"I'M COMING WITH YOU."

Honestly, I'm not even surprised by anything anymore. That Varek has changed his mind and is insisting on joining me and Kael is not typical of him exactly, as I have to hand it to the guy, he's usually steadfast in his decisions. But—

"With Zeyv no longer around to cause problems"— my lips twitch despite the gravity of all that's happened, but beyond Varek rolling his eyes at me, he doesn't pause—"Shanae can handle things here."

She steps forwards, lips parting I suspect to argue with our fearless leader. The shake of Varek's head stops her, though.

"If the library does exist, between us, we can find it."

Fair point.

"I still don't know how you have info that Kael

doesn't," I say, squinting at Varek like I might be able to read the answers off his shimmering purple face.

He simply offers a tight-lipped smile. "You'd be surprised how many secrets come to light when people think no one's listening."

Cryptic. Great. I also know that long before he founded this rebel group, he'd been captured by the royal guards and spent time in the queen's palace. I just don't know for how long or what his purpose was. It's something I know I should never ask. Nor is it anything anyone here really gossips about.

Kael's fingers brush against mine—subtle, grounding. It's enough to make my nerves tangle a little looser, but not completely. Because this? This still feels a little like jumping into a firestorm with nothing but a wet rag and good intentions.

I look over my shoulder at Dawson and Aelith. Iris stands between them, her posture rigid but hands gentle as she adjusts the monitoring equipment. Her mate, all mist and menace, lingers nearby like a living shadow. If either of them shifts so much as a toe, I know he'll be there.

"They're stable," Iris says without looking up. "For now. I'll let you know the moment anything changes."

That "for now" feels like a blade against my spine. I nod, swallowing past the tightness in my throat.

Solan and Jack arrive, tension written across their faces. Jack's gaze flicks to me, Kael, then the medical beds. He exhales hard. "We heard what happened. Heard it was bad."

"It was," I say, not bothering to sugar-coat it. And whether he's talking about the fight or the medical status of Dawson and Aelith seems inconsequential. It's all bad.

Solan steps up beside him, nodding. "We'll stay here. Watch over them."

"And Shanae?" Varek says, glancing over at her.

Shanae's jaw is clenched, her lips slashed in a tight line. She nods, remaining silent—a testimony to just how pissed off at Varek she really is.

"She'll have backup." Solan gestures towards the door where the two unconscious bodies are secure.

A beat passes. Kael straightens beside me, his armour whispering against itself as he shifts. There's steel in his stance now, not just physically but emotionally. He's made up his mind. "The queen's healers won't help. Even if they could, they'd use it as leverage. She'd want something in return."

"Like her son's head on a pole," I mutter.

Kael doesn't deny it. "What's happening between Aelith and Dawson is beyond medical science. This is something else. Something... older."

"Something fated," Varek says. "Something buried."

I glance at Kael again, searching his face. "And you really think we'll find answers in some dusty, maybe-imaginary archive?"

He meets my gaze evenly. "If I didn't, I wouldn't let you go." His voice is low, but it strikes with purpose. That does it.

I sigh, rubbing a hand over my face. "All right. Let's go dig through some ancient scrolls and hope to the terrifying deities of Terrafeara that this isn't a massive waste of time."

Kael's lips twitch. "Your optimism is inspiring."

"I try."

Then the air shifts. Thickens. I don't need to look to know what's coming. The temperature drops. Shadows bleed across the floor. A hiss like the rattle of a thousand bones sounds behind us.

And there he is.

Henny.

The Hendroy appears in a swirl of mist and malevolence, his towering form even more imposing inside closed quarters. His head tilts, glowing eyes zeroing in on Kael with no attempt to hide his distaste.

He doesn't speak, but I feel it—a brush of his power skimming across my mind like a warning. Kael steps half in front of me. Reflexive. Protective.

Varek, unbothered, gives a nod. "We're ready."

Henny extends an arm, palm up, fingers tipped in wicked claws. The mist coils tighter, forming into a vortex of spinning black-and-violet energy.

My stomach flips. "Oh, fuck me," I whisper.

"Later," Kael murmurs through our bond.

My startled snort breaks the tension, and I shoot him a sideways look as we step towards the portal. *"As much as I love you, I hate you a little right now."*

"You love me?" Kael says—asks?—through the bond, quiet, awed.

I freeze. *Shit.* That wasn't supposed to slip out, but I don't take it back.

"Unfortunately," I say, because sarcasm is safer than sincerity, and I'm already halfway undone.

Kael doesn't reply, but the flare of heat and emotion through the bond is unmistakable. He heard me. Felt me. All of me.

The vortex pulses beside us. Varek moves first. Then Kael. Then me.

As I step into the swirling dark, my heart thudding against my ribs, I send one last thought into whatever dimension fate is listening to. *Please let there be answers on the other side.* Because if not, I think we'll definitely be royally fucked. Maybe even here in this black void that wipes away my vision.

I barely have time to take a breath, though, before we land hard. Like, arse-meets-stone, ungraceful-as-hell hard.

The ground beneath me is cool and rough, the scent of moss and distant smoke catching in my throat. I sit up, disoriented, the mist still curling around my shoulders like ghostly tendrils, until it's gone—vanished as though it never existed.

Panic grips my chest. "Shit," I mutter, spinning. "Did no one think to talk about where we were actually going?"

Kael appears beside me, already upright, hand on the hilt of his blade. Varek is standing, too, brushing dust from his coat like he didn't just get yeeted into another part of Terrafeara via a scary-as-fuck mist vortex.

"Is it safe here?" I ask, scanning the area. It's... eerily quiet.

Stone structures rise around us—weathered buildings with jagged spires, smoothed by time and the subtle thrum of energy that hums beneath the surface. The stone itself almost seems to pulse faintly, like it's alive. Or maybe that's just the panic making my brain short-circuit.

No Glowranth in sight. No crowds. No chaos.

Just empty, watchful silence.

My arm aches suddenly—sharp, hot. I wince and glance down. "Uh. What the—" A mark glows faintly on my forearm. Ink-black with hints of purple, it spirals into a rune I don't recognise, sleek and otherworldly.

Kael's eyes land on it and narrow. "It's from the Hendroy. His tracker. A tag."

"Great," I say, flexing my arm. "Mystic LoJack."

His lips twitch. "We're close to the citadel. The palace is further east."

"Define 'close,'" I urge. "Close enough for guards to

skewer us, or just 'hey, we're in the neighbourhood' kind of close?"

Kael's eyes flick to the tallest spire visible in the distance. "Too close. But not immediate danger. Yet."

"Comforting," I mutter.

Varek steps forwards, his expression unreadable. "We're not wandering blind."

Kael arches a brow. "You know where to start?"

Varek nods once. "I have a contact. We'll begin there."

"Care to elaborate?" I ask.

"No."

Of course not, but we follow him anyway.

The pathway is uneven, cut into the stone itself, bordered by sleek walls that glow faintly with etched runes. The further we walk, the more I notice: floating lights that seem to be contained in orbs overhead, illuminating the streets like lanterns with minds of their own; doorways that seal with a press of energy, a quiet hum echoing as they slide shut; strange vehicles— hovering, low-slung transports that glide silently past alleyways, disappearing before I can fully focus on them.

It's different, sure. But also... familiar. Like Earth and Terrafeara had a drunken one-night stand and this was their weird, beautiful, slightly terrifying baby.

"The tech," I whisper. "It's getting more advanced, right?" At least that's what I heard. I suspect the multitude of species who are finding their way here, bringing their knowledge with them—as well as patches of their homes—will have helped significantly with that.

Kael nods. "The queen's been pushing development. Integration from rift remnants. Borrowed tech. Stolen in some cases."

I have a feeling the "stolen" here refers to species' knowledge rather than an inanimate object. "And the energy manipulation?"

"Still the foundation," he says. "It powers everything. Machines, defences, even transportation. Without it, this city wouldn't function."

Varek doesn't comment, just keeps walking. Fast. Determined.

We continue to follow, but I can't help but wonder what kind of contact Varek has in the heart of enemy territory. But one thing's certain—we're not here by accident. I can't imagine Henny bringing us to a place we shouldn't be.

"Where are we going?" I whisper, matching Kael's quiet steps as we trail Varek.

"To someone who owes me a favour."

That's ominous and not at all encouraging.

We wind through side streets, ducking under archways and past stone pillars etched with softly glowing sigils. No people. No movement. Just the eerie sense that something's watching.

"Wait." Kael's hand shoots out, stopping me as we near a narrow alley. "Someone's nearby."

Varek doesn't pause. "We're close."

We follow him down a tight passage that opens into what looks like the back of a stable or a transport station. Varek gestures for silence. There's a building ahead—low, squat, more like a storage structure than a house. A heavy stable-style door sits partially ajar, faint light spilling through the gap.

Voices carry out. First in Glowranthian—low, sharp, clipped. I pick up a few words, mostly due to Varek's tutoring, but the dialect is fast. Three voices. Maybe more.

Then English.

My brows shoot up. I lean towards Kael. "Did you hear that—"

Light explodes through the door. The wood jerks open with a creak, and a tall, brown-skinned man steps into the alleyway, eyes wide and mouth open. He's human, wearing the robes of a Glowranth native, but clearly not military. My heart pounds, and Kael steps in front of me instantly, his body going taut, hand already near his sword.

The man curses, low and vicious.

I grab my dagger. Kael goes for his blade.

And then—

The guy charges. Not at us. At Varek.

He grabs the massive, horned rebel by the collar, yanks him down, and kisses him. Hard.

I blink. "Uhh."

Kael stills beside me, completely silent while the kiss lasts forever. Or maybe a few seconds. It's hot. Intense. Messy. Then the human rears back—and punches Varek square in the nose.

Crunch.

"Ow." I wince.

Varek's head snaps back, blood trickling down his face, but he doesn't move to retaliate. Doesn't even flinch.

"What the actual fuck?" I whisper to Kael. "Is this foreplay or interdimensional retribution?"

The moment we're inside, Kael doesn't relax. Nor does he answer me. His palm stays firmly on the hilt of his sword, his posture rigid as his eyes scan the cramped interior.

I, on the other hand, am busy processing approximately fifty things at once. Like the building—half stone, half whatever that is—and the man who just delivered the most feral welcome I've ever witnessed. Not to mention the two other Glowranth now standing awkwardly to the side like they're deciding whether to bolt or throw hands.

We're ushered in with all the subtlety of a bar fight. Kael stays between me and the others, a wall of gleaming metal and protective vibes. His glowing markings pulse faintly, which does nothing for my heart rate.

The man—Varek's mystery kisser/puncher—launches into a furious tirade in thick Glowranthian, his voice sharp and musical, like he's singing insults at a very aggressive tempo. Every now and then, English words filter through: "betrayal," "idiot," "what the fuck, Varek."

I blink. My lips twitch.

The two other Glowranth watch with wide eyes. One of them steps forwards as if to intervene, then hesitates when he catches sight of Kael. His eyes widen further. He whispers something to the other, and I swear I catch "royal guard."

Great. Fan-fucking-tastic.

Things go from awkward to nearly combustible. Kael's markings blaze like warning lights, his entire being locked and loaded. The mystery man finally tears his attention away from Varek to snap something at Kael. It's half growl, half snarl, and a hundred percent threatening.

"Okay!" I announce, stepping forwards and raising my hands like a referee between rabid wolves. "Everyone, take a breath. Or ten. Preferably before someone else gets kissed. Or punched. Or both."

The Glowranth blink at me. Kael blinks at me. Even Varek blinks like he's only just remembered I exist. And the bloke, he studies me hard, assessing, but some of the initial fury bleeds from his expression.

"Seriously," I add. "Whatever I just walked into, we can sort it out after we figure out how not to let your prince die and maybe, maybe save a few hundred lives in the process."

The silence is thick.

Then the puncher—who I'm now mentally calling "Kisspocalypse"—lets out a string of vicious-sounding Glowranthian. It's definitely not polite.

Varek drags a hand down his face and mutters, "This is going well."

Understatement of the year.

Kael shifts closer to me, his energy brushing mine in a silent pulse of reassurance. I have no idea what's happening. But judging by the look on Varek's face, he's perhaps reconsidering his plan to come here to claim a favour.

I clear my throat. "Can we do this in English?" I ask. "I mean, yeah, I suck. I'm privileged. I'm the worst. But I'd love to actually know what the hell is going on."

Kael's voice slides into my mind, smooth and calm. *"The human—his name is Pax—is furious. Varek promised never to come back here."*

"Like, promised how?" I murmur in my mind. *"Are we talking a 'my word is my bond' kind of promise, or a 'magical vow with actual painful consequences' thing?"*

He hesitates. *"We'd know if it was a binding vow. He's still alive."*

"Oh. Yay."

Meanwhile, Pax is still pacing, dark eyes blazing. His skin is rich brown, warm toned, marked with intricate tattoos that twist around one bicep and peek up past the collar of his shirt. There's a scar running from the corner of his left eye to his temple. Thick muscles flex as he moves, and yeah, he's got a bit of a dad bod thing going on, which shouldn't be hot—

Kael growls softly beside me.

Right. Focus.

The other two occupants, both Glowranth, are still watching Kael like he's about to draw his sword. One of them murmurs something low and urgent in Glowranthian, and I catch the word "heir."

"Wait," I say, snapping my gaze to Pax. "You know Prince Aelith's missing, right? Like, probably dying?" Which of course they don't know the latter beyond my verbal diarrhea, but still, this shit right here is tedious. "And his unbonded fated mate is human. Dawson. He's barely hanging on either."

Shock ripples through the room. Pax stiffens. Then he snorts. "Of course it's a human." His mouth curls into something almost cruel. "The prince. The one who demanded Riftborn be shackled the moment they stumbled into Terrafeara. The heir to a throne built not just on the bones but the backs of those they enslaved. Who sanctioned cruelty and collars and turned entire species into property. And now his life is tied to a human?" The laugh that follows is bitter. Harsh.

And it pisses me off.

"Okay, yeah, sure," I snap. "The prince was a raging arsehole. Not denying that. But he's also barely alive. His mate, Dawson, who's a really nice fucking guy, is worse. So maybe show a little fucking compassion."

That earns me a blink and then a slow, assessing look. "Huh."

"What?"

"You're mouthy."

"Thanks."

"And Aussie." He bobs his head. "A refreshing surprise." Before I can respond, he turns back to Varek, eyes narrowing. "You haven't told them, have you?"

Varek doesn't move. Doesn't flinch. But I can feel the change in him. He's stiff. Closed off. Like a man preparing to break.

I frown. "Told us what?" Pax's laugh this time has no humour. "Care to share with the class?" I add, annoyed.

He crosses his arms and tilts his head at Varek. The silence stretches. Then Pax sighs and looks me dead in the eye. "Varek is my fated mate."

My jaw drops. "Wait. What?"

No one answers me, which I get, since I suppose I'm

not the most important person in the room, and Pax simply continues shouting shit in Varek's direction.

Varek looks like he's been gutted. At first, Pax's cold cruelty seems to roll right off him, but then I see it—the tightness in his jaw, the twitch in his fingers. He's not immune. He's just holding it in.

And Pax doesn't let up.

"Shouldn't have come," he snaps, turning his back on us. "I'm not interested in your excuses or your mission. You're on your own."

My chest clenches. I glance at Varek. The guy looks... defeated. And it makes something twist deep in my gut. I suppose Pax has every right to be angry—but this level of venom? It's cruel.

Kael, sensing the shift in me, gently brushes his energy against mine. It's soft, steadying, and I lean into it instinctively.

"Pax," I say, voice firmer than I expect. "You might think you're justified, and maybe you are, because abandoning your fated mate, it's shit. I know what it's like to be left behind. And honestly?" I shoot Varek a sideways glance. "I have no idea why Varek did that to you—"

Pax turns, eyes flashing. "You have no idea what you're talking about."

But Varek doesn't lash out. Doesn't rage. Hell, he doesn't confirm, deny, or even explain. Instead, he looks gutted—utterly wrecked. Like the ground's crumbled beneath him, and he's still trying to stand.

"I wanted it to work," he says quietly, pain threading every syllable and surprising the shit outta me. "I didn't come here to fight. I came because I thought maybe... maybe you regretted turning me away."

My brows shoot high at that. Holy shit. Apparently, we all have ulterior motives.

Pax's jaw clenches. His eyes darken, something volatile burning there.

"You didn't even give us a chance," Varek continues, voice low, almost pleading. "You didn't ask questions, didn't want to hear anything. You demanded I leave, and I did—because it's what you said you wanted."

The room pulses with silence. Bloody hell. I got that wrong, then. Varek didn't abandon Pax at all. Guilt shifts uncomfortably in my chest that I immediately thought a human would be the one wronged. And that I thought Varek was the shitty party—the person who I trust and owe my life to—I think that makes me a shitty friend.

I watch on as Pax's face twists into something venomous, his voice sharp enough to wound. "You killed my husband."

The revelation drains the room of heat, of sound. I stop breathing. Kael tenses beside me.

Ho-ly shit.

Varek's head jerks back as if struck. He opens his mouth—then closes it again, clearly struggling. "I didn't know," he rasps, agony hollowing out his features. "All I saw was a man. A human. Hurting you."

Fuck. We shouldn't be hearing this. This is too personal, too raw.

I step closer to Kael, heart hammering, and he pulls me in tight, grounding me. Neither of the Glowranth in the room say a word, but their expressions have shifted, wariness giving way to something deeper. Understanding, maybe. Or dread.

Kael's the one who breaks the silence. "Enough." His voice isn't loud, but it cuts clean through the room. "This isn't the time. Whatever history you have, whatever pain, put it aside. If you don't want to help us, fine. But let us take a breath and figure out our next steps before we leave."

His tone is so rational, so kind and resolute, that even Pax seems caught off-guard. Kael's thumb brushes against mine, reminding me he's here. That we're here. Together.

"We're searching for a hidden library," Kael adds. "There are rumours it's somewhere in the citadel, but it's never been confirmed."

That gets the attention of the other two Glowranth in the room. They exchange looks, and one of them finally steps forwards. "You think that's where you'll find the answers?" he asks, voice measured. "About the prince and his fated?" he clarifies.

He seriously sounds calm and not even puzzled over the barely there information we've dropped on his lap.

"Yes," Kael says simply.

"And what's in it for us?" Pax's voice is all sharp angles again.

"I don't know," I say honestly. Am I also kinda disappointed he's gone there? Maybe, which is foolish of me. Naïve too. "Maybe nothing. But if we can save the prince and Dawson, we might change everything. And not just for Riftborn. For everyone."

Pax exhales hard, running a hand down his face. It's the first time he looks less like a stone wall and more like a man unravelling. "I'm still not over what happened," he mutters before swallowing hard, and I think he's pointedly not looking at Varek. "But I'll get you started. No promises. No guiding hand. But I can get you into the citadel."

"Why are you still here?" I ask before I can stop myself. "I mean, if you're not with Varek...."

Pax arches a brow. "I've got my uses. Let's just say I keep things running down here. Someone has to."

It's the "down here" that makes me think of shady dealings in the club I used to work at. "And them?" I nod towards the two Glowranth.

"They owe me."

Not exactly the reassuring answer I was hoping for, but it'll do.

Kael shifts beside me, his presence warm and steady. We're not out of the woods yet—but at least we're moving forwards.

And if there's one thing I've learned in Terrafeara, it's that momentum is everything.

CHAPTER
SEVENTEEN

MOMENTUM APPARENTLY MEANS WE'RE MOVING right now. I don't even get the chance to take a piss since Pax made two things crystal clear. One is that he wants us gone and never to return. And yeah, so many warm and fuzzies are coming from him that my heart really hurts for Varek. What the hell is fate thinking, pairing them together? And two, we have to move now if we want to get into the citadel undetected and without getting dead.

Fun time all around for sure.

We're outside, the bright day not giving us any cover. Varek and I are wearing pretty daggy cloak-like clothing, though, to stop us from standing out too much. It's itchy, and I look ridiculous. It's just a good thing Kael already loves me is all I'm saying.

Tension clings to the air, thick as smoke. Pax has

made it clear that this window of opportunity is short—shifting patrol schedules and some upcoming ceremonial procession mean the usual guards will be thinned out around the perimeter of the citadel for a brief stretch. That's the only reason we'll be able to get close without drawing attention.

Kael keeps glancing upwards at the tall silver-white spires jutting from the citadel's crown, as if expecting something—or someone—to appear. His jaw is tight, his eyes constantly scanning. We're close now. I can feel it.

"Why here?" I whisper to him.

He doesn't answer immediately, just adjusts the cloak over my shoulders before speaking into my mind. *"The citadel was once the seat of ancient Glowranth wisdom. Long before the queen, long before the divide. If the library exists—if it's real—it's here. Hidden beneath what the monarchy built on top of it."*

Right. Because of course it's under a fortress that's probably crawling with potential death.

We make it to the edge without being spotted. My nerves are riding me hard, gut tight and mouth dry. I know it's not just anxiety—I can feel the pulsing of energy beneath my skin, like it's drawn to something here. Maybe Kael's glowing cum jump-started something—not the actual reason, obviously, but hey, if I can't crack a joke while edging towards a complete meltdown, who even am I?

The four of us crouch at the edge of a shadowy wall, a giant stone facade looming ahead like it's daring us to enter. The structure is breathtaking and terrifying all at once—arched windows, tiered stonework carved with ancient sigils, its smooth grey surface pulsing faintly with stored energy.

I glance at the others. Varek is silent, jaw clenched. Kael stands at my side, a calm wall of strength, though I can feel his unease churning beneath the surface. Pax is the only one who moves.

"Double date adventure?" I murmur, voice low. The joke drops to the ground like a stone. No one reacts. Not even a blink.

Tough crowd.

Pax pulls a massive key from the folds of his cloak —seriously, where the hell has he been hiding that?— and then a small rectangular device that hums with a faint buzz. He inserts the key into what looks like a flat slab of stone embedded into the floor at the base of the wall. With the device held against the stone, a pulse of light shoots out, tracing patterns into the slab. Something clicks. The stone slides back, revealing a staircase that descends into darkness. A wave of cold air rushes out.

But it's not the chill that makes me shiver. It's the feeling in my chest.

Kael goes rigid beside me. His energy pulses hot and sharp. "That device," he says, voice like iron. "It's charged with Glowranth energy. Captured." His anger hits me like a shock wave through the bond.

Pax glances back, unfazed. "You want in or not?" And for the first time, I hear a twang of Aussie in his otherwise English accent.

I step closer to Kael, placing a hand on his arm. "We don't have time. We need to find whatever's down there."

Kael's jaw flexes, his fury simmering just beneath the surface. But after a beat, he nods.

We descend into the dark. And whatever waits for us below? It better have answers, because if I'm going to shit myself, there needs to be a legit reason for it.

The door hisses shut behind us, sealing off what little light we had from above. It's instantly cold—damp-air, stone-walls, crypt-vibes cold. I blink, trying to adjust, but everything is shadow and dust.

"Welcome to the world's creepiest cellar," I mutter, my voice echoing off the arched ceiling.

The basement of the citadel is... vast. Like, could-host-a-Gothic-rave-level vast. The ceiling stretches high, disappearing into darkness, and the walls are lined with strange etchings—glyphs carved into the stone, their meanings lost to time or magic or possibly someone's incredibly angsty teen phase. Columns support the space at intervals, some cracked and worn, others looking sharp enough to pierce armour.

Kael steps closer to me, his glowing eyes scanning

the surroundings. "This was once a hall of record. Glowranth scribes stored knowledge here before the royal libraries were established."

"Before? How old is this place?" I ask.

"Centuries," Kael says. "Maybe more."

"Right," I whisper. "So... basically the last place anyone wants to be if they've got even a hint of claustrophobia or mummy-related trauma."

Pax, who's clearly over our existence, strides towards the far side of the room and stops at a stone doorway I hadn't even noticed. It's built seamlessly into the wall—one of those annoying magic things you wouldn't know is there unless someone showed you or you smashed into it by accident.

"This way," he says, voice gruff.

We follow.

The doorway leads to a spiral staircase made of narrow stone steps that look like they were designed to trip people with poor spatial awareness. The kind that were probably a hit before handrails were invented.

"Down," Pax says unnecessarily and starts descending.

"I'll go first," Varek says, brushing past both of us. "In case there are traps."

"I'll guard the rear," Kael says immediately, shifting behind me.

I snort. "Tempting to make a joke, but honestly, I don't want to tempt fate right now."

Kael's quiet chuckle echoes in my mind, a warm flicker even as the walls close in.

We move. Step after step. The spiral feels endless, a winding descent into the bowels of the citadel. A couple of landings come and go, marked by doorways we don't enter. Not yet.

"How deep is this place?" I pant, because I am in fact a human and not a giant lizard-fae-warrior with endless cardio.

Kael thinks for a beat. "I don't know in your measurements."

Pax doesn't even look back. "About a hundred feet. Maybe more."

So, roughly thirty metres. "Cool," I mutter. "That's... terrifying."

The air grows thicker the deeper we go, charged. My skin starts to prickle like it's preparing for a sunburn, but inside out.

We finally get to the bottom. One last landing. One last door.

I pause, reaching out and grazing the stone wall. The moment my fingers connect, the air hums. Something thrums beneath the surface. It zings along my skin, shooting straight to my chest like a tether being pulled taut. "Kael?" My voice cracks.

He's already swearing under his breath. His markings are glowing brighter, his expression sharp and unsettled. "Do you feel that?"

"Like my insides are trying to do jazz hands? Yeah."

Varek steps closer to the door but doesn't react. Pax arches a brow. "You feel something?" he asks Kael.

Kael nods tightly. "Energy. Wild, unhinged energy. So does Sonny."

Pax's frown deepens. "Really? No one else has ever reacted. Not even Glowranth."

"Well, I hate to break it to you," I say, dragging in a breath through my teeth, "but something down here is getting real personal with my nerve endings."

"The bond," Kael murmurs. "It might be... amplifying."

My bond. *Our* bond.

Right.

So, this room, whatever's behind that door, isn't just old stone and secrets. It's something more. Something wild—and it's calling us.

We go through the door, and honestly, I'm not sure what I expected. Maybe glowing tomes. Floating relics. A room full of ancient scrolls that whisper forbidden knowledge in seductive voices.

Instead? Bugger all.

It's dusty. Dim. Bare as Kael's chest the first time I saw him, minus any of the appeal. There are a few rickety old shelves, warped from age and weightless from lack of books. A couple of broken chairs, one of them with a leg missing and slumped over like it gave up on life mid-meeting. The air is still thick with that strange, electric energy, but visually? This place is a dud.

My shoulders slump. "Well, that's... anticlimactic."

But Kael? My hunk of a mate is already moving. He steps further inside, his gaze distant, tracking something invisible. "It's still here," he murmurs. "The energy. It's beneath us."

I frown, following. "Beneath?"

He nods, his eyes glowing faintly, his steps slow and deliberate. "Like a river, flowing under the stone. I can feel the current. It's strong here, stronger than anywhere I've ever felt it. Even stronger than... than the bond."

That stops me cold. Because if this is more potent than our bond—which just nearly exploded both of us into blissful stardust—then yeah, this is serious.

Kael moves towards the back of the room, where a wall stretches floor to ceiling, carved with faded markings. He presses his palm to the stone.

Nothing happens.

"It's here," he says again, firmer this time. "But I don't know how to open it."

I join him, reaching out and brushing my fingers over the surface. It's cool. Solid. Unmoving. But there's a thrum underneath, like a distant heartbeat. My skin tingles. The bond in my chest flickers to life in response, like it's perking up with curiosity.

Varek and Pax hang back, watching silently. Waiting.

"Great," I mutter. "So, we've got a magic energy river under an ancient floor and a wall that probably opens into Narnia but won't respond to any of us."

Kael's mouth twitches at the reference, making me wonder if there were some good fantasy books he managed to read, but his eyes remain on the stone. "We're missing something," he says softly.

No kidding. And whatever that something is, it's right on the other side of this wall.

"Wait, wait—hold up a sec." I turn from the stone wall and wave my arms vaguely around the mostly disappointing basement-looking space. "You think this is it? The secret library 'nobody' whispered about like it's the bloody Holy Grail of Terrafeara?"

Kael glances at me, brow arched. "It's hidden."

"Sure," I say, spinning in a slow circle. "So hidden that we managed to find it on the first try. No scavenger hunt. No cryptic riddle. Not even a single cursed artefact trying to eat my face."

"Technically," Varek mutters, voice flat, "it's not the library yet. It's antechamber five from memory."

I blink. "There are four others?"

"Destroyed," Pax replies, leaning against a shelf that definitely wasn't built to support his weight—or his mood. "This is the last one. Maybe."

I point a finger between them. "See, this is exactly

what I'm talking about. Everyone keeps referring to this as *maybe* the library. We don't even know if we're in the right place."

"The energy is real," Kael says, his voice quiet, eyes still fixed on the wall like it's holding secrets in its stone.

I sigh and rub the back of my neck. "Sure. I feel it. But is this the magical answer to our problems or just some weird underground foot spa for energy-sensitive Glowranth?"

Pax snorts but doesn't look at me. He hasn't looked at anyone much—except Varek, and even that's mostly out of the corner of his eye when he thinks no one's paying attention.

Spoiler: I'm paying attention.

Varek's still silent. Still coiled tight like a spring that's been bent too far.

"Do you know what this place really is?" I ask, stepping closer to Pax.

He lifts his eyes to mine—dark and unreadable. "No. Only what I was told. That if there was any place in the queendom where the truth might still exist, it was here. Whatever was too dangerous or too inconvenient to make it into the official records? It ended up down here."

My gaze sharpens. "Conveniently vague."

"It's all I have."

"It's more than we had yesterday," Kael adds, finally turning from the wall to face the rest of us.

I sigh again and glance at Varek. He hasn't moved. His fists are clenched at his sides, knuckles pale beneath purple-blue skin. He looks like he's holding himself together with willpower and grief. And Pax? Still hasn't so much as offered a shred of kindness.

Except... except I saw it. That one glance, quick and sharp and full of longing, when Varek looked away. The tiniest flicker in Pax's expression before he crushed it under a scowl. Like maybe—*maybe*—he's not as indifferent as he wants to be.

Bloody hell. Fated mates, am I right? You either burn for them or burn because of them.

"All right," I say finally, stepping between them and towards the stone again. "Let's assume this is the entrance. Let's also assume the universe isn't just trolling us with a bad basement and a funny feeling. How do we open it?"

Kael steps up beside me, brow furrowed. "That's the question."

Behind us, Pax murmurs something in Glowranthian under his breath. Varek stiffens, a breath caught in his throat. His gaze lifts, meets Pax's for half a second —and Pax looks away. Again.

I glance between them, then sigh. "This is gonna be a long day, huh?"

Kael's fingers ghost over mine. *"Longer if we stand around waiting."*

I smirk. "Good point, lover."

He looks vaguely pained.

Pax looks vaguely disgusted.

Varek finally cracks a smile.

Progress.

Kael moves first, tracing his glowing fingers along the smooth grooves of the wall. His power pulses, syncing with something unseen. I watch, heart in my throat, as faint lines of energy appear—curling symbols that rise to the surface like they're being drawn from thin air.

"Well, that's not ominous at all," I mutter, inching closer. "Just your casual glowing ancient glyphs reacting to blood magic and destiny. Totally normal Friday." Because you never know, it *could* be a Friday.

Kael flicks me a look. *"Be ready."*

"Be ready for what? For it to open?" I lean in, a little too close, my shoulder brushing his arm.

Click.

"Oh, bugger." The floor under my feet shifts with a low groan. Before I can step back, a sudden whoosh of air hits me from below—like the world just inhaled—and the ground drops.

"Sonny!" Kael roars as the platform beneath me disappears.

I fall—but only for a second. A flash of light engulfs me and Kael both. Something grabs us, maybe energy, maybe fate just being a dick again, and swoop—we're flung sideways, slamming through a separate wall of light like it's been waiting for two idiots in love to stumble into it.

When we land, I roll into Kael, limbs tangled and breath knocked clean out of me.

From somewhere above, I hear Varek shout, "What just happened?"

"Oh, you know," I call back, gasping. "Just taking the scenic route through Deathtrap Alley!"

Kael groans beside me, already on one knee, scanning the chamber we've crash-landed into. It's a long, narrow hall made of old stone, etched in strange script that glows dimly with every step we take.

A grinding noise sounds above us. I spin, eyes wide. The ceiling is sealing shut. "Kael—"

"I see it."

Too late. *Boom*. The ceiling wall finishes its closure with a satisfying stone-on-stone thunk. And we're alone. Fantastic.

He glances at me, tension bleeding through our bond. "I shouldn't have let you fall in."

"Excuse you?" I say aloud, brushing dust off my already-daggy cloak. "I distinctly recall you being right there beside me. Pretty sure gravity had beef with both of us."

He huffs. Possibly a laugh. Possibly exasperation.

"Varek? Pax?" I yell towards the sealed ceiling. Nothing. No response.

Great.

"This is fine," I say to no one, turning a slow circle as the hall stretches out ahead. "Just trapped in a potentially ancient death corridor with the hottest Glowranth boyfriend in the world. What could go wrong?"

Kael touches the nearest wall, and symbols begin to light up again—responding only to him, it seems. The energy here is stronger. Buzzing. Alive.

My fingers twitch with the echo of it. "Okay," I mutter, straightening. "I'm not saying I want to be Indiana Jones, but if a giant boulder starts rolling at us, I'm punching fate in the dick."

Kael sends me a look over his shoulder.

I grin. "Don't worry. I'll still protect your beautiful face."

He groans again. "You're impossible."

"But charming."

"Debatable."

My humour fades as we start walking. We press forwards, the corridor curving into deeper shadow, lit only by the soft glow of Kael's palm and the occasional flicker from the runes embedded in the wall.

Each step echoes too loud. My nerves are frayed, the high from earlier gone, replaced by something colder. My thoughts keep looping—what if we're trapped, what if this isn't the library, what if there is no library and this is some elaborate, cruel trap? What if we're too late and Dawson dies, and the prince dies, and it's all on us?

My breathing shortens. Tightens. Kael's hand in mine grounds me—but only a little.

"I don't get it," I whisper, voice edged with panic. "Why are we the ones to find this? How does something like this even exist? Secret libraries are great in books, sure, but in real life, they don't just appear conveniently after a death match and a weird dimensional leap. It's too much. It's—"

"Sonny."

I snap to him. Kael's eyes are glowing low and steady. He steps close. One hand rests against my chest, right over my heart. His voice enters my mind like a balm: *"Breathe. With me."*

I try.

It takes a second, but our bond helps regulate the spiral. My pulse starts to match his. One thrum. One rhythm. Our hearts beating as one. Handy feature, really. Then Kael leans down and kisses me. Slow. Firm. The kind of kiss that doesn't rush, that doesn't promise anything except *I'm here. You're safe. We've got this.*

My lungs finally expand properly. "Okay," I whisper, forehead pressed against his chest. "I'm good. I'm not *good* good, but I'm... better." I nod. "Let's go find whatever bloody secret was left down here like a twisted escape room prize."

We pass into a wider space. Rows of shelves line the room, though most are broken or bare. A few scrolls remain, as well as dusty tomes and scattered bits of parchment. The air smells of old knowledge—paper and time and something a little metallic.

"This is it?" I murmur, stepping forwards. But it doesn't feel right. Too empty. Too... easy? "This can't be it, right?" I whisper, turning in a slow circle.

Kael's hand tightens around mine. His expression is wary. "You're not wrong."

Then I feel it. That same thrum of energy. But this time it's not from Kael—it's from the ground. The pulse hits my boots and vibrates up my legs like a silent alarm. Kael stiffens beside me.

"It's beneath us," he says.

We both look down. To anyone else it would look like the same stone flooring as before. But there—right ahead—is one tile. A different shade. A little too clean. A little too deliberate.

He steps towards it, dragging me with him. His sword shifts into his free hand.

The moment his foot lands on the tile, light explodes. Bright sigils spiral outwards from beneath his boot—etched into the tile in the same sharp, elegant lines as Kael's own markings. They glow bright, identical to the faint pulse of bioluminescence that travels up his arms. He gasps—and I feel it before I even see it. A shock of burning power races through our linked hands.

My scream catches in my throat. I shove up my

sleeve just in time to watch his markings etch themselves into my skin in glowing blue and gold.

"Oh fuck—Kael, what the hell is this—"

He looks at me, stunned, his mouth moving, but I can't hear him. There's a ringing in my ears, sharp and high like pressure building inside my skull. Then comes a burn on my shoulder—hot, fierce, biting—and I collapse to my knees with a strangled cry.

Kael drops with me, holding me tight.

I see his lips move again as my name appears aloud and in my mind. *"Sonny."*

But everything else? White-hot light and the sound of my pulse, my breath, the crackling roar of energy rising.

This isn't a library. It's something more. Something ancient. And whatever we've just activated... we've crossed a line we can't uncross.

The tile vanishes beneath Kael's boots. Just gone—like some twisted trapdoor in a nightmare—and with it, we fall.

A-fucking-gain.

"Shit!" The scream rips from my throat as we plummet into open air, no wind, no up or down, just black and endless.

I can't even think—I only feel Kael's grip, his hand crushing mine, our fingers laced so tight, my knuckles grind together. My other arm flails, useless in the void, my hand still gripping my dagger. We're just falling. Fucking falling.

This is *Alice in Wonderland* bullshit on steroids. And then—light.

Not a lot. Just a faint pulse where my sleeve's shoved up, a soft glow bleeding out of the sigils carved into my skin. Kael's are glowing, too, jagged and bright and electric, like living veins of light along his arms.

My eyes adjust and then—oh fuck. No, no.

Below us. Fast approaching. A jagged, impossible mess of ground—dark metallic rock, with shards like broken glass, like a blade-toothed basin ready to swallow us whole.

Kael sees it too. His fear spikes, hot and sharp, crashing into me like a wave through the bond. *"I love you,"* his voice says inside my head, clear, intentional.

"No—don't—" I try to twist to look at him, to say it back, to do something, but I can't move. His arms clamp around me, iron and desperation, pinning me to his chest.

I can't breathe. I can't think. I feel him twist, his weight shifting, rolling in midair. Then—

We hit.

It's brutal.

My body jars with the impact, but it's cushioned. All the pain—all the sound—hits Kael first. And he takes it all. His grip loosens the second we land. Just enough for me to scramble back with a strangled sound stuck in my throat. My knees skid on the floor, slick with something I pray isn't blood.

"Kael?" My voice cracks.

He's sprawled on his side, his body twisted at an angle that makes my gut roil. His chest is rising. Barely.

I crawl to him, my heart hammering wildly in my ribs. Light flares around us—faint, from slits in the walls. Not natural, not powered by anything I've seen before. Just... presence. Like the room knew we were coming.

But I can't even look at it. All I see is him.

He coughs. Blood sprays across his chin, glistening and wrong. His markings are dim, barely glowing. His skin is pallid, like the light inside him is leaking out too fast.

"No. No, no, no," I whisper, cradling his face, pressing my hands to his chest, desperate. "You are not doing this. You are not leaving me."

His eyes flutter, meeting mine for the briefest soul-shattering moment. And fuck, all I feel in the bond is love. Bone-deep, galaxy-wide, soul-warping love.

"Kael." My voice breaks. "Stay with me. I love you. I love you, and you're not dying. Do you hear me?"

I shake him gently. Then harder. "I just got you," I whisper. "You don't get to be my fated mate and die before we even figure this shit out. I need you, you stubborn, perfect idiot. I need you."

And still, he fades. His energy's draining away, like

sand through a sieve, and the terror in me crystallises into something cold and determined.

I don't know what to do, but I know I'm not letting him go.

Not here.

Not now.

Not ever.

As I press my hands to Kael's chest, still trying to stop the bleeding, something snags beneath my palm.

My dagger.

No.

No, no, no.

It's mine. The hilt, the edge—I'd know it anywhere. Lodged deep in Kael's gut like a sick joke, like a betrayal I never made.

"Kael," I whisper, my voice so broken, I barely recognise it.

He doesn't answer. Not with words. Just that same faint smile on his lips. Serene. Fucking serene, like he's floating on some peaceful cloud while I'm being ripped to pieces from the inside out.

I swallow a scream and wrap shaking fingers around the hilt. "Sorry," I breathe. "Sorry, sorry, sorry—"

And I pull.

It comes free with a slick, awful sound, and the blood—fuck, the blue blood bubbles out thick and fast, too fast, too much. He doesn't flinch.

"Stop smiling," I whisper, pressing my hands to the

wound again. "You don't get to look like that. Like you're ready. You're not ready. I'm not ready."

His eyes flicker open—barely. His voice is a rasp. "I love you."

"No," I whisper, tears sliding down my cheeks. "Don't say goodbye."

"It's okay," he says. "You'll be okay."

"The fuck I will!" My voice rises. "If you die, I die, remember? We're fated, bonded—tied together in this twisted, beautiful thing, and we've only fucked once, Kael. Once. I've only had your cock in my mouth once. Do you really think I'm done?"

His face twists—not in pain but in something closer to horror. The peace vanishes. "No. No, I—"

"Exactly." I shake him, voice cracking. "So stay. Don't you dare leave me, Kael."

He gasps, barely audible. "Heal me."

"I don't know how!" I scream.

But my hands are already glowing. Not like before. Not a flicker. Not a pulse.

It's like my soul has been pulled from my chest, turned inside out, and pushed into my palms. Gold-and-blue light floods from my skin, straight into his. I pour everything I have into him. Every drop of love. Every ounce of rage. Every breath, thought, memory—

But his heart... it's slowing. Mine isn't.

"What the fuck?" My voice shakes. "Why isn't mine stopping too?"

Why am I still here if he's leaving?

Tears pour down my cheeks. My arms tremble with the force of energy burning through them. His wound isn't sealing. The bleeding slows, but he's still fading.

Kael's voice brushes against my mind—weak, frayed. *"You were always stronger than me."*

"No," I growl. "We are strong. Together."

The bond pulses. Hard. Then again. I scream as I push harder, as the energy inside me threatens to tear me apart. I feel my own strength draining, my limbs going cold, but I keep going.

I have to.

He's mine.

And I refuse to let the universe take him from me.

The bleeding doesn't stop. My hands are slick with his blood—his fucking blue blood—and I keep pressing, keep begging, but his eyes keep sliding shut. The glow in his markings is fading, and his grip on me loosens by the second.

"No. No, no, no—Kael." My voice breaks, ragged and thin. I'm losing him. And I can't.

I can't.

Tears blur my vision. My body shakes as I lean over him, fingers slipping in blood and panic. I'm supposed to be his mate. Fated. We're supposed to be stronger together. That's what everyone keeps saying. That we're rare. Precious. Some fucking miracle.

But what kind of miracle lets this happen?

"Come back," I whisper. "Please, Kael. Please."

I kiss him. His lips are cool. Still. He doesn't kiss me back.

My tears smear between us, my nose pressed awkwardly to his. I'm a mess. A snotty, broken, ugly mess, and I don't care. I want him to feel me. Hear me. Need me.

I need him.

And I realise—suddenly, painfully—what this is. What he did. What the prince did for Dawson. He gave him his life.

His life force. Piece by piece, breath by breath, he kept his mate alive.

That's what I need to do.

I pull back, frantic, scanning the space as if I'll find instructions etched into the stone, a glowing how-to manual hovering in the air.

Nothing. No answers. Just Kael. Pale. Still.

Too still.

I crawl over him, straddling his body, lowering myself carefully so I don't cause more damage. My arms curl around him, my hands splayed across his ribs and the back of his neck. I press my forehead to his, squeezing my eyes shut.

"Come back to me," I whisper, trembling. "Take what you need. Take everything." My heart thrums wildly in my chest. I imagine that rhythm sinking into him, like a thread. A rope. Something real.

"I give it to you," I breathe. "All of it. Whatever it takes. My life, my strength, my soul—Kael, I'm yours. Always."

The bond flares. Hard.

A white-hot light explodes behind my eyes. Energy surges through me like a tidal wave. The burn is instant and blinding, my body locking up, like something ancient has snapped into place and is demanding I surrender.

I feel it leave me. My life. Thread by thread, it flows from me into him. I'm shaking, gasping, my lungs struggling for air. My pulse slows, my thoughts start to drift —soft, quiet.

It's working. I think. Maybe.

Kael's markings pulse once, faintly. His lips part. A breath escapes him.

My body collapses. My mind unravels. I sink into darkness, the last thought in my head not fear, not regret—

Just love.

"Come back to me."

CHAPTER
EIGHTEEN

I WAKE TO HEAT AND STRONG ARMS. IT'S NOT AN unfamiliar position—one I've been in before—but this time, there's no calm, no bliss. Just panic. I jolt, adrenaline punching through me as I try to sit up—

—but the arms around me are too strong.

"Sonny." Kael's voice is soft, hoarse, but real.

My breath hitches.

"You saved me," he whispers, and there's so much rawness in those three words that my eyes sting before I even realise I'm crying.

"I saved us," I murmur, burying my face into his neck, clutching at him like he might disappear again. "Don't ever do that again, you arsehole."

He chuckles—fucking *chuckles*—and kisses the top of my head, loosening his grip just enough for me to sit up and grab his face. My lips crash to his. The kiss is frantic, possessive, a jumbled mess of teeth and desperation, and when our bond surges to life again, I don't even bother with words.

"I love you. I want you. I'm not losing you again."

His thoughts flood mine in return—*"Mine. Always. Forever."* Raw, unfiltered emotion washes over me—his gratitude, his awe, the utter reverence in his love.

But then he groans. Not the good kind.

I pull back fast. "What is it? Are you hurt? Where—fuck, your wound—" My hands are already fumbling at the buckles of his armour. "Take it off. Now."

There's amusement in his eyes, but he obeys without argument, stripping down until his bare chest is exposed—beautiful and strong and not at all the distraction it usually is. Because my eyes zero in on the place where I stabbed him.

The cloth beneath is ripped, darkened by dried blood—but the skin underneath? It's healed. A clean, angry scar sits puckered just above his hip. I let out a breath that nearly breaks me.

"It really worked," I whisper, brushing my fingers over the mark in awe.

"It did," he murmurs, gaze never leaving mine.

I kiss the scar. Hard. Then I sit up properly, still straddling his thighs. And yes, okay, my brain definitely goes there. His chest is bare, he's alive, I'm alive, and it's been a shit day, and we've earned a little inappropriate post-near-death celebration.

I grin down at him. "Do you think we have time to get off?"

He blinks. "What?"

"You know. A quickie. Life-affirming orgasm. We literally just died, Kael. That kind of thing requires celebratory sex."

His lips twitch, that luminescent glow in his eyes sparking with laughter. "Literally, huh?" He snorts. "You're unbelievable."

"Hot. You mean hot."

"I mean distracting."

"Still hot."

He groans again, but this time it's paired with the subtle lift of his hips beneath mine. "Five minutes?"

"That's all I need," I shoot back smugly, but a flicker of light catches my attention. I turn, and shock slams into me like a punch to the gut.

The wall of light is gone. In its place... is a library.

Like, an actual motherfucking library.

"What the hell?" I whisper.

Kael sits up, gaze narrowing as he follows my stare. His armour is back on in seconds—rude, but I get it. Priorities. I stare dumbly as he steps towards the trail of faintly glowing sigils on the floor, tinged with smears of blood.

"They lead all the way to... where the door should be," he says. "We found it."

I gape. "We're so much faster than Indy or Lara

Croft. Fuck, Kael, when all this is over, we should be treasure hunters or some shit."

He looks amused, but the expression shifts quickly into something more serious. "Just because this is a library," he says carefully, "doesn't mean it's the one."

I scoff. "Mate, come on. Hidden for centuries? Secret sigils? Floor panels that eat you alive? What, you think it's the local public reading room?"

Still, he narrows his eyes at the space ahead. "Let's just stay focussed. If this place has anything about fated mates, or a way to help Aelith and Dawson... we have to find it."

I nod, the weight of everything slamming back into my chest. "All right," I say. "Let's go crack open some ancient secrets."

The moment we cross the threshold into the library, the air changes. It's thick. Heavy. Laced with something that tastes almost metallic, almost electric. Like the hum before a storm.

The space opens out far wider than I expected. Columns stretch towards the domed ceiling, their surfaces carved with unfamiliar markings—some similar to the glowing sigils I've come to associate with Kael, but others older, rougher, like they've been etched by hand over time. The floor is stone, cool beneath our boots, lined with inlaid paths of dull metal veins that seem to pulse faintly as we move.

Shelves stretch in all directions—some wooden,

some stone, some suspended in ways that don't make any kind of architectural sense. A few float several metres off the ground with no visible supports. I eye one that's swaying slightly like it's daring me to question it.

Kael walks beside me, one hand brushing my lower back. Protective. Steadying. Which, honestly, I need, because this place? It's straight out of a fantasy novel. A creepy, majestic, very possibly haunted fantasy novel.

"I don't get it," I mutter, running my hand across a dusty ledge. "If this place has been hidden for centuries, how the fuck does it look like this? Like... like someone was here yesterday."

He doesn't answer right away. His gaze is roving the space, tense but calculating. "Some energy fields are self-sustaining. If it's bonded to ancient Glowranth sigils... time might not move here the same way."

I blink at him. "Okay, Gandalf."

He smirks. "You said you wanted treasure hunting."

"Yeah, I was thinking more Indiana Jones and less 'cursed *Labyrinth* meets *Stranger Things*.'" Still, my fingers tingle. The bond hums between us, reacting to the energy like it's recognising something in the air. Something important.

We walk deeper.

A massive table—no, altar—sits at the centre of the space. Books and scrolls are scattered across it in a way that feels less forgotten and more left mid-research. Kael's hand tightens on mine.

"This is it," he murmurs. "Someone's been here."

That jolts through me like a shock. "Wait. Like recently?"

He crouches, fingers skimming one of the scrolls. A smear of red—dried blood, fresh enough that it hasn't turned black—edges the parchment.

"I don't like this," I say immediately. "Who the fuck was bleeding down here, and why does it feel like the beginning of a horror movie?"

Kael stands, his eyes scanning. "I think we're alone."

Before I can fully spiral, my gaze snags on a worn leatherbound tome tucked beneath a stone weight. I lift it carefully, coughing as dust clouds up in a plume. The cover is marked with the same symbol that shimmered on the floor beneath Kael—the same pattern that's still faintly glowing on my arm.

I crack it open.

The pages are handwritten in neat but archaic Glowranthian. I recognise some of it, not because I'm fluent—please, I'm still trying to master rolling my *R*'s —but apparently my kick-arse bond with Kael comes with special privileges. Enough to catch phrases like:

Bonded energy transfer—accelerated healing, transmutation, life-for-life preservation.

I look up. "Kael," I say hoarsely. "I think this is it."

He's beside me in an instant, eyes scanning the page,

his breath catching. "It speaks of what the prince has done."

"And what I did for you," I whisper, my voice suddenly too small in this huge, ancient room.

We share a look. The weight of what we've found is slowly dawning.

There's a rustle behind us. My heart slams into my throat—but it's just air shifting. Or... maybe not just air. The sigils on the far wall flicker to life, casting the whole room in soft golden light.

"Okay," I breathe, clutching the book. "Let's keep going. I've got a good feeling about this." It doesn't mean I'm not still creeped out, but I'm trying on the whole "stay positive" vibe.

Kael nods, the tension in his jaw easing just enough to let the faintest smile through. "Together," he says.

"Always."

We step deeper into the library and work in near silence, my fingers brushing against ancient bindings, rough parchment, and the occasional scroll so brittle, I'm terrified to breathe near it.

He reads quietly for a few moments more before he finally speaks, voice low and deliberate. "I think I found something."

I straighten. "Please say it's not a story about Glowranth mating with space dragons or whatever."

Kael tilts the book slightly, showing me an illustration—faded, almost erased by time. It's a crude figure surrounded by what looks like swirling shards, stepping through a tear in the sky.

The title beneath it reads *The First Breach of Terrafeara*.

A chill rolls down my spine. "The Shardwalker."

Kael nods. "This must've been written long after the events. But it aligns with what I told you. A Glowranth royal... bonded to something—someone—not from this world. When they joined, their bond didn't just change them. It tore open a rift that never fully healed."

I run my hand over the page, reverent despite myself. "That... doesn't sound like something you casually shelve and forget."

His expression hardens. "They didn't. It says here the council of that time—not yet a queendom—buried the heart of the rift's power source beneath what would eventually become the citadel."

I blink. "So, this place isn't just hiding a library. It's hiding the rift?"

"Or its remnants," Kael says. "Whatever was left."

Suddenly the energy in the air makes more sense. The odd pulsing. The ache in my arm where Kael's markings now live. Maybe we're not just here to read about history. Maybe we're sitting on top of it.

"Does it say what happened to them?" I ask. "The Shardwalker and his mate?"

Kael's mouth flattens. "No. Just that they were powerful. Unstoppable. And dangerous."

I swallow. "Sounds familiar."

His eyes lift to mine, something sharp and worried flickering there. "It's a warning. These scrolls… they weren't meant to be kept as knowledge. They were meant to contain it."

A beat passes. I reach for the nearest bundle of texts and start tying them off. "Cool. Let's take it all anyway."

He huffs but doesn't argue. We'll need help translating the rest. Iris, Shanae, and even Varek, if he can pull his head out of his tortured romance for five seconds. We'll have to get all this back to Dathanor. Quietly.

We move fast.

There's no time to sit and read, no matter how much Kael's fingers linger reverently over the spine of each book he selects. I'm stuffing scrolls into the pack like we're looting a magic version of Officeworks. A twinge of guilt hits me—like maybe the ancient Glowranth of lore would rather we read their life's work than treat it like takeaway—but survival trumps manners.

Kael lifts a bundle of aged parchment and slides it into his satchel. "We need to prioritise the texts that reference the Shardwalker, fated bonds, and the original breach. Anything that connects it to the citadel."

"No shit, Sherlock," I mutter, not for the first time. "Although if I ever meet the ancient Glowranth equivalent of Arthur Conan Doyle, I'll personally deliver a glowing Yelp review."

He arches a brow. "That was a sentence."

I shrug, even as my mind races. "I've got questions, Kael. Lots. But one of them won't shut up."

He stops, glancing over.

"I get that the current rifts are different," I say, my voice low. "They come in storms, right? They rip through and vanish. Slice a bit of a world and stitch it onto Terrafeara. But this? The one we're apparently standing on? The very first one—it didn't seal on its own. It was open. Wide. They had to close it manually and then build a damn citadel on top of it."

Kael nods, tension tightening his jaw. "It had permanence. Like a doorway instead of a tear."

"Right," I say, grabbing another scroll. "So whoever's creating the new rifts now—they're doing it differently. More erratic. Temporary."

"And harder to trace," Kael murmurs.

I pause, straightening. "You think they're doing it from here? This location?"

His gaze sharpens. "I don't know. But the energy down here—it's not dormant. It's alive. And it responded to us."

"You think it's a fated bond thing?" Something that Varek mentioned earlier.

"I think... I don't have all the answers," he admits, "but someone must. And if they're manipulating rifts now, they might have learned how by coming here."

I shudder. "Great. So we just waltzed into the tutorial zone of Rift-Tearing 101."

He doesn't smile.

"I'm serious, Kael. This could be it. The place it all started. But that also means it could be where someone's coming back to. Using."

Hesitation slices across his features. He wants to stay to discover the truth. Find answers and potentially put a stop to what's going on. His emotions are crystal clear.

"We can't stay," I say quickly. "Dawson and Aelith need us."

His jaw clenches, but he nods. "You're right."

"But we know where to return to, yeah?"

"Okay."

"Okay," I agree, relieved he's focussed on the most urgent thing. Slinging the last of the scrolls into my pack, I say, "I guess we're walking back to Varek and Pax? Through the trappy hall of doom?" Assuming we can of course. There has to be a way out of here.

Kael glances towards the dark exit. "We'll have to find another route. I don't trust the one that collapsed on us. And we don't know if it was designed to separate us intentionally."

"Well, if it was," I mutter, dusting off my hands, "whoever built this place can kindly suck my—"

"Sonny," he warns, even as amusement slips through the bond.

"Fine. Let's just not die on the way back, okay? I've nearly died enough this week. Honestly, my quota's full."

Kael pulls his sword again, light pulsing from his palm, and offers me his other hand. "Then stay close."

"Always."

I take it, and we begin our search for the way back.

CHAPTER
NINETEEN

IT TAKES A WHILE TO FIND OUR WAY OUT. HOW long exactly or what the route is that we take, I have no idea, but as we finally escape through a door after climbing a narrow staircase that's so steep, my calves are burning, I'm ready to collapse and get the hell out of here.

But first we need to locate Varek.

We venture through a room, one that I think is familiar. So much has happened since we entered the citadel that, honestly, it's difficult to recall the details. Another door and another room and Kael pauses.

"Okay?" I ask, not sure if I could speak aloud without panting heavily. Thank Christ for our ability to talk mind to mind.

"This is where we last saw them."

It is? Though from his tone, Kael doesn't sound

convinced either. I glance around. Nothing's familiar. There's definitely not a gaping hole in the floor. I take a couple of steps, though, gaze finally landing on the off-colour tile. It's intact, looking innocent, and no doubt ready for its next victim. "So, what do we do?"

Kael's jaw ticks. "Step around it. Carefully."

"Thanks for the top-tier strategy, General." But I obey, because that tile and I are never becoming friends.

We move slowly through the space, doubling back through the winding corridors of stone and faded glory. Eventually, we reach the chamber where we last saw all the sigils on the walls. Empty. No burnt furniture. No broken walls. No bodies, which... honestly feels like a win.

"Do you think they made it out?" I ask, my voice low. "As in, they haven't been captured or something?"

Kael gives a short nod. "There's no evidence of that."

That doesn't really answer the question, but I go with it.

We keep moving, each turn and shadow making me tenser. The air feels tighter the higher we go. And just when I think we've looped back again—

Light.

Actual, blessed daylight spills in from under a door, and Kael cautiously pushes it open. We step into a small stone antechamber—one I vaguely recognise from earlier—and creep to the outer doorway that'll take us outside.

Kael places a hand on the handle, halts. "Stay behind me."

He eases the door open a sliver. A shaft of sunlight slips through, and he leans forwards, peering through the gap. His breath catches.

I shove closer, careful not to make a sound. And when I finally see what he's seeing, my stomach bottoms out.

There are people. A lot of people. Locals, soldiers. Royal guards, their armour glinting with the telltale flashes of orange, swords sheathed but visible, posture coiled like vipers ready to strike.

Kael pulls back, letting the door close softly.

"Well?" I whisper.

His expression is grave. "We can't go out there."

I don't argue. "They'll recognise you."

He nods once. "I trained half of them."

"Cool, cool. So walking out means instant recognition. Maybe arrest. Maybe death." I run a hand through my hair. "Love this for us."

Kael steps back, pacing a short line. "They'll assume I've betrayed my post. That I've abandoned the prince."

I want to argue that anyone with eyes could see how loyal he is, but I also know how Terrafearan politics work—not well. Plus, there's the whole thing of the prince being AWOL.

"So, what do we do?" I ask again, louder this time. Sharper.

He looks at me. I feel the flicker of his thoughts before he speaks. *"We summon the Hendroy."*

My mouth opens. "You want to call Henny?"

Kael gives me a dry look. *"Do you have a better plan?"*

"Yeah," I deadpan. *"Run screaming and hope I get mistaken for a street performer."*

He doesn't laugh. Neither do I.

"But what about Varek?" I ask after a beat, glancing back towards the depth of the citadel. *"What if he's not out yet?"*

Kael hesitates. "I don't think he's here."

I can't argue with him. If they weren't waiting for us where we left them, it's unlikely they were hiding elsewhere. Which means Varek felt the need to leave. He wouldn't abandon us... me without cause.

"I think they made it out of here," Kael adds. "They've likely gone to the warehouse where we found Pax. The guards out there aren't on high alert. They would be if Varek had been found."

I nod slowly, throat tight. "Then we call in Henny and hope he's in a good mood."

He reaches for the rune mark still glowing faintly on my arm. "You remember how?"

"I say his name and try not to shit myself?"

Kael's lips twitch. "Something like that."

I step back into the shadows of the room, take a breath, and press two fingers to the rune. It warms under my touch. And then, loud and clear, I whisper, "Hendroy."

The air thickens, and then it rips. A plume of smoke and shadow swirls into existence in the centre of the chamber. The temperature drops. My skin prickles. I barely have time to breathe before he appears.

The Hendroy.

Massive. Monstrous. Otherworldly. Nothing's changed.

His form towers, vaguely humanoid but too fluid, like a shadow made flesh. Barbed edges coil around his limbs, and that voice—a low, distorted growl that seems to crawl straight into your bones—vibrates through the room.

"We need you to—"

"No."

"Wait, what?" I blink. "You're not even going to hear the request first?"

Kael reaches for me, but it's too late. The vortex slams around us—black mist closing in from all directions. Cold and force and some kind of unrelenting pressure shoves against my skin, and then—

Light. Noise. Alarms.

We're not in the citadel anymore. I'm still opening my mouth to argue—to demand he take us back to find Varek—when the sound truly hits me.

Sharp. Urgent. Terrifying.

I spin, taking in the familiar room. The medical wing. "Why the fuck are we—"

Then I see them.

Dawson. Aelith.

Chaos explodes in my chest.

Kael's already moving, tearing towards the bed where his prince lies pale and deathly still. Iris is bent over Dawson, her hands pumping compressions against his unmoving chest, her face carved with panic.

He's not breathing. He's not moving.

Oh shit.

I rush forwards, my heart in my throat, bile rising. The room swims, and I barely register Kael's hoarse shout. "Sonny—"

I trip over my feet, scrambling to his side. I hear him before I feel him—Kael's devastation, his pain, pouring into me like a flood. His hand is splayed on Aelith's chest, eyes wild, jaw clenched.

Iris lifts her head as we reach her, sweat dripping down her temple, hands trembling. "He's crashing. We're losing them both. Do you have something? Anything?"

"We have—" I lift the satchel, the weight of scrolls and books barely registering. "We have books." It sounds so fucking weak.

Kael's hand finds mine. He doesn't say anything out loud—but the pull is immediate. Urgent. I understand.

He wants me to help. To connect. To try.

I glance at him sharply. "We better not die doing this."

His lips twitch, but his eyes are full of grief. "I don't intend to."

"If I do," I mutter as I grab his hand, "I swear to God, I will haunt you for the rest of your afterlife. I will endlessly rearrange your weapon racks and whisper awkward sex dreams into your ear at every opportunity."

His shoulders shake. It might be a laugh. It might be a sob. I take his hand anyway, then press my other palm flat against Dawson's bare, unmoving chest.

Cold.

So, so cold.

Iris flinches but steps back. Her faith—or desperation—keeps her from intervening.

Kael closes his eyes. I mirror him. And then I open myself.

The bond flares to life, white-hot, rushing like a storm through every vein. Kael feeds it to me, and I send it into Dawson. Like with Kael before, I give. I pour everything.

And pray it's enough.

My new sigils flare almost immediately. Not just a shimmer but a flash—brilliant, searing, as though something deep within me is waking up for the first time. I don't understand it. Don't control it. But Kael's presence grounds me. His energy wraps around mine, his mind brushing mine.

"*Stay calm.*" His voice threads through my skull, velvet and steel. "*Focus. Just like before. Heal—but don't give too much.*"

Easy for him to say.

The brightness behind my eyes grows. My breath shudders as something pulls from inside me. Not just energy—life force. Kael's and mine are tangled together now, strands woven tight. I feel his love for his prince, the weight of their years, their bond—not romantic but bone deep. Loyalty. Honour.

And it pours from us, rushing out in a stream of light, wild and thrumming and alive.

I can't see it exactly, not with my eyes squeezed shut, but I feel it. It dances over my skin like fire without heat, like electricity without pain. It's Kael's strength. My stubbornness. Our bond, our will, our everything—

And then it changes.

A shift, sudden and absolute, slams through me like a shock wave.

It's Dawson. His energy—so faint, but there—reaches up to meet ours. A gasp rips from my chest. I open my eyes. I expect to see blinding light. Some mystical glow. Instead—

All I see is my hand, trembling, pressed to Dawson's still, too-pale skin.

No movement. But then—a mark. Right beneath my

palm, a sigil begins to form. Black first, then pulsing deep violet. It isn't Kael's. Not even close.

It's Aelith's.

My head jerks towards Kael.

He's crouched beside his prince, hand on Aelith's chest, eyes half closed in absolute focus. The markings across his skin pulse in waves, casting him in surreal, celestial light. He looks like a warrior from another world.

Because he is.

And fuck me, he's the most beautiful thing I've ever seen. I swallow hard and turn back, forcing every shred of energy, attention, and will into Dawson. He can't die. Not now. Not when we've come this far. Not when Kael is giving everything.

Not when I finally understand how much this means.

My limbs tremble. My vision swims. But I keep going.

And then—colour. A flush blooms across Dawson's chest. The blue fades from his lips. His breathing hitches, once, then twice.

Iris is there in a flash, checking vitals. "It's working," she breathes, awe and disbelief tangled in her voice.

I force myself to wait one more second before I pull my hand away. The light fades. The sigils dim, and Kael lets out a shaky breath. I reach for him, grab his wrist, and tug him back from Aelith.

"Sonny—"

I turn to him, seeing the fight in his eyes—until they land on me. Concern swallows the glow in an instant.

"Are you okay?" He cups my cheek, eyes scanning every inch of me.

I must look like absolute hell. "I'm okay." I lean into him. "Just... tired."

He nods and then pulls me into his arms. No hesitation. Just warmth. Safety. Exhaustion, threaded through every breath. I feel his weariness, the deep ache in his bones. We're barely standing. My muscles scream, and my soul feels frayed.

"I think we need to sleep for at least forty-eight hours," I mutter.

The steady beep of the monitors cuts through the quiet, and we both turn.

Aelith lies still, but colour's returned to his face. His markings pulse, faint but sure. Dawson lies next to him, his chest rising and falling again. And right there, covering the centre of his chest, glowing faintly violet—

The same sigils as Aelith's.

I gape. "Is that...?"

Kael exhales, voice rough. "It looks like a full bond."

"Did we start it or... finish it?" My words wobble, tired and stunned. "Because that looks final to me."

He doesn't answer. Neither of us knows. But what we do know—without doubt—is that they're alive. And for now, that's enough.

We leave the medical wing without fanfare. No triumphant music. No fireworks. Just tired legs and heavy hearts and the faintest flicker of hope that things might—finally—be okay.

Dawson and Aelith still aren't awake, and Shanae is waiting for us outside. We explain everything to her—what happened in the citadel, the library, Varek, Pax.

She's quiet for a long moment before she says, firm as steel, "You're not going back for him."

I stiffen immediately. "Excuse me?"

Her eyes are kind, but her voice leaves no room for argument. "He knows what he's doing, Sonny. And you —both of you—are no good to anyone if you collapse trying to play the hero."

"But—"

"No." One word. Final.

And I hate it. Every part of me screams that we should do more, fight harder. But Kael's hand finds mine, grounding me. And I realise... I have nothing left to give. Not tonight.

The walk back to our room is quiet. The kind of quiet that rings a little too loud in your ears. Either the storm's passed—or it's still waiting just around the corner. But those are problems for tomorrow.

Inside our quarters, we don't speak. We strip without ceremony, clothes dropped in a trail from the door to the bed. I sink onto the mattress, muscles aching, every nerve in my body raw and tender. Kael moves towards the wall of piping and returns a minute later with washrags, still warm from the basin.

He kneels beside me and begins to clean me. It's not meant to be sensual. He's careful, methodical, quiet. Wiping the dried blood from my skin, dabbing gently around my temple, where a faint bruise is forming. His touch is reverent, almost devotional.

But my cock still stirs, twitching with attention. The exhaustion tries to smother it, but I've spent the whole day dancing between life and death, and right now my body just wants to feel something.

Kael notices—of course he does. He smiles, small and soft.

"We need a proper bath," I mumble, half embarrassed. "This is like some ragged battlefield spa day."

He chuckles, low and warm. "Tomorrow. Today... this is enough."

He finishes wiping me down, then himself, and tucks me beneath the sheets like I'm something precious. The move alone almost undoes me. No one's ever done that. Not for me.

I blink up at him, heart thudding unevenly. "I don't think I can sleep. I'm too wired."

"I'll help." He presses a kiss to my temple, then my jaw, then my lips—slow and sweet, deep and sure. It's not a kiss meant to arouse. It's a promise. But when his mouth travels lower, and he slips beneath the covers, I feel him smile against my hip.

His tongue flicks. I gasp. The kiss he presses to the head of my cock is maddeningly gentle. Worshipful. Then he takes me into his mouth—and I forget everything.

Stars burst behind my eyes. My hips jerk, muscles tightening, heat flooding through me. His hand anchors my thigh, holding me down, teasing as he sucks with the kind of focus only a bodyguard could bring to a mission. And fuck, is it effective.

It takes maybe two minutes. Maybe less. I explode with a choked gasp, my hand buried in his hair, my mind blissfully blank for the first time in hours.

My orgasm washes over me like an ocean. And then... I crash.

I can barely roll over. I don't even reach for the sheets. I just lie there, blinking at the ceiling, boneless and reeling and wrecked. Kael crawls up beside me, pulling the covers over us both. His arms wrap around me, protective and warm, and he presses a kiss to the back of my neck.

"You should come," I mumble. "I didn't mean to... just... fall asleep on your—"

"Hush." He tugs me closer, chest to my spine, breath in my hair.

"We have all the tomorrows," he whispers. "You can make it up to me then."

And secure in his arms, against the quiet thrum of our bond, I believe him.

Tomorrow will be better. Dawson and Aelith will wake. The books will hold all the answers, and Varek will appear at the gates. And even if none of that happens, we'll be okay. Together. Because Kael and I saved two lives tonight. Four if we include each other's.

All of that has to mean something.

I release a soft sigh and press a gentle kiss against Kael's arm.

Yeah, we'll continue to make every day and moment count. Together.

KAEL

I'VE LIVED IN WAR. I'VE WALKED THROUGH blood, followed orders that tasted like ash, and stood at the edge of a thousand choices that weren't mine to make.

But this? This stillness—this moment in a too-small bed, with Sonny's heart beating steadily against mine—is the most terrifying and beautiful thing I've ever known.

His breath is warm on my skin. His body tucked against mine like he belongs there. Because he does. Every inch of him. Loud-mouthed, sharp-tongued, reckless, and brave—he's mine.

Fated. Claimed.

Loved.

Even if I haven't said the word aloud again yet. I

will. I will, a hundred times. When the world stops trying to eat us alive.

I shift slightly, careful not to wake him. He made a sound earlier, something soft and content. He gets that way after orgasms—limp and smug and impossibly vulnerable. I love that version of him.

I love all versions of him.

My hand drifts to his chest, brushing over his heartbeat, and my own markings glow faintly in response.

They're not supposed to glow without power being summoned. But that's Sonny. He breaks the rules just by existing.

The room is dark, but our bond is light in my mind. I can feel the echo of his exhaustion, the way he still worries even in sleep. About Varek. About Dawson. Even the prince I don't think he quite hates anymore. About whether we'll have to fight for our lives again tomorrow.

He doesn't know it yet, but I'd burn the world for him. I already tried to die for him. And he... he brought me back.

I press my forehead to his temple and just breathe him in. He smells like salt and energy and a life I didn't think I was ever allowed to have.

When I first saw him, I felt the bond like a blade—sharp and terrifying. It would've been easier to ignore it again. To walk away like I did when the lightning struck my heart and changed my destiny.

But nothing worth protecting has ever been easy.

He shifts in his sleep, murmuring something unintelligible before curling closer around me.

My arms tighten around him instinctively. Always. For the first time in years, I don't feel like a weapon waiting to be used. I feel like something more.

A protector.

A partner.

A mate.

And in this moment, with the whole world waiting on our next move—I let myself have one perfect, quiet truth.

I am loved, and I love him. There's nothing more important for me than that.

If you've yet to read Solan (Monsters & Mates #1), now is definitely the time to do so, but let's talk about *Kael*! Gah! I hope you adore my guys and miss them already. If you do, you can read three fun bonus scenes in any of the following three ways. No purchase necessary.

1. The link found in the pinned post in my Facebook group.

2. Over on Patreon (it's free to follow)

3. By SUBSCRIBING (or already being a subscriber) to my NEWSLETTER

FB & Patreon links can be found on the **About the Author** page.

You can also preorder Varek right now!

Looking   for   more paranormal/supernatural reads? Be sure to check out my Fangs & Felons series, starting with book 1, **Thicker Than Water**.

BONUS SCENE

BATH TIME WITH A BEAST

"You're not going to fit."

Kael blinks down at the bathtub, then at me. "I can make it work."

"No, babe. That's not optimism. That's delusion."

We're in our quarters—finally upgraded, thank fuck —and staring down at what some very well-meaning but clearly size-oblivious builders thought was a "luxury bath." It's deep, sure. Wide even. But Kael is... Kael.

And Kael is huge.

Not just tall, not just muscular, but celestial-guardian-turned-death-sword-of-justice huge. With shoulders that could block the sun and thighs that deserve their own postcode.

He tilts his head. "If I fold my legs—"

"Oh my God, you'll get stuck like a crab. Or worse,

dislocate a hip. What's the emergency protocol for 'royal guard trapped in tub'?"

Kael sighs, amused. "We could try you first."

"That's what you said last night."

His lips twitch. "And you didn't complain."

Fair.

With dramatic flair, I slide my pants off and lower myself into the water, sighing as heat wraps around me. "Mmm. See? One perfect-sized human. Happy. Uncramped. Not folded like an origami fortune-teller."

Kael watches me for a long second, then strips. Slowly. Purposefully.

And damn it, I'm not proud of the way my brain immediately short-circuits. "Okay... you're hot. Still doesn't mean this bath is built for Boss-Level Glowranth."

He steps in, one leg at a time. The water sloshes over the sides like we're reenacting the Great Flood.

He tries to sit.

Fails.

Tries again—this time with a twist. There's a thud as his knee smacks the side. "Ow."

"I told you!" I squeak, both horrified and wildly entertained. "Do not break your ancient death-guard kneecaps because you want to bathe with me, you big idiot."

He grunts. "I want to hold you."

Okay. Rude. Now I'm melting like a chocolate in the

sun. I scoot forwards, curling my legs up and patting my lap. "Fine. We're doing this my way."

Kael snorts. "You want me to sit on you?"

"No! You'll break me in half. Sit behind me. Like, very awkwardly. One leg out of the tub if needed. We'll call it... a modified bonding soak."

He actually manages it. Sort of. His knees are halfway up the wall, one leg sticking out like he's signalling for landing clearance, but his arms curl around my chest, and I lean back into him with a satisfied sigh.

"See? Logistics. Solved."

"Barely," he mutters.

"Still counts."

He presses a kiss to my temple. "You're ridiculous."

"And you love me."

"I really do."

The water settles. Our heartbeats sync. And for the first time in what feels like months, we just... breathe. Peace. In a glorified soup bowl. With a Glowranth limb hanging over the side.

Romance? Conquered.

Spatial awareness? Optional.

BONUS SCENE

TERMINATOR TROUBLE

"I'll be back."

The words come out of Solan's fang-filled mouth in the deepest, most gravelly accent I've ever heard him attempt. And he pairs it with a stone-faced expression that would make actual statues jealous.

I choke on my drink. "Did you just... are you doing Arnie?"

Jack groans next to him, dropping his head into his hands. "Don't encourage him."

Kael, seated beside me, tilts his head like a confused golden retriever. "Who is Arnie?"

Solan perks up immediately. "The greatest warrior Earth has ever produced."

Jack splutters. "He's not real! Okay, the man is, but you know...." He waves his hand around in the air.

Solan ignores him entirely, eyes glowing faintly as

he looks at Kael with terrifying solemnity. "He is called Schwarzenegger. I have studied his works. His physique. His one-liners. They are sacred."

Kael looks to me, alarmed. "Is this a human king?"

I wheeze. "No! He's an actor. From movies. He just... plays action heroes."

Solan leans forwards. "No. He becomes them."

Jack rolls his eyes so hard, they might escape orbit. "He kinda watched Arnie movies to learn English. Now he quotes *Commando* like it's scripture. Help me."

Kael still looks confused. "So, he isn't real... but he battles predators?"

"Apparently," I mutter, wiping my eyes. "But wait—Solan, how many Arnie movies have you watched?"

Solan puffs up proudly. "All of them. Twice. And the animated one. It was... confusing. But his power endured."

Kael's eyebrows furrow. "He fights in many different times. And places. Yet his face is the same?"

I nod. "Welcome to Earth cinema."

Solan isn't done. "In *The Running Man*, he defeats an entire death game. In *Conan*, he wields a great sword of destiny. And in *Jingle All the Way*, he... secures a doll for his young. It was very moving."

Jack is sliding further down in his seat. "I love you, but you're a menace."

Solan curls a massive, clawed hand around Jack's waist and tugs him onto his lap with all the subtlety of a boulder rolling downhill. "Say what you want. But when I flexed in the mirror this morning and said, 'Hasta la vista, baby,' you moaned."

Jack turns beet red.

Kael nudges me. "Should we watch this Arnie?"

"Oh, absolutely." I grin. "But only if you do the voice next time you save me from a beastie."

He looks thoughtful. "If I say... 'get to the choppa'... what does it mean?"

I howl. "We have so much to teach you." And apparently, he's already been having some aside conversations with Solan.

Kael leans in close, his breath warm against my neck. "Then teach me. And after, we can... practice."

Oh. *Oh.*

Solan notices my expression and flashes a sharp-toothed grin. "The mating rituals of Arnie are sacred."

Jack groans again. "I regret everything."

BONUS SCENE
TRAINING... SORT OF

Kael says I need more practice.

Not because I suck—well, not in a sword fight anyway—but because, according to him, "Your stance leaves you vulnerable. Your shoulders are too tight. And you pause when you pivot left."

Rude.

"I pause because I'm calculating," I say, rolling my eyes and swinging the practice blade in a wide arc that would've made a five-year-old proud.

He catches the blade mid-swing with one hand.

One. Hand.

"I'm calculating how long I can get away with this before I distract you enough to pin you down," I add with a smirk.

Kael's luminescent eyes flicker. "You're not supposed to tell me your strategy."

"Where's the fun in that?"

We're in a private section of the training field. No audience. Just me, him, and the low hum of our bond buzzing under my skin like an energy drink made of want.

He tosses the blade aside like it weighs nothing (show-off), then steps forwards, closing the distance between us in a heartbeat. His chest brushes mine. I swear I hear my knees threaten to file a complaint.

"You should focus," he says, low, close, voice pure temptation wrapped in thunder.

I blink up at him, oh so innocent. "I am focussed. On strategy."

"Which strategy?"

"This one."

I slide my hand down, grab his butt—firm, muscular, a work of art—and yank him against me. He stumbles, barely, his control slipping just enough for me to pivot and press him against the tree behind us. His back hits bark with a thud. My blade is gone, but my hands are busy.

"You're weaponless," he murmurs, grinning now. "Pinned me without even trying."

"Who says I'm weaponless?" I lean in and up onto my tiptoes, nipping at his jaw. "You've met my mouth."

He exhales a shaky breath.

I may be shorter, slighter, and nowhere near his

level of lethal grace, but I have technique—and Kael. Which means I'm not losing this round.

His hands catch my hips. "You're cheating."

"Just using the tools God gave me."

"And your arse."

"That too."

He flips us without effort. My back hits the tree next, his body pressing me there. I gasp, laughing.

"Still think your strategy's working?"

I grin up at him, breathless. "Is your sword still sheathed?"

Kael groans. "We're not getting any training done, are we?"

"Depends how you define 'training.'"

He huffs out a laugh and leans in, kissing me like I'm the only victory he ever wants.

Spoiler: I win.

ABOUT THE AUTHOR

I live and breathe all things book related. Usually with at least three books being read and two WiPs being written at the same time, life is merrily hectic. I tend to do nothing by halves, so I happily seek the craziness and busyness life offers.

Living on my small property in Queensland with my human family as well as my animal family of cows, sheep, chooks, and dogs, I really do appreciate the beauty of the world around me and am a believer that love truly is love.

HEAD TO MY WEBSITE:
BECCASEYMOUR.COM
HTTPS://LANDINGMAILERLITE.COM/
WEBFORMS/LANDING/R9FD14
JOIN MY FACEBOOK GROUP:
WWW.FACEBOOK.COM/GROUPS/ROMMANCE
WITHBECCALOUISA

patreon.com/BeccaSeymour

facebook.com/beccaseymourauthor

instagram.com/authorbeccaseymour

bookbub.com/authors/becca-seymour

tiktok.com/@beccaseymourwrites